# Until You BELIEVE

An Until You Novel

Book Four

# D.M. DAVIS

# About This Book

**Some scars are hard to forget. Some wounds, too deep to heal.**

**FIN:**
Family means everything.
Slotted to become CEO of his family's tech company, he lives, breathes, and sweats family.
But his commitments are crushing his hopes of starting his own family.
Margot lights up all those ignored desires and unspoken dreams.
She is what he wants—exactly what he needs.
It's not a matter of *want*. It's a matter of who he lets down.
Which ball will he drop if he decides he wants more from life than a job that *is* his life?

**MARGOT:**
Family means disappointment, broken hope, and reinforced insecurities.
It's not a sanctuary to seek, but a tie to break.
Fin represents what family could mean. What it would be like to be loved despite her flaws.
Her goals are tested when she desires to have *more* with a man she shouldn't want, yet can't resist.
But she's hiding a secret from the world—her bubbly personality, a mask she wears well.
When Fin decides to make Margot a priority, will she unburden her secret for a chance at love?

D.M. Davis' Until You Believe is the fourth book in the *Until You* series and is a poignant, emotionally raw, friends to lovers, sexy, contemporary romance.

# Note to Reader

*Until You Believe* runs concurrent to *Until You Books 1-3* and beyond. Therefore, it is highly recommended that you read Joseph and Samantha's story (Books 1-3) before reading this book, Until You Believe, to avoid spoilers and to ensure the most positive reading experience possible.

XOXO, D.M.

# Playlist

*Starving* by Hailee Seinfeld (feat. Zedd)

*Sad Eyes* by James Arthur

*Put a Little Love On Me* by Niall Horan

*Where Were You in the Morning* by Shawn Mendes

*Goodbyes* by Post Malone (feat. Young Thug)

*What a Man Gotta Do* by The Jonas Brothers

*Lay Me Down* by Sam Smith

*Quite Miss Home* by James Arthur

*Love Me Anyway* by Pink

*Scars to Your Beautiful* by Alessia Cara

*I Won't Back Down* by Ryan Star

*Love You 'Till the End* by The Pogues

# Dedication

Scars are a badge of honor. A sign of the pain you've endured.

Proof you survived.

This is for all the survivors.

Whether your scars are on the outside or on the inside,

wear them proudly.

And if you can't—fake it *until you believe,*

as some scars are hard to forget.

Some wounds, too deep to heal.

# Until You
# BELIEVE

# One

## December

I'M HAVING TROUBLE BREATHING. THE TIGHTNESS in my chest…I'm too fucking young to be having a heart attack. If I believed in fairy tales, I'd think I'd been struck by Cupid's arrow, zapped by a love spell…or found my other half right here in this dive in Austin, Texas.

But I don't believe in fairy tales, cupid, love spells, or soulmates. I believe in family, working hard, numbers—they never lie—loyalty, and truth.

Yet here I am about to lose my shit over a girl I haven't even met, don't even know her name or her availability. All I know is she radiates like the sun, her dark hair shimmering like her very life force is woven into every strand that flows around her shoulders and frames the most refined face I've ever seen. Her bone structure could only have been molded by God himself.

Am I losing my everloving mind? My drink must have been spiked or poisoned. I'm too damn busy to consider dating—even someone whose sumptuous lips, straight nose, and large doe eyes beckon to me in a haunting, make-me-yours way.

I flew to Austin to check up on Joe, my baby brother. He's heartsore over a girl he wants more than he believes he has a right to.

And now, I'm going to die. Right here in this restaurant. In front of God and everybody who's not too drunk to notice, including the waif of a girl who stole my breath the second I spotted her and is too selfish—or oblivious—to give it back.

Fucking figures I'd go out this way.

I pride myself on my calmness. I don't freak out. I'm the fixer, for God's sake. Yet, here I am about to keel over due to my inability to draw a life-sustaining breath.

*Breathe! Close your eyes and breathe.*

"Have a drink, Brother. You look like you've seen a ghost." My ever-intuitive, could-be-my-twin, youngest brother urges.

An apparition, a fairy, whatever it is—whatever she is—she's haunting me nonetheless.

His smile eases the tightness in my chest. I catch a full breath and drink half my beer, reality coming into focus. I'm here for my brother. He needs me, and I've managed to get a few smiles and laughs out of him.

We laugh over stupid shit and drink our beers, lightening the weight on my shoulders. It's good to see him give his sadness a break. Make no mistake, he's sad as fuck. But for the moment, our burdens ease, and he can forget his twenty-one-year-old ass has fallen in love with his best friend's younger sister.

Joe's light demeanor goes out the window on his next breath, turning serious and putting me on edge. "Why didn't you tell me Samantha interned at MCI last summer and has plans to return next summer, and to get a job with us after she graduates? She wants to work in *my* department. Don't you think I should have known that?"

I flinch as his disappointment hits me like a punch. I sigh, putting down my beer. "You're right. I should have told you. Trusted you enough to handle it with decorum. But the other side of that coin is—you aren't VP yet, and Uncle Max agreed, given your friendship with Jace—and Sam's request to fly under the radar—that perhaps there was no harm in letting it slide."

Green eyes the same shade and shape as mine stare back at me as he contemplates before responding, "I can see your point. But it still pisses me off."

"I know, but would you be nearly as pissed if you didn't care for her like you do? If it were just one of your other friends' kid sisters, would you be so upset?"

"No," he admits on a drawn-out breath.

"It was a clusterfuck of secrets all woven to be sure she received no special treatment."

He frowns with a far-off look in his eye. "She loves MCI like it's her family heritage too."

"Maybe it's supposed to be. She wouldn't have needed the strings anyway. She was a rising star, received rave reviews from her manager, and was instrumental in getting two of our new key products out of research and development and into production."

Joe smiles at that, taking a deep breath as if his chest is filling with pride.

"Are we good, Brother?" I ask.

"Of course. Just don't keep things from me again, especially when it comes to her."

"Understood."

Another round of beers and another hour of laughter later, and while I've forced myself to ignore the tug from across the room, I can no longer pretend she doesn't exist.

Except when I finally scratch the itch and look directly at her, she's looking directly back—*at my brother.*

I motion with my chin to her table where she's sitting with another woman. "I think you've got an admirer. The dark-haired chick over there can't keep her eyes off you. It's too bad. She's more my type than yours." And by *type,* I mean I've somehow already claimed her as mine despite having never met her and her focus being solely on Joe.

*You're not looking, remember?*

I'm not *looking,* looking. I'm just *looking.* I can appreciate a fairy goddess when I see one. My life is too hectic as VP of Accounting & Finance for MCI as well as being my brothers' keeper. The sad sack in front of me is a strong deterrent. Who has time for heartache? Besides, my pixie looks too innocent with those big brown eyes that beseech me to teach her things I have no business considering.

I take a sip of beer to keep from saying something stupid like *she's mine!*

*Jesus, I'm a head case.*

"You're in luck then, as I'm off the market," he throws out without even looking, without even seeing the remarkable creature she is. I'm almost pissed he's discounted her so quickly, yet happy he has.

"You're going to have to tell her that. She's on her way over, and she's brought a friend." I smile, hoping my casual words disguise my excitement over meeting the waif who's gotten under my skin without even looking my way.

Joe groans his disapproval seconds before they reach us.

"Joe?" Her all-too-feminine voice greets us as she stops beside our table.

Well, hell. I guess she does know him. Did he sleep with her? I frown at the thought.

"Margot?" Joe lights up and is quick to stand to give her a hug.

He's awfully happy to see her. Fuck, he did sleep with her, and by the looks of it, he wouldn't mind doing it again. She, on the other hand, doesn't seem too sure. Good.

"Hey. How are you?" Jesus, could Joe's voice seem any happier? He seems to have gotten over Sam pretty fast..."What are you doing in Austin?"

"I'm good." Her eyes barely meet my flagrant stare before darting back to my brother.

"I'm visiting my sister." She gestures to the woman next to her who looks familial but not as petite. "Jenny, this is Joe. He's Jace's roommate and Sam's... Uh... Hmm... Friend, too."

God, that was painful. I try not to laugh at her shitastic introduction, which perfectly summarizes the state of Joe's relationship with Sam, and also made me forget for a split second that my brother may *possibly* know this pixie in the carnal sense.

Joe scowls but brushes it off valiantly as he offers his hand to Jenny. "It's nice to meet you. This is my brother Fin."

Already on my feet, I all but dismiss Joe and Jenny, my eyes glued to the dark-haired beauty in front of me.

Joe nudges me. "Fin, this is Margot. She's a good friend of Samantha's." Samantha, the woman my brother is completely devoted to.

More relieved that I should be, I shake their hands—Jenny's first so I can linger with Margot. Yeah, not creepy at all. "It's nice to meet you both."

Margot's shy yet mischievous smile captivates me as she slowly pulls her hand from mine, my palm burning from the contact. I bury my hands in my pockets to keep from snatching her up and putting her in there instead.

*Down, boy. This one is not for you.*

"Would you like to join us?" Joe and I offer at the same time.

God, he's going to bust my balls about this later. I can feel his eyes boring into my skull.

*Stare all you want, Brother. I'm just happy she's Sam's friend and not your ex.*

# *Two*

## March

DART AROUND A MASSIVE OAK TREE, MAKING myself as small as possible. Why is Bobby even at Sam's Dad's funeral? He barely knows Sam; there's no way he knew her dad. It never even crossed my mind Bobby would be here. His presence is wrong. It's such an emotional day. I'm not prepared to deal with him and the weight of his disgust and sour attitude.

I dry my tears, take a cleansing breath, and glance around the tree. I don't have the energy to deal with the inevitable confrontation, should he see me.

He'd never miss an opportunity to make me feel as small as possible.

A hefty hand grasps my shoulder. I jump, smack my hand over my mouth to silence my uncontrolled and inappropriate-for-where-we-are yelp, and spin around to find Victor, McIntyre Corporate Industries' head of security.

"You okay?" His furrowed brow deepens as he takes in my emotional state.

I nod, glancing at the people making their way to their cars, having paid their respects to Sam, her mom, and her brother, Jace, after the conclusion of the graveside service. Fidgeting with my tissue, I meet Victor's stare. "Yeah." I fake a smile I'm all too good at hiding behind. "I'm peachy. All things considered. How are you doing?"

"Good." Victor's steely-eyed visual investigation of me is interrupted by Fin joining us and completely blowing my hiding spot out of the water. It's impossible to hide behind anything smaller than a tank with these muscled giants. I should have known Victor's bestie wouldn't be far behind. They stick together like bookends.

I haven't been around them all that much. Fin more than Victor, and Michael, whom I met at the hospital when Sam was shot. Victor fights for that best friend slot with Michael, an FBI agent. Needless to say, these guys are an imposing bunch.

Fin rarely goes unnoticed—particularly by me. But get these two together, and I swear the earth's gravitational pull changes to accommodate the sheer force of their combined presence. Add in Michael and Fin's brothers, and I'm surprised we aren't thrown into the ice age or the apocalypse. These guys don't think the earth revolves around them—it just does.

But that's not what gets me. It's my racing heart, sweaty palms, and the desire to both run away and climb Fin that makes him the biggest threat to my sanity. My heart trips over itself whenever he's near. It darn near does it if I let myself even *think* about him. And think about him, I do, entirely too often.

It's only been three months since I met him in Austin when I was visiting my sister, and he was visiting Joe. I tried to hide my attraction to Fin. I have no idea if I succeeded. I just know I have to keep my cool. He's a man, and I'm just a silly high schooler with a crush. Unfortunately, my heart, my soul, or whatever it is inside me that makes we *want* this man, isn't giving up. Its hold has only grown. And now, here I am, face to face with him again, hiding behind a tree so my ex doesn't see me and point out to Fin what I already know: I could never be his. If he knew my secret, he wouldn't even acknowledge my existence.

I'd nearly forgotten how impressively distinguished Fin looks in person. Besides being ungodly handsome, he has an air about him like royalty. Where Joe might be the charming caveman, and Matt the unfairly charismatic Lothario, Fin is all class and finesse. Not a hair out of place. Perfectly tailored suit. Reserved coolness that's softened by his heated gaze and tantalizing smile. He could charm a girl out of her panties in .001 seconds. *If* he had the mind to. But he's not a player, which makes him even more attractive and doubly dangerous to my quivering heart.

"What's wrong?" Fin matches Victor's scowl and piercing gaze. My head's going to explode if I don't get their attention off me pronto.

"It's a funeral." I shrug as if that's explanation enough as to why I'm holding up a tree nearly big enough for Victor to hide behind. Nearly. Did I mention he's built like a house? I'm fairly minuscule, but I think his neck is bigger than me.

Fin steps forward, tipping my chin till our eyes lock. His touch sears my skin. He's barely touching me, and it's like the world closes in, and he's breathing life into me, feeding hope, and soothing my worry. And those green eyes—so much like his brother's yet entirely different when they're focused on me.

"What's wrong, Margot?" He leans in. "The truth."

I stifle my ready-made lie, bite my lip, which his eyes flash to before returning to mine. I shake my head and step back. If I can't tell a fib, then I have no reply. I avert my eyes, spotting Joe. Sam's tucked under his arm; he's consoling her as mourners and well-wishers greet them one by one. His parents are close by. Sam's mom and brother resemble statues rather than grieving widow and son.

Who am I to judge? I haven't lost my dad—at least not physically.

"Pixie?"

I jerk to Fin, startled by the softness of his voice and the nickname. My brows pinch as I contemplate his size-defining term. Is he making fun of me?

He simply smiles. "If you can't lie, you've got nothing to say?"

I offer the only truth I'm willing to share. "It's good to see you." A truth I probably should *not* admit.

His smile grows. "It's good to see you too. I wish it was under better circumstances."

"Me too." Like dinner and a night of hot sex.

My skin heats at the thought. I turn, stepping farther from the tree and away from his gravity. I can't hide here all day. Sam needs me. Or I like to think she does, but maybe Joe has her covered.

I catch a ghost of blond hair and blue shirt in my periphery. My heart skips. *Please don't let it be him.*

"Margot?" Sebastian's voice greets me from behind. If he's near, then Bobby isn't far behind.

I cringe, closing my eyes briefly before turning, not missing the concern on Fin's and Victor's faces. I need to do a better job of hiding around those two. They're entirely too observant.

"Sebastian." I lean into his hug. It's always good to see him. "I'm glad you were able to make it. I know it means a lot to Sam."

He squeezes before releasing me. "I would've quit before missing being here for her." He gives a nod to Victor and Fin and a quick glance over his shoulder. "How are you?"

"Hmm…" I swallow the knot in my throat as I consider his question nearly as much as the guy looming behind him. "Fine."

Sebastian gives me an apologetic smile and mumbles to his friend—the blond and blue ghost, "Don't be an ass."

*He can't help it. He just is,* races through my thoughts. I have to clench my fists at my sides to keep from stepping behind Fin and Victor. I'm not above running to avoid a confrontation with Bobby, especially here of all places. I chance a glance at Fin, considering my options, and find he's already watching me—reading me.

Before I can move, the ghost steps forward with a curt nod, focused solely on my chest. "Margot."

"Bobby." I nearly kick myself when my hand hovers over my chest as if he could see what's hidden below. Like he doesn't already know, hence his look of revulsion.

Fin steps to my side, pulling me to him as he places his arm around my waist, a menacing stare locked on Bobby. "I don't believe we've met."

I lean into Fin, letting Bobby think we're an item. *Take that!*

Victor steps to my other side, arms crossed, glare in full force.

Wow. These two are intense. And I'm thankful for their support as I attempt to stare down the guy who left me more scarred than he found me—emotionally, at least.

Sebastian, accurately reading the situation, laughs it off, handing Bobby the keys. "I'll meet you at the car."

With a final lip-curling sneer, Bobby scurries off without a word.

*Jerk.*

Sebastian studies me with concern. "I'm sorry."

Does he know? Did Bobby tell him? I search for pity in Sebastian's eyes, but there's only the apology on his lips and a hint of embarrassment for his jerk of a friend.

"I'm really sorry about him." Sebastian pats my arm with a gentle smile.

He's a good egg, unlike Bobby. "You need better friends." Another truth I'm willing to part with.

"I'm realizing that." He kisses my cheek. "Don't be a stranger. Call me if you or Sam need anything," he says before shaking Fin's and Victor's hands and departing.

"Who the fuck was that?" Victor asks.

"What was that?" Fin asks at the same time, looking down at me but not removing his hand from my back, which I'm not a bit sorry about.

"Bobby. Sebastian's friend." Also true. I'm on a roll.

Fin adjusts so he's facing me. "Who is he to *you?*"

"No one." Not the truth. I just wish it was.

*No one* my ass. One look at Victor has him pulling out his phone and following said *no one.* Margot's distress over seeing this Bobby character has her shaking in her dainty, strappy heels. I swear everything about this woman screams out to me to protect her, keep her safe, and banish every soul who dares look at her crossways.

I shield her body with mine, crowding her to the tree so she can lean against its strength if she won't let herself lean against mine. Her soft gasp beckons me to meld my body with hers. Arms at her sides, palms splayed on the cool bark, she keeps her distance when all I want are her hands on me.

Fuck. I can't, but, God, I want to. I want to kiss the naked fear out of her eyes, the tremble from her chin, and the uncertainty in the cower of her shoulders. "Would you tell me if you needed help?" *Will you at least give me that if I can't have anything else from you?*

"I... It's..." Her head falls forward.

Fuck it. I pull her to me. She wraps her surprisingly strong arms around my middle, under my suit jacket. The warmth of her seeps through my shirt. Jesus, she's warm for such a little thing. Like a fire burns deep inside her, giving her strength, and making her radiate tantalizingly bright. Like a fairy—like a sprite. My Pixie.

"Guuurl." The slurred word hits me from behind.

Margot goes rigid, and I swear her heat fades. But it's not until she extricates herself from my grasp that I feel the stark coolness of her absence.

"Dad." Her eyes dart between me and the man swaying on his feet before us.

"Youuuur mom had to go to werrrk," he states with sloppy elongated pronunciation, answering a question we didn't ask.

Margot's shoulders sag impossibly lower as she wraps her arm around her father's arm, fighting to steady him.

I step forward. "Let me—"

A quick hand stops my advance. "I've got this." She offers a reassuring smile that I don't believe for a second. "Please tell Sam I..." She catches herself. She was going to offer up a lie. Yet, I've asked her for truth.

It's apparent Margot is used to padding the truth to mollify others' concerns. "I'll tell her you had to see your father home."

She rolls her bottom lip in and nods, moisture forming in her eyes. "Thank you." I see the words on her lips more than I hear them.

"Call if you need anything." *Any fucking thing at all.*

Her dad grumbles something, turning and forcing her to move with him or lose her grip on him altogether. She glances over her shoulder, giving me that damn fake smile again. I'll have to tell her those are also lies. I wave, but she's already turned away.

I watch as long as I can. The sorrow of the day seems heavier now I've seen my Pixie and witnessed the weight she carries. I have no doubt it's heavier than just the remnants of these two jackasses—Bobby and her father. Though, I doubt she normally lets it show. Today was an exception. She was all bubbly light at the hospital, doting on Sam and doing anything she could to help out. But even then, I saw through her façade. I've heard a bit about her ass of a father from Joe. Yet, you'd never know it based on Margot's demeanor and temperament.

With a deep sigh, I survey the gravesite. The weight of my own responsibilities seems more burdensome today as well.

Maybe that's what I'm attracted to in Margot. Her need to take on the troubles around her, and her ability to carry them as if they're nothing. We're kindred spirits.

I straighten my shoulders, crack my neck, and run a hand down the front of my suit. Here's to *nothing…*

It's time for me to tackle my own load. My family needs me. And I will never let them down.

# Three

**M**Y PHONE CHIMES WITH A TEXT FROM MY PA, Angela, as I step into the elevator to my penthouse in MCI's Alpha Tower, advising dinner will be delivered shortly. It's been an unusual day that started by Joe flying into town at the ass-crack of dawn to check on his ex-girl, Sam. She broke up with Joe after her father's funeral, fearing for his safety. Her father's killer is still at large and seems to think Sam can help him obtain what he's after.

It's crazy drama that I've only seen on TV and in the movies, but there I was beside Joe and Michael, my best friend and her FBI protector, knocking on her door trying to convince her to let us in.

Yesterday was her eighteenth birthday, and she spent it alone. Alone. That sweet girl who'd never hurt a fly, who lost her father, her mother is so deep in grief she's not functioning, and a manwhore of a brother who can't be bothered to be the man of the family, spent her birthday alone. When Joe found out, all hell broke loose. Understandably.

Now, my parents are taking care of Sam's mom, Eleanor, and Sam will be living with me for the foreseeable future. I volunteered. Victor's team at MCI is the best. He'll continue watching over Sam in addition to the FBI. It's redundant, but no one is willing to take that chance with Sam's life, especially not Joe. He put Victor on her tail the second he figured out why she broke up with him.

That was this morning. After a few hours spent on getting the ball rolling with lawyers to take care of Daniel Cavanagh's estate, and a property manager to take care of the house, I made it back to the office and managed to get some solid hours in. But I'll be working late—after dinner. I'll need the distraction. Margot is coming to dinner. My suggestion. Joe's execution. Sam doesn't know. It's a surprise. I'd like to say it's purely altruistic on my part and I was only inviting Margot for Sam's benefit. But that'd be a lie.

The ding of the elevator has me stepping out and glancing at my brother Matt's penthouse door. I'd invite him, but he's got other plans of the female persuasion. His status quo for after work or most evenings, really. Rarely is my middle brother without a girl on his arm or in his bed, so to speak, because he never actually brings them back to his bed.

I pause at my door and consider knocking for a half second, unsure of what I'll find on the other side. I'm close to Joe, but the last thing I want is to walk in on them during an intimate moment. Plus, Sam would be horrified, I've no doubt.

*It's my damn house.*

With that reminder, I square my shoulders and unlock the door. "Honey, I'm home," I holler my attempt at humor and also a warning.

Joe's growl reaches me before he pops his head over the arm of the couch, a scowl to accompany him shushing me.

Bypassing him cuddling Sam on my couch, whispering words I'm sure I don't want to hear, I grab a water from the fridge and head to my office to drop off my laptop. I pop my head out, garnering his eyes. "Dinner will be here shortly."

A curt nod is all I get before he continues to soothe a sleeping Sam.

I cut my gaze from the pair. How those two don't know they're in love is beyond me. But witnessing it is not for the faint of heart. It sets off ideas about a woman I shouldn't want—Margot. She'll be starting college in Austin this next semester. Then medical school, God knows where. She doesn't have time for a relationship any more than I do. Plus, she barely acknowledges my existence—beyond flirting glances and goosebumps that are hard to ignore. She's Sam's friend, which makes it complicated if things implode. Then there's the irrefutable fact that I have no room in my life for a relationship that is anything more than sex.

Sex. Jeez, when was the last time?

I scrub my face, set up my laptop and ban all thoughts of romance—*sex*, not romance—in lieu of work.

My head jerks up as soon as the door opens to Fin's apartment—penthouse. I'd almost hoped I was in the wrong place. I'm not sure I'm capable of having dinner with Fin and remaining cognitively coherent, not tripping over my own feet, or drooling all over him. It's only been a few weeks since the funeral, but I swear I suffer from hot flashes from the mere thought of his piercing green eyes.

Sam is here, but she has Joe and her own troubles to deal with. She doesn't have time to be a buffer between me and a man I have no business wanting. Fin could end up being Sam's brother-in-law. Someone I'll have to see for the rest of my life if Sam and I remain friends, which I hope we do.

Though, lately I'm not sure she feels the same about our friendship status. She lied to me about her birthday. Her *eighteenth* birthday. It's a milestone—one she shouldn't have spent alone. She hasn't come right out and confessed that fact, but I've produced enough of my own to recognize a lie by omission when I see one.

"Pixie," Fin's nickname for me flies easily from his gorgeous mouth, bringing me out of my thoughts and into the reality of having dinner with *him*.

I smile when I want to frown.

I offer a warm salutation when I really want to ask him to stop making fun of my size.

I let him kiss my cheek when I'd rather feel his breath flutter across my lips before he presses his to mine.

We can't always get what we want. I know that all too well.

Fin touches the small of my back as he motions me forward. "She'll be happy to see you."

I try to hide the shiver his touch produces. My traitorous body won't listen to reason. We can't want *him*. We just can't. "Will she?" I wonder out loud when I know I shouldn't.

His contemplative frown falls from my view when I step out of his reach and into the living room to a smiling Sam, who rushes me into a hug that practically cracks my ribs.

"Oh my god! I can't believe you're here. I'm so happy to see you."

She pulls me farther away from Fin. I should thank her, but parts of me don't want to leave the comfort his nearness affords. Which is exactly why I need to stay away from him. He's too sexy, too handsome, too rich, too successful. He's *too everything* I'm not. I'm too *me*. I'm too small, too plain, too poor, and entirely too damaged for one Finley *Whateverhismiddlenameis* McIntyre, current VP and someday CEO of MCI.

Yes, I know more about him than I should. All of the McIntyre heirs are famous in Dallas. They're as handsome as they are rich. Texas-bred royalty. Texas proud.

At Sam's dad's funeral, I had to hurry my dad away from Fin before he recognized him. Dad would've made a stink—one I wouldn't been able to live down. He'd either put me down in front of Fin, or worse, get onto Fin for being privileged and having more money than God. It might be true—the more money than God part. But I know they work hard for everything they have. It's not like someone gave them a fully functioning, successful company. Three generations of McIntyres have poured their lives into MCI—they live, breathe, and eat it. My dad wouldn't have a clue how to work hard for the money he doesn't make since he's jobless. He *lost* his bigtime CPA job years ago because of his drinking. He can't hold down a job—any job—because he can't stay sober.

Except this is where my anger ends, where it fizzles out and the blame turns inward. He drinks because of me. My family is broke, in debt, because of me. My family is broken, damaged, dysfunctional because of my inherent flaw that cost them everything.

"We'll be back," Sam shouts over her shoulder.

"Dinner is ready," Joe's gruff voice trails behind us.

"We'll be *right* back. I promise." She giggles and rolls her eyes. "That man."

I smile and nod like I have any clue what it's like to have a man who's so in love he skips school to fly home to move you from your lonely life at home to live with his brother. Her family is broken. *That* I can relate to. But this *thing* between her and Joe is inconceivable.

He called earlier to arrange dinner and for me to miss school tomorrow to spend the day at the spa with her. It's a surprise. She's so lucky, and she has no idea.

"I'm sorry," Sam blurts as soon as the door closes to the bedroom. *Her* bedroom, by the looks of the suitcase on the floor.

"You don't need to... For what?" My mind reeling from my darker thoughts about my situation, it takes me a minute to switch gears to focus on the train wreck of her life instead of my own. Then, of course, I feel guilt for not already knowing how hard her life has been since her dad passed. What kind of friend am I? She didn't share the details, but I didn't push. I didn't notice or follow up. I didn't show up on her doorstep yesterday to be sure she didn't spend her birthday alone.

She's sorry? I'm the one who should be apologizing.

"For lying about my birthday." She pulls me to the couch in the sitting area in her room. A. Sitting. Area. Yep, too darn fancy for me.

"You could have told me you didn't want to spend it with me. I would have understood. Or I would have *tried* to understand."

"God, no." She squeezes my hand. "It wasn't that I didn't want to. I just... Couldn't bear the idea of faking a celebration. I still can't. I'm eighteen. Big whoop. My dad is dead. My mom is catatonic. My brother is MIA. My dad's killer is after me. I broke up with Joseph to keep him safe—a fact he believed enough to sleep with someone else—until he figured it out and rushed home to drag me out of my hell and bring me here." She motions around the room. "To a penthouse, for God's sake." She takes a deep breath and locks eyes with me. "Who does that?"

"Apparently Joe does."

She smirks on a laugh. "Yeah, apparently he does."

*Wait.* "Joe slept with someone else? You really broke up with him?" I had no idea I was so far out of the loop. I'm nowhere near the best-friends zone. I'm in the barely-know-you zone.

"Long story. Don't be mad at him. I broke up to protect him, but I didn't tell him that. He got drunk and, well, he slept with some chick. He's really upset about it." She shakes her head. "*I'm* really upset about it. But I don't have a right to be. I did it to him—to us."

Her voice breaks, and I immediately feel bad about my tiny problems. Here I am thinking about myself when she's been going through so much. Life-and-death kind of so much.

"I wish you'd told me." I hug her as best I can in our side-by-side position on the couch. "I wouldn't have had a clue how to fix any of that, but I could have listened. Been there for you."

"I know." She swipes at her tears. "Ugh, I'm so tired of crying."

I stand. "Then let's not." I point to her door. "There are two hunky men out there waiting to feed us. What are we making them wait for?"

Her smile is pure Sam. "Not a damn thing."

# Four

"**W**HAT DO YOU MEAN YOU DON'T GO IN THE water?" My reaction is entirely too strong for such an easy-going topic, but I'm at a loss. I don't understand her aversion to swimming, intense to the point she won't even consider going to the lake house for the view and the company. The company! I'm a catch. Seriously.

For a guy with no time to date, I'm sure trying to have a lot of quality time with Margot.

"Well, I don't wear swimsuits, so I don't go in the water." Margot's voice is sweet, soft, and full of discomfort. I should give her a break, but I'm stuck. I need to understand this creature who has taken ahold of me, crawled under my skin and nested, and invades my thoughts, my dreams, my focus. She's stolen my calm. If I can just *understand* her, I'll find my center—my calm.

"Ever?" She doesn't go in the water? My unease grows with each passing second. Is she trying to subtly let me know she's not interested?

Somehow, the vision of the four of us going to our family lake house is stuck in my head, and I can't shake it free. The idea of watching Margot bask in the sun, glowing like the sprite she is, getting a glimpse of her undone and relaxed, hammers in my head and brings a warmth to my chest.

Yet, she looks none too pleased or even mildly interested. In fact, she looks downright uncomfortable as she squirms in her chair and flicks pleading glances at Sam as if she asking for help. Help to escape a conversation with me. Me! Not that I blame her. I've never been so completely incapable of charming a woman in my life. In fact, I'm not sure I've worked so hard for a woman's attention when I'm not even sure I want it.

Okay. I want it. But I shouldn't. And still, here I am working for it. Hard.

Margot flashes another pleading glance at Sam as she forks a bite a sumo wrestler couldn't manage. When she notices, she discretely removes half the food on her plate from her fork and starts again.

I have no fucking idea what's going on. Is she pleading to change the subject, or pleading to get away from me?

Joe, my useless brother, laughs, not helping me in the least. He's enjoying this entirely too much. I don't ruffle, and Margot has me beyond ruffled. She has my head spinning.

Samantha smiles at her friend and then throws out casually, "She's sensitive to sunlight, so it doesn't make much sense to hang out at the lake or the pool."

Okay. Photosensitivity is a real thing, but there's shade at the lake too. Maybe her unease is more embarrassment in sharing a detail she's not comfortable with. "But do you swim?"

"Uh… Yes." Margot shimmies uncomfortably in her chair.

So she knows how to swim. Maybe she had a bad experience once, nearly drowned or lost a friend that way?

I catch Joseph's all-too-knowing gaze. *Yes, yes, I'm interested in her, okay?*

"Do you go to the lake often?" Sam asks, glancing between Joe and me.

"I think we could stand to go more often, particularly if you two joined us." It's obvious this is a dead topic for Margot, and Sam is trying to save her friend. In that light, and to retaliate against Joe for not helping a brother out, I spill the surprise. "Sam, we thought you and Margot might like to take a spa day tomorrow."

Joe glares at me before taking Sam's hand. "You're off the rest of the week, and it's been arranged for Margot to go with you tomorrow if you're up for it. We thought you could use a day of pampering and relaxation."

Sam's gaze ping pongs between the three of us. "Seriously?" Her smile grows with each passing second. She's nearly vibrating out of her seat.

Joe fills her in on the details about tomorrow. From there it's a series of hugs all around and gratitude. As the girls get lost in talking about tomorrow, I collect our dinner plates and start to clean up.

Joe follows me into the kitchen. "You like her."

I grunt in response, not willing to entertain this discussion while said subject of the discussion is half a room away.

"You do. I can tell," he pushes.

"What?" I turn on the disposal, drowning out his next words.

He bulldozes me out of his way, turns off the disposal, and takes over washing the dishes. "It's okay if you do." His gaze flashes to the girls laughing as they walk to the balcony. "She's been through a lot for almost-twenty." His eyes flash to me. "But you already knew that, didn't you?"

"I know no such thing." My skin pricks at the lie. Victor shared his findings about that guy Bobby who rattled Margot at the funeral. He is a friend of Sebastian's as Margot advised. What she didn't say was the fact that they dated for a while. It was hot and heavy and then nothing. Cold turkey. I don't know the details. I'd rather hear them from her. Victor doesn't believe Bobby to be a threat to Margot or anyone else beyond being an ass. Therefore, I didn't ask Victor to go deeper. That could change.

But in his investigation, he also found out she's nearly a year and a half older than Sam, and in the running for valedictorian with her. Margot is incredibly intelligent.

So why is she nearly two years behind in school?

I have no doubt that's a detail Margot would want to tell me herself in her own time. She's private. Hiding behind her pep and practiced smile. She's cute as a dark-haired Tinkerbell, but rivers run deep under her façade of happiness. There is more to Margot than a fairy-like stature and staged joyousness. Her big brown eyes beg me to get closer, to find the crack in her armor and bury myself deep inside until it shatters at our feet.

The problem is, if she lets me see her cracks, does that mean she'll see mine too?

# *Five*

*14 Months Later*

## ⼀ **August** ⼀

I DON'T HAVE TIME FOR THIS. I SHOULD TURN around and go home. I have more packing to do to be ready to leave for UT Austin on Friday. It's my second year, but like Sam, I busted my booty in high school to graduate with an associate's degree, which makes me a college senior this school year.

Summer school has helped as well. I finished two more classes last week, giving me a leg up this semester. I'm determined to graduate as early as possible. I need to start my life. Be out of my parents' house—out of their hair, and them out of mine. But I still have to graduate with my bachelor's degree in the spring, pass the MCAT, get into medical school, graduate…and then *start* my residency…

My heart races at the stress of all that. It's going to be a hot minute before I can even think about moving out on my own. I've worked, saved, and scrimped, getting by on my savings and my scholarships. The saving grace this past year was living in Austin rent-free thanks to Sam and her McIntyre connection. I lived with Joe and Sam in the house his family has owned since Fin went to school there.

Which brings up my current issue. Joe graduated in May, and Sam is not returning to UT but finishing up her degree at SMU, here in Dallas. They don't need the house any longer. I'm hoping Mr. and Mrs.

23

McIntyre will give me a few weeks to find a new place to live before booting me out of the house I'm sure they'll be selling now that they have no more kids living in Austin.

Our usual Wednesday night happy hour locale is swinging tonight. Sam texted me after I'd already caught an Uber from my parents' home, advising she wouldn't make it tonight, so I'm surprised to see Joe in deep conversation with Michael before he darts out the door without even a *hello*, barely five seconds after I walk in.

I'm starting to feel like the unwanted stepchild here.

Sam and I have barely hung out this summer, besides these happy hours. She's been busy with her MCI internship. When I'm not working, I'm tied up with summer school. We thought we'd have this school year to catch up. Plus, we'd be living together. But as best laid plans go, it hasn't worked out that way. Seems like as you get older, plans become guilty calls and texts saying, "Sorry I've been MIA! We need to hang out!" and they say, "OMG same! We'll do better!" and then never hanging out.

Now, I'm leaving in a few days, having barely seen her. She's not coming tonight. And I'll be all alone in Austin.

Pity party for one, please.

"Hey, Margot. You made it." A forced smile from Michael as he glances past me to the door Joe just swept through doesn't bode well for my confidence in being accepted here without Sam.

I step back and point over my shoulder. "I think I'm going to head out."

"You just got here." He urges me forward. "It's good to see you. You have to stay. At least one drink. I'll even let you have a sip of my beer." He kisses my cheek, then motions to the door. "Don't let Sam and Joe not being here scare you off. The guys will be happy to see you."

*Will they?* I doubt it until I see Fin's face light up as if seeing me just made his day.

But that can't be. I've seen him, all of them on and off over the past year and a half. Mainly when they come to Austin to visit, or here at the happy hours when I'm in town. I love these guys. They're like my big brothers. Except for Fin. He's nowhere in the brother zone for me. He's a secret wish, hidden desire that never seems to let up. After all this time, you'd think my want of him would diminish, but the heat in his eyes only stokes the flames I've tried so hard to extinguish.

"Margot!" Victor sweeps me into a robust hug. My feet swing freely as he spins. "You doing okay?" His smile is genuine as he sets me down, hands on my shoulders until he's sure I'm steady, for which I'm thankful, since my head is still spinning.

"I'm good, Victor. How about you?"

"Great." He elbows Michael, giving himself room to turn me around to face Fin, who's moving in fast, his beaming smile replaced by a glower at his best bud. "But I'm even better watchin' man of steel here get his panties in a bunch." Victor laughs in my ear, barely releasing his grip on my arms before Fin's hand captures mine.

I focus on not blushing as heat sails up my arm from his touch. Jeez, this man.

"Pixie." His easy use of his nickname that I used to hate but now don't mind makes me all too giddy when I really should be upset about him mocking my size.

*Maybe he doesn't mean it that way.*

"Fin," is all I can manage until I get a grip on my running thoughts and dangerous emotions.

His smile grows, showing a single dimple as he pulls me to their table. "What are you drinking?"

"Oh, um… I'll have a coke." These guys have an air of worldliness beyond their years. I'm not sure turning twenty-one in two months will change the fact I feel like an inexperienced babe around them.

Fin nods to Michael, who gives a quick tip of his chin and heads for the bar.

"He doesn't have to do that. I could get it myself or wait for the server." I follow Michael and Victor with my gaze as they slip through the crowd.

"They were getting refills anyway. Our server seems to have disappeared on us."

"She obviously doesn't know who you are," pops out of my mouth without any forethought. My eyes widen in horror, hoping he doesn't take offense.

He laughs, sitting back in his chair. "She's new." He winks over the rim of his glass as he finishes the last of his beer.

Wait. Beer? "I thought you only drank Macallan."

His empty glass hits the table, his chin down, and his eyes meet mine. "I guess you know me." The gruff in his tone sends shivers down my spine. His smirk belays he knows that even after all this time, I still want him. But the heat of his stare means I'm not alone in my attraction.

I don't know what's changed. He's flirted with me more this summer. Near kisses fraught with second thoughts. Maybe it's because we're alone, which is rare, or maybe because I'm leaving town. He has nothing to lose by hitting on me. I'm not sticking around to get attached.

Though, who's to say I'm not already *attached*? Two years is a long time to want someone.

"A little." My voice is a wisp of its normal volume.

He leans in. "I'd like you to get to know me a whole lot, Pixie," he says, low and soft in my ear.

My breath hitches, and our eyes lock for a split second before Michael and Victor return with our drinks and take their seats. Fin's arm rests across the back of my chair, not making contact, but I can feel the heat radiating off his skin, only visible from the rolled-up cuffs of his crisp white button-down. His normal jacket and tie are missing, but the air of a man with money and influence remains.

*Is it getting hot in here?*

I nearly moan when his fingers graze my back. His touch is subtle and bold with his friends sitting right here with us.

Her laugh is infectious. I'm not sure if I've ever seen Michael and Victor laugh so much without a crude joke involved. Michael swipes at his eyes, actually laughing hard enough to tear up. That makes me laugh even harder. He was upset about something earlier. Something involving Sam and Joe, but a phone call later, his shoulders are less tense, and he's enjoying our company. Or more pointedly, Margot's company.

We all are. Me, probably more than any of them realize, and more than I should. But she's leaving for Austin this week, and I don't feel like waiting another year to make a move, to find out what those lips of hers taste like, what kind of sounds she makes when she comes.

I don't have time for forever, but I sure as fuck can give her a night. Maybe two.

My fingers, of their own volition, started teasing her hair and the back of her neck an hour ago or so. Her shivered responses are tantalizing, her stuttered words, perfection, and the goosebumps on her arms make my cock and mind jump to conclusions on how this night could end.

Her nipples are hard. Is she wet for me? All dangerous thoughts I've spent entirely too much time contemplating about the woman next to me. She plays it cool. But when I remove my arm from around her chair, her hand miraculously finds my knee. It takes me all of two seconds to lay my hand over hers to keep her close—to keep her hand on me. A connection of some sort, confirmation she wants this—she wants me. Victor and Michael have no idea, or are doing a great job of ignoring my slow, savored seduction.

I see my Pixie for who she is. A woman with secrets she's not ready to share, who hides it better than most, but not quite enough to fly below my radar. My signal is tuned to her wavelength, and she's broadcasting at full digital.

Matt shows up late and talks Victor and Michael into hitting a club they like to frequent. Thankfully, Margot seems to miss their masked remarks.

With them out of the picture, I'm more at ease asking what I've wanted to suggest all evening, "Would you like to get out of here and grab a bite to eat?"

"Sure," her reply is all too easy, almost as if she hoped I'd ask—or been about to, herself.

Once outside, I move to hail a cab. I walked here from the office, but dinner may take us farther than she'll want to walk in her heels. "Any place in particular you'd like to go?"

"Anyplace?" Those doe eyes of hers slay me with their inquisitive innocence.

"Anywhere your heart desires."

She smirks and drops her eyes. "Your place."

*The fuck?* I manage to pick my chin up off the ground before she meets my shocked gaze.

"If you're okay with that." She holds my stare this time.

Giving up on a cab, I drop my arm and stalk toward her, pressing forward until she's flush against the building, her face tipped to mine. "Pixie, I am more than happy to give you whatever you want." *...whatever you need.*

Her quickening breath skates along my jaw, and I tense from the effort to not take her mouth for a practice run right here, right now.

"So, you're not hungry, then?" She bats those long eyelashes of hers like she's not testing my steely resolve—on purpose.

"Oh, I'm plenty hungry." I lace her fingers with mine and pull her to my side. As we start to walk the few blocks to my apartment on top of MCI towers, I lean in and catch her gaze. "I'm ravenous, Pixie. Absolutely ravenous."

# *Six*

MY MOUTH CONSUMES HERS THE SECOND WE step in the elevator. I corral her to the corner, my back to the surveillance camera, her hidden from view of the electronic eye. She climbs me like a kitten on a tree, and I happily sink my fingers into her ass, holding her securely as she lashes my tongue with hers like she's greedy for everything I'm dying to give her.

How long have I dreamt of kissing these lips, feeling her in my arms, waiting for our timing to be better? Nearly two years? The fantasy of her doesn't compare to the reality.

Jesus, I'm hard as fuck. I need to slow down. Take my time.

The elevator dings with perfect timing. I tear my lips from hers and walk to my door, not bothering to set her down. She's pocket-sized and perfect for carrying. Though, by the strength of her legs wrapped around my waist, I'm not sure I could pull her off me if I wanted to. Which I don't.

Inside, I make it as far as the entryway table, dropping my keys, phone, and wallet in the basket, and set her tight little ass on the edge, the perfect fucking height. I suck her bottom lip, pulling until she whimpers.

"Have you wanted this as much as I have?" I breathe against her sultry mouth.

"Yes." She claws at my shirt, wrapping her legs around mine. "Now."

I can do *now*. But first— "Need to feel you."

"Oh, gosh," she gasps.

29

I smirk into our kiss. Yeah, my Pixie can't even cuss. There's something even hotter about that too. She works on the button of my shirt as I flip off her heels and work her skirt up around her hips—not even considering the precious time it would waste to take it off. We're all hands, moans, and desperate kisses that freeze the second I find her hot center. Her head falls back, her hands tug at my hair and shoulders in the most feral of ways that'll probably leave bruises I couldn't care less about.

I latch onto her neck and slip my fingers past her panties to her decadent, dripping heat. "Is this for me? Or are you always this wet?"

"You." She buries her reply in my shoulder as I stroke into her with less care than she deserves for our first time together. I promise to make it up to her. But her leaning back and pulling me closer as she spreads her legs only makes me crazier as she shows me what she needs. Deeper. Harder.

I give exactly what she needs, sucking on a nipple through her simple white t-shirt and barely-there bra. Her breasts are small but perfect. I can't wait to see, tease, and taste those rosebuds, skin to skin. Soon.

But first, she's going come for me. Spectacularly by the way she's writhing, her muscles tensed, her breathing stuttering, and her elated moans and gasps. Yeah, my girl is going to come hard. The idea is making my cock press painfully against its confinement in my slacks.

I rub her clit as my fingers play her insides, where I can feel the little ridges of her g-spot. Gotcha.

"Fin!" she cries my name as her body locks in release, shaking with tremors, moisture coating my hand.

*Jesus, she's the sexiest thing I've ever seen.*

My first thought as she catches her breath is, I want to do that again. And again. And again.

"What..." she pants, trying to catch her breath.

My forehead rests on her shoulder. "Yeah?"

"That..." Her breath hitches. "What... How? Oh, God."

I'm not sure which surprises me more: her using the Lord's name or her question about what just happened. I rise up to see her eyes locked on the ceiling, my thoughts turning darker the longer she avoids eye contact. "Please tell me that wasn't your first orgasm."

Her eyes flick to mine. "First?" She shakes her head. "No, but..."

I ignore the fact that she just clenched around my fingers still buried inside her, exactly where my cock wants to be—is begging to be. "But?" I'm not going to like whatever she says next.

"Never like that. And never by someone's else's hand."

I capture the back of her neck, sitting her up as I stand. Her forehead is warm when mine touches hers, our eyes locked. "Are you a virgin?"

Instead of being shocked or insulted, her hand slides up to rest over my heart, and her lips don a soft smile. "No, I've just been with idiots, apparently."

"Apparently." Relief floods me that I don't need to worry about being her first, but I can't help the steel in me that says, *I'll be your last.*

"You have lost orgasms to make up for." I sweep her into my arms, and she giggles at my exuberance as I head to my bedroom. "Let's remedy that."

"I can't," I pant.

His green eyes shine with determination and want as he stares up at me from his position between my legs. "Yes, you can. One more. Then I'll fill you with my cock." The thought has me squeezing around his fingers. "That's it. Keep thinking about my cock."

"You keep saying that." I clutch the covers in my hands, my body reacting to his every breath, gaze, word, touch, lick, and suck.

He chuckles. "I mean it every time, then you come, and I just want to drive you over the edge again." He licks my clit and pops his head up, the lower part of his face covered in evidence of his hard work. "I swear. This time—one more orgasm—and my cock is all yours."

31

He's made me come so many times, I can't even count. I think some of them ran together, piggy-backing on the one before, or the one after. I don't even know. I don't see how I can have another, but the idea of his cock—and seeing this magnificent man naked is all it takes to have my body racing again.

"Just like that, beautiful," he mumbles against my most private parts. Parts no man has ever made sing like he does. He's a maestro, and I'm his devoted instrument. He strums, and I sing. A perfect chord of harmony and mastery.

When it hits, I nearly stop breathing, my heart ready to explode in my chest, but instead, it's my orgasm that detonates and has me arching off the bed, a scream ripping from my lips, and the man between my thighs grips me tight to keep me locked to his sucking embrace as he takes me over the edge, and then eases me down with gentle kisses and tender caresses.

"Fuck. You're a dream." A naked Fin settles over me. My shirt's still on—I insisted—but I'm naked from the waist down. His hand fists his impressive condom-covered cock. "You sure?"

Is he kidding? The man just gave me a million orgasms, and still I want more. "You promised," I remind him.

"That I did." He slides in on a groan, his eyes on our connection before they glide up to mine. "I'll always keep my promises to you, Marguerite."

"Oh, fudge." The way he says my name with such reverence has me gripping his shoulders as he fills me to the brim. My eyes water. It's too much. *He's* too much.

"Breathe, baby." He kisses my cheek and along my chin until I get a full breath.

Finally, I meet his gaze and nod.

"Okay?" He wants my words.

"Yeah, you're just a lot to take." And I don't mean just physically. He's the perfect man. But he can't be mine. I have to remember this is just physical. It's just sex.

"You're good for my ego." He swivels his hips, making me gasp. "You're so fucking perfect."

His words ring in my ears as his mouth seeks mine. If he only knew how not perfect I am.

I'm wrapped in his arms, our kiss never breaking, his hips thrusting at the perfect rate and angle to fuel another orgasm. How in God's name is that even possible? His groans become guttural and his movements jerky. He picks up the pace, chasing his release.

The thought of this man of steel coming apart for me has my eyes pricking with tears and my orgasm ratcheting up with his. Each thrust, each moan, each tremor as my hands traverse and knead every part of him I can reach, has him losing more and more control. I feel powerful with him.

He groans into our kiss as he jabs his release into me, sending me flying so high I fear I'll never land safely again. When I come, he's there, feeding my release, stretching it out, holding me tight, kissing me deeper. Every ounce of this man is focused on me. And the topper, he catches me as I fall with tender strokes and slow kisses, his racing heart coaxing mine into submission.

This man. He can't be human. No one can fuck this beautifully and be so present. It's a gift. It's a dream.

I need to wake up.

I don't ever want to wake up.

# *Seven*

I JERK FROM SLEEP, MY ARMS EMPTY. PANIC HITS ME like a sledgehammer. I didn't wait nearly two years for my girl to have her disappear on me. I glance at the dark bathroom. Hearing only silence, I throw off the covers and grab my slacks, forgoing underwear. I don't plan on having them on long once I find her.

I stride from my room, noting her clothes are missing—those she let me remove. I don't know what's up with her keeping her shirt on. I can only assume she has body image issues or is embarrassed by her small breasts? They were heavenly to me—even through the fabric, I still enjoyed the hell out of them.

Across the living room, I spot her slipping from the hall bath. The light highlights she's dressed and ready to escape before she plunges us in darkness when she flips the bathroom light off. She hasn't spotted me. Silently, I step into the living room, watching her creep to the entryway.

"Going somewhere?"

She yelps, her hand flying to her chest. "Joseph and Mary! You scared me."

I stifle my chuckle at her G-rated cuss. "You were sneaking out. Why?" I cross my arms and wait. I don't want to make this easy on her. I want her to feel my disappointment.

Two years of flirting around our attraction led to the best sex of our lives, and she's running out on that like a thief in the night?

Instead of hiding in the dark like I thought she might, she steps

34

forward and flicks on the kitchen light, bathing herself in a halo from above. "I didn't figure you'd bargained for a sleepover."

*Bargained?* She's right. She's not at all what I *bargained* for. She's much more. Breathtakingly so. I step into the light and pull her to me, my hands clasped around her waist. "No? What part of last night made you think I was ready for you to leave?"

When she doesn't answer, I prop her on the island, set her purse aside and slip between her legs, forcing her skirt to ride up her thighs. My eyes caress her creamy skin seconds before my fingers blaze a trail to the promised land. I suck in a breath when I find her bare. I guess she couldn't find her panties I stole on my second trip to the bathroom to dispose of the condom and get a washrag to clean her up.

"Was it the way I licked you that made you think I wanted you to leave?"

"No," she answers, whisper-soft.

"Hmm." I push two fingers inside her, my cock going rock hard at the feel of her, wet and welcoming. "Was it the way you came on my fingers over and over again?" I stroke her, my thumb on my other hand teasing a nipple beading below her shirt and bra.

"No." Her head falls back, her eyes closed.

I nibble her ear and breathe, "Maybe it was the way my cock was buried inside you, then?"

"Fin." Her eyes meet mine.

"Yeah, baby?"

"Please."

I tease her clit. "Please what?"

"Inside me," she pants. Her hands rest behind her as she leans back, spreading her legs.

Fuck she's beautiful.

"I am inside you." I finger fuck more aggressively in case she's forgotten.

Her shoes hit the floor as she reaches for my unzipped slacks. My cock sticks straight up, waiting for permission to come out and play.

"This." She grabs me, unable to wrap her hand completely around my shaft. I hiss from the pleasure of her touch.

"You want my cock, Margot?" I lean forward and kiss her hard. "Take it out and put it inside you." I pass her the condom I snagged on my way out of the bedroom. A guy's gotta be prepared.

"You're so dirty," she mewls.

I step out of my pants when she slides them down, my cock falling into her hand. "My girl likes dirty." I bite her neck and suck lightly as she strokes me, and I pull her skirt up her hips. Her bare ass hits the cold marble counter.

I help her out with the condom she seems shy about. But I won't let her off the hook on the other thing. "Put me inside you. Show me what you want."

She shudders and grips me, teasing herself and me with my cockhead at her entrance.

"Margot," I growl with impatience.

When she slides me in, I grip her hips and slam home, pausing, eating up her reaction as she squirms to adjust. I've been inside her three times now, each time better than the last. "Okay?"

She nods but catches my glare. "I'm good. Really," she confirms what her body is telling me. I needed her words all the same.

Just like I needed her to put me inside her. I could do it, of course, but she needs to admit what she wants. I don't want her regrets. I want her participation. Her passion. Her fire. Her body writhing below me as I pound our release free.

"Does it feel like I want you to sneak out on me?" I drill my point home.

"No. It feels… Ohhhhh," she moans.

"No more sneaking out, right?"

"Yes."

Her one-word answer turns to screams of "yes" as I nail her to the counter, wringing a couple of orgasms out of her before I find my own release. Then I carry her back to my bed, wrap myself around her, and keep her where she belongs for as long as I can.

I arrive at the office with the taste of her on my tongue.

I showered and dressed, but I couldn't stand the idea of leaving without saying goodbye. She leaves tomorrow. Returning to Austin. Alone. A state I'm not too happy with, but I understand why Sam decided to transfer to SMU. It's what's best for her and Joe, but it's not what's best for Margot. I sense her hurt. Her disappointment.

Maybe as a consolation prize, I woke her up the nicest way I could imagine—my mouth on her pussy.

When she cried out my name and came like the sexy goddess she is, I did it again. Then as she fell back asleep, I washed my face, brushed my teeth and left her snoozing in my bed.

My cock has just returned to its suitable-for-business state when my phone rings. Margot's name and smiling face pop up on my screen. I took a picture of her at the funeral. She has a way-off look in her eyes as she stares into the distance, her dark tresses lightly blowing in the wind and the sun kissing her cheek. It's a picture that says so much about the depth of the woman I just had the best sex of my life with.

"You're awake already?" I thought for sure she'd sleep for another hour or so. "I must not have done a good job."

Her laugh is lightning in a bottle. "You did just fine." She sighs as if she's envisioning me between her legs. My cock stirs, and I try to think of anything but her. "Better than fine. It was amazing. All of it."

So much for not thinking of her. "It was. I'd like to see you again before you leave."

"I… I don't know if I can."

I grimace when Joe walks in my office. Putting my back to him, I lower my voice. "I understand. It was great to see you."

"Same." She's quiet a moment. "Maybe I can. I'll let you know. But if not, please know I really enjoyed spending time with you."

"Me too. I'm sorry if I won't get to see you again before you leave. But... I'd like to... Check in... See how you are from time to time."

"Maybe you could make a booty call to Austin."

I laugh despite not being crazy about her seeing herself as just a hook up. "Yes, I'd like that."

Joe clears his throat behind me.

"Joe just walked in."

Margot chuckles. "Tell him *hi.*"

"I don't think that's wise."

"I suppose not." I hate the disappointment in her voice. But I can't be flaunting what happened between us around my family—they'll put pressure on it, and it's too delicate. It's too new, and I'm not sure how it'll all play out. She'll be in Austin for at least another year. Maybe longer, depending on where she applies to medical school. Shit, she could be moving across the country in pursuit of her dream of being a heart surgeon in whatever city she ends up... Maybe another country. How often am I likely to bump into her if she's working for Doctors Without Borders somewhere deep in South America?

I bridle the unease building in my gut. The thought of never seeing her again doesn't sit well with me.

"I should get dressed and get out of your hair."

"No rush. Take your time. Victor will give you a ride home when you're ready. Just text him."

"That won't be awkward or anything."

"He's expecting your call." He's head of security. Plus, I want to cut off any ribbing with telling him upfront what he'd find on the security footage. He reviews the tapes daily to ensure we don't have any breaches.

"Got it. I guess I'll see you when I see you."

God. I hate the sound of that even more. "Soon," I promise.

"Bye, Fin."

"Goodbye." Marguerite.

When I turn, my brother's observant stare is already on me. I'd forgotten he was in the room.

How much did he hear?

Does he suspect?

If he does, he doesn't let on.

We jump right into the reason for me summoning him to my office. But my mind drifts to the top of MCI's Alpha tower where Margot is lying in my bed or using my toiletries or my shower as she gets ready to leave.

A thought that both thrills and saddens me.

# Eight

"**Y**OU LEAVING ALREADY, GIRLY?" MY DAD'S appearance at my door isn't surprising. What *is* surprising is the fact he's sober.

"Yeah, I have to get back to Austin and find a place to live." The harsh reminder that I'm basically homeless has me wanting to hide under a rock instead of facing the next year alone.

It's a somber thought. Time to make new friends.

"Need any help loading up your car?" The glimpse at the dad he used to be has my eyes glistening and wishing I was sticking around to enjoy this rare moment.

"Sure." I point to my suitcase. "That's the last one." I've loaded everything else in the trunk already. "Then that's it." I glance around my childhood room. Pink and yellow tapestries scream at me from a youthful place of wanting to feel sunshine and spring all year round. Flowers, patterns, it didn't matter. If it was yellow and pink, I plastered it to my wall, hung it, or threw it on my bed. It still makes me smile. I still love sunshine and spring and flowers, most of all. New life, blooming at its peak of life.

*Have I missed my bloom?*

Ignoring that thought, I make one last check for any missed items. Finding nothing, I catch my reflection in my dresser mirror. My high ponytail shows off my neck that's supporting my halter sundress of— you guessed it—yellow and pink. I smile, not realizing I'd dressed to match my room, carrying sunshine and flowers with me as I leave.

Quick goodbyes—my forte—and barely a wisp of a tear, then I settle into my car, praying it makes the drive to Austin without incident. My Mustang may be old, but she's been good to me—and she's a classic. *Just another year, baby. You can do it*, I urge as I start her up. A little encouragement never hurts.

She roars to life with a satisfying rumble. She'll never go out of style, and I'll never give up on her.

I call Mom as I merge onto the highway, leaving her a voicemail to let her know I love her, and I'm hitting the road. She works the early shift most days. She doesn't mind. She loves her NICU babies and doting on their parents. She was a nurse before I was born. She's the reason my sister, Jenny, is in nursing school and why myself and my brother, Zeke, want to be doctors. Though, I have added reasons as well.

Rubbing my sternum, I let out a breath. *Should I call him?* I'm still tender from my night with Fin. I knew he was a man to be reckoned with, but I never thought the buttoned-up charmer would be a sex god. The things he did to my body. I had no idea. Not a clue.

He's educated me now. Only, I'm sure no man could even come close to his perfection. He's not perfect. I know that. Still. There's something so perfect about a man who can make my tone-deaf body sing in perfect harmony with his.

I jump when my phone rings, but nearly freeze when I see Fin's name. I blush as if he could read my thoughts.

"Hello?" Jeez, could I sound any more timid?

"Margot." His voice is the kind of husky that makes me believe he was thinking of our night together too. "Where are you?"

I smile at his no-hello phone skills. "I'm in my car. Heading to Austin."

"You were leaving without saying goodbye?" His tone infers we've already covered how he feels about me sneaking out on him. But I'm not sneaking.

"I've left town many times, *Finley*. You never cared before." I can give *tone* just a good as he can.

If I could see his confident face, I've no doubt he'd be wearing his one-dimpled smile. He doesn't mind my sass, and I love giving it to him—when I'm not feeling shy and self-conscious.

"I know how you taste, Marguerite."

*Holy moly.* I swallow the saliva that just pooled in my mouth.

"I know how you moan and shake right before you come."

*Oh, man, I wouldn't mind that right now.*

"I know how your tight pussy strangles my cock when you fall apart for me."

*Joseph and Mary, this man.* My walls contract as if he's inside me.

"Come tell me goodbye. Now," his bark is nearly as delicious as his bite.

"Ask nicely." I fan my face, heat blooming… Everywhere.

"I'll be waiting at my place. Come say a proper goodbye, Pixie. Please." He hangs up.

Which is good because the only reply I have is the moan that escapes as goosebumps ripple across my skin.

With shaky hands, I take the exit to MCI Towers.

I might have been too harsh. But the idea of her leaving without even a phone call rubs me the wrong way—and makes me want to rub her in all the right ways so she remembers whose touch she's going to miss.

My cock, doing its man of steel impression, is difficult to ignore, but ignore it I do. I order in lunch. Set the dining room table. And wait.

I'm not much for waiting, though my calm exterior would beg to differ. I'm a patient man, normally. I've waited for Margot for nearly two years. Timing is still not perfect, but if I've learned anything from Joe and Sam's relationship woes, there is no such thing as perfect timing.

There is only now.

Tomorrow is not guaranteed, and even if it were, it might not be what you expect.

I pace to the wall-to-wall windows in my living room. Below, Margot's classic yellow Mustang is just parking out front. A satisfied warmth fills my chest.

I should have told her to park in the garage. Next time. I'm too eager to suggest it now.

My Pixie's knock sounds a few minutes after lunch is delivered.

*Perfect timing.* The irony is not lost on me. Perhaps it exists; it's just rarely accommodating.

Opening the door, the sight of my girl in a yellow sundress with pink flowers has a smile teasing my lips. It's perfect. She's a ray of sunshine in my all-too-gray existence.

"I'm glad you stopped by." I catch her warm hand and pull her inside, brushing my lips across her cheek. *Fuck, she smells like sunshine and honeysuckle.*

"Not that you gave me much of a choice." She squeezes my hand before setting her purse on the entryway table, her fingertips sliding across the marble top as she coquettishly glances back at me and slips into the living room.

*Yeah, I remember what happened on this table, my sprite.* I get hard every time I look at the damn thing.

"You always have a choice, Pixie."

"Something smells good." She ignores my statement.

I'll have to reiterate my point later. She jumps, her breath hitching when I graze her back, urging her forward. "I ordered lunch, hoping you'd be hungry."

The wattage of her smile lights me up in unexpected ways. "I'm famished." She looks relieved, as if she expected me to rip her clothes off the moment she walked in the door.

Not that I hadn't considered it.

Seated with our plates full of roasted chicken and vegetables, Caesar salad, and crusty bread, I watch as she digs in and groans her delight. She might be slender, but she's not shy when it comes to food. I appreciate her enjoyment; so much so, I have to look away before I become inconveniently hard.

"Are you looking forward to school starting? What's your plan when you get back?"

Her eyes widen like she hadn't expected small talk.

"I'm... I am looking forward to school starting. Though, I don't feel like I've had much of a break with summer school. But it's necessary. I want to finish my bachelor's degree this year, and as long as everything goes as planned, it should happen."

*Goes as planned.* Life rarely does. "Let me know if there is anything I can do."

She sets down her fork and wipes her hands across the cloth napkin in her lap, nervousness riddling her demeanor. "I... Uh... There is one thing." She clears her throat. "I was hoping you could talk to your parents about giving me a few weeks to find a place to live—"

"What do you mean?" The back of my neck prickles.

She takes a drink of iced tea. "When I came home for the summer, I didn't realize... I hadn't *planned* on moving. So... I need to get back, find a place to live, and get my stuff packed up. I assume someone will come get the rest of y'all's stuff." She motions round the room. "The furniture and stuff. I, uh, think Sam and Joe even have clothes there still. But I'll know for sure once I get home. If I could just get a few weeks, I'd appreciate that." Her gaze bounces around the room and lands on her fidgeting hands.

She's out of sorts, and I don't like it. "Margot, did someone say you need to move out?"

"No... I... Well, Sam's not going to be there and..." She motions to me. "Y'all have all graduated. I assumed your family would be selling the place, or at the very least expect me to move out for new tenants."

I could strangle Joe and Sam right now. Did they even stop to consider what it would mean to Margot when Sam decided not to return to Austin? I know they're busy being in love and planning their wedding, but they need to take other people's needs into account. Namely, Margot's.

Scooting my chair back, I motion to her. "Come here, Pixie."

The tentativeness in her movements has me fighting frustration upon frustration. When she's fully on her feet, I snag her around the waist and pull her on my lap, garnering her eyes with a finger under her chin. "You don't need to move."

"But—"

"No buts." I cradle her cheek, my fingers sliding over her silky hair, wishing it was down for my fingers to sink into. "I own the house, Margot. Not my parents."

Shock widens her already large and expressive eyes. "What... You?"

"You can stay there as long as you want, even if it takes you ten years to finish school."

She laughs and swats my chest. "Don't jinx me, Fin. I have to finish this year. I. Have. To."

I chuckle at her adamancy and relish her relaxing in my hold. "However long it takes, you will always have a place to live. I don't want you to worry about it. You have enough on your plate. If this is one thing I can do for you, I'm more than happy to."

"I'll pay you rent."

"No. No, you will not." There's no compromise here. "And before you think my generosity comes with strings. It doesn't. What happens between us will not affect your living situation. You have my word on that. I'll even put it in writing if it'll make you feel better."

"I trust you." Her eyes seek mine, and I gladly lock onto hers.

"I'm happy to hear it." Her trust means everything. "But I'm serious. No rent or payments of any kind are expected or needed."

She nods. Her hands slip up my chest. "Shall we kiss on it?"

Want rushes through me like a tidal wave. I clench my jaw and fist her dress to keep from slamming my mouth to hers. "As long as it doesn't give you the wrong impression. I don't expect sex as payment."

Her smirk is devious. "Understood." She leans in, her breath teasing my lips. "Kiss me, Finley. Give me a proper goodbye."

My growl can't be helped. I've been patiently waiting to taste those lips again, to feel her against me, under me, shattering around me. "Pixie." I nip at her lips. "A proper goodbye will take hours." Days, if I had my way.

"Then what are you waiting for?"

Nothing. Absolutely nothing.

The crash of our joining is voracious, devoid of conscious decisions other than making her come as many times as possible before I have to let her go.

And let her go, I shall.

For now.

# *Nine*

## September

THE FIRST FEW WEEKS OF SCHOOL HAVE ME second-guessing my medical school aspirations. Beyond obtaining a bachelor's degree in science, I'm not sure I'm cut out for twelve more years of school, residency, and a specialized training fellowship. Maybe being a nurse like my mom and sister could be enough. Maybe even going with my first career choice, a teacher, would work too. I could be done in two more years and still be in my twenties instead of being in my thirties before I can even think of starting my own practice.

Medical school is no joke. Besides the cost, the life commitment is not something I'm sure I'm willing to give anymore. What kind of life will it be? I don't picture me being able to maintain a relationship, much less get married and have babies. Two things I desperately want. I know doctors are mothers too, but I have no doubt they sacrifice heavily for it. I've seen it. I've experienced it from the child's perspective, and my mom is a nurse—nowhere near the same level of educational commitment. I'm not sure I could do that to my theoretical children I'm not even sure I'll be blessed with.

If I'm having doubts before I even begin, how will I feel once I'm up to my neck in MCAT prep, medical school, and residency?

I look up from the stacks in the Life Science Library and catch the sight of a familiar face I haven't seen since school let out in the spring. Chills race down my body as he scolds me with his gaze. He's no Fin,

47

but jinkies, Raymond Burns does something to me. Something dirty and desperately needed right now. A distraction. A release.

Leaving his football buddies behind, he moves with determination and a look that tells me if I don't hurry and pack up my stuff, I'll be leaving it where it sits.

"You look good, Margot." He licks his lips and whispers, "Real fucking good."

"You don't look half bad yourself, Watt."

His face softens with a teasing smile. He loves it when I call him by his nickname, Watt, short for Wattage because he turns on like the flip of a switch, electricity zipping through his legs, making him run like lightning on the field. He's the team's fastest wide receiver. No one can catch him.

Sequestered in a secluded study room, out of sight, but not completely safe from discovery, his hands run down my body, squeezing and teasing, till he has my skirt hiked up and his cock nudged between my ass cheeks.

"You gonna let me kiss you, Margot?" He trails kisses up my neck, nipping and sucking.

I claw at the wall, need racing through me like I've never felt with Watt before.

It has to be the Fin effect. He knocked something loose, turned a switch, and now my motor is revved to a whole new speed.

"Not on the mouth," I remind him of my rules. No kissing. No beds. No face to face. I soften my delivery by pushing back and sensually rubbing against him.

"Someday, baby girl. You're gonna let me take you out on a date, kiss you till your lips are swollen…" He pulls my panties to the side and rams his cock into me in one fluid motion. "Fuuuuck!" He groans, his fingers digging into my hips, holding me securely as he thrusts at a speed that would have never made me orgasm before, but now—post-Fin—I'm about to come without any clit or nipple play.

Slipping his hand into the front of my drenched panties, he circles my clit. My legs start to shake. Breathlessly, on a silent scream, nearly balled up, wrapped in his arms, around his cock, I come. So. Hard.

"Gaaaah! Fuck, Margot. You're so fucking hot, turned on like a damn race car." He nips at my ear, still thrusting. "So fucking hot," he repeats over and over again until I come again, and he stabs his release into me, muffling his cries in my shoulder.

Things are always easy with Watt. It's just sex. Random hookups on campus. No pressure. No commitment. We have each other's numbers but never use them. We see each other, we fuck. If we don't, I'm sure he finds someone else. I don't know for sure, but I hypocritically wrinkle my nose at that thought. He was my exclusive fuckbuddy until school let out. Then no one until Fin.

"Something happened." Watt eyes me as he disposes of the condom, tucks himself away, and helps me right my clothes. "What changed?"

I shrug. I know what happened, or better yet, *who* happened. But I don't know why or what to make of it. And now, even in my post-orgasm haze, I feel like I just cheated on Fin. But I didn't. We made no promises. No claims. It's just sex.

But still. Guilt. Eats. At. Me.

"Let me take you to dinner." Watt pushes through my thoughts.

Shaking my head, I grab my bag. "I can't." I meet his gaze. "We can't."

Looking like I just stole his last piece of candy, he squares his shoulders. "Got it."

He doesn't have a clue.

I move until I'm looking into his blue eyes and notice his longer, shaggier hairstyle for the first time. "I don't date, Watt. I don't have time."

He brushes his thumb across my lips. "I just want a kiss, Margot." And then his smile grows as he admits, "And dinner, and to fuck you in a bed, chest to chest, skin to skin."

I pat his massive chest. He's not as tall as Fin, but he's solid and broad in the same way Fin is.

Something must flash across my face. "Who is he?" Watt asks, stepping back, his hands falling to his sides. He seems hurt by the idea of there being someone else, like he's not dipping his dick in every girl he can.

I shake my head. "No one." I motion to the door. "I have to go."

"Yeah, I see that."

Backing out of the room, I give him my best cheerful smile. "I'll see ya when I see ya."

"Ya, Margot. See ya when I see ya." His smile dims, never reaching his eyes.

As I walk out of the library, I can't help the feeling I left a part of me behind. Not a part that belongs to Watt, but a part that belongs to Fin.

But that's crazy.

I don't belong to Fin.

I don't belong to anyone.

I'm Margot. The bouncy girl who's friendly to most, but friends with few.

The girl you see and then forget just as fast.

The girl with the secret.

The scar I can't forget.

The wounds too deep to heal.

# Ten

THE HUM OF THE ENGINES LULLS ME INTO A STATE
of calm the ribbing from my brothers knocked loose. I didn't admit
anything, but when they found out about my trip to Austin, they
knew—suspected—Margot was my destination, not the city itself.
They're not wrong.

The flight from Dallas is quick, barely any time for work, or to
figure out what I'm going to say when I knock on her door. I own the
house, but I'd never enter without her permission. And now that I'm
nearly there, I'm not confident in my decision to surprise her with a
weekend visit. What if she has plans with someone else? What if she's
not even in town?

I scrub my hands over my face, knowing I just fucked up my hair,
and adjust the crease in my pants, thinking it'll ease the knot in my
stomach. It doesn't. I'm still in my suit, didn't want to waste time changing. Now I question if a more casual look would make my unannounced
visit more palatable.

My Pixie has me tied up in ways I'm not sure I can ever unravel.
I'm out of my comfort zone. Advice is my forte, fixing other people's
problems, a gift. But my own... Well... My charmed life hasn't left me
with much time for anything for myself. Stealing away like this is rare.
Spending an entire weekend with a woman, a new adventure. Wanting
to make a woman mine in every way possible, scary as hell.

But it's been over two years, and this feeling hasn't gone away.

The silver and black BMW i8 my assistant, Angela, has waiting for me at the private airfield would normally be enough to put a smile on my face and a swagger in my step. But even this sleek beauty can't touch the darkness of my thoughts.

What the hell am I doing?

*Living. Fucking living, for once.*

I don't have time for a relationship.

*Life is passing you by. Get onboard or be satisfied with window shopping.*

Fuck, I hate window shopping. I buy to experience, not fucking imagine how something would fit if I *might* buy it.

Jesus, I sound like Joe, arguing with himself before he decided to go for it with Sam. No, I wasn't in his head, but I might as well have been. Though four years apart, we have a unique connection, like twins. We think alike. Similar in more ways than we differ.

I pull into the driveway, next to her Mustang that's seen better days. I'd love to get my hands—my mechanic's hands—on her baby and get it fixed up for her. It's a classic 1965 Ford Mustang GT Fastback in godawful yellow, but it makes me smile. The color is so her, bright and cheerful, despite its weathered look.

Knocking on the door, I wait in anticipation, shaking off my nerves, praying she didn't witness it through the peephole. Then I frown—can she even see through the peephole? Seconds pass. I hear nothing, no footsteps.

I ring the bell and wait.

Nothing.

I pull out my phone and call her.

It rings and goes to voicemail.

Her car has a flat tire on the passenger side. I took her car being here as a sign she's home. Obviously, that was an inaccurate assessment. My scowl deepens as I wonder how long her car has been sitting here. A day… Two… Weeks? How has she been getting around?

My phone ringing floods me with relief when I see it's Margot calling me back.

"Pixie."

She sighs as if hearing my pet name for her was all she needed to ease her stress. She hasn't even said a word, yet I know her car not being drivable is adding to her already overburdened life. "It's nice to hear your voice. What's going on?"

"Where are you?"

"Just getting home. Why?"

I pace. "How are you getting home? You have a flat."

"I... Wait. How do you know that?"

"I'm on your front porch."

"What?!" she screeches as a beat-up Toyota pulls up to the curb. The back door opens and my girl steps out, a bag slung over her shoulder. The phone still pressed to her ear, she stares at me, not moving even when the car that dropped her off drives away. "You're really here."

The shakiness of her voice has me on edge. "What's wrong?"

She just shakes her head, biting her lips, and her hand holding the phone falls to her side. She sways like a stiff breeze might knock her over, and a lone tear slips down her cheek. And then another. Then another.

Fuck. Me.

Oh my God. What did I do?

I'm paralyzed. Stuck on the sidewalk in front of my home—no, not mine, his—staring at the man I think entirely too much about. The man who's going to turn around and leave the second he realizes what I've done.

The sight of him glazes over as my vision blurs with tears, but the pounding of his footfalls alerts me to him closing in on me.

He wraps me in his arms. "Margot, you're scaring me. What's wrong? What happened?"

I shake my head. "You…" I step back, my hand on his chest. "Can't…"

His hand grips mine on his chest. "I can. I promise you." He brushes my cheek. "Are you okay?"

The pained determination on his face hurts to my core. I continue to shake my head. "No." I'm not making any sense, but I can't find the words. My brain is riddled with shock and guilt, and I can't make heads nor tails of a single frigging thought. Other than the one pure, lightning-clear realization that I'm so happy to see him.

Before I know what's happening, Fin sweeps me in his arms. His lips press to my temple. "Whatever's wrong, Margot, we'll fix it. I promise."

"You can't fix this." I shudder a breath and sob, then bury my face in his chest, ashamed of falling apart before him. We aren't in *that* place in our relationship. We don't even have a *relationship*. And he sure as heck won't want one, much less be able to look at me, when he finds out.

Inside, he drops my bag on the kitchen table, then envelopes me in a hug. A hug so tight and safe, I almost believe it's possible. A hug that threatens to be everything I've ever wanted but feared could never be mine. A hug that could wash away my past, my scars, my uncertainty, and even my use of sex as a coping mechanism.

No, his magical embrace couldn't possibly do that.

"Pixie." He holds my face in his hands, his thumbs swiping at my tears, his soft gaze locked with mine. "Why do you smell like sex?"

# *Eleven*

SHE CRUMPLES. RIGHT BEFORE MY EYES, SHE SLIPS from between my hands and falls to the floor in a mass of tears and sobs.

Jesus, fuck, my girl smells like another man, but I can't for the life of me keep my anger burning. I want to. I want to be so fucking mad at her. But she's devastated. Like she cheated on me when we both know that's not the case.

We aren't together.

We never made promises of fidelity—or any promises, for that matter, except no lies.

And yet she's undone like she broke something between us.

"Margot, baby." I pick up her noodle of a body and carry her to her bedroom and straight to the adjoining bathroom, setting her on the counter.

I move back enough to see her cast-down stare. Her tears still come, but she's more settled... Or resolved.

Tipping her chin, I capture her gaze. "Pixie."

She blinks, clearing her vision.

"I need you to focus on me. On what I'm about to say."

She nods, her chin trembling under my touch.

"As much as the idea of another man touching you pains me—angers me."

Her tears pick up speed.

"Baby, listen." I kiss her wet cheek. "I'm not angry." Except, perhaps, at myself for not putting parameters around our relationship. *Relationship?* Fuck, I don't have time for one of those. "We didn't label what it is we're doing. We made no promises."

"No." Her voice seems small, but not doubtful.

"I surprised you." I slip off her shoes. "I should have called. Given you a heads-up." I kiss her nose and brush her hair off her shoulders. Her tears dry up as her big brown eyes follow my every movement. "I won't make that mistake again."

She frowns.

I clarify. "Next time I'll ask. I won't just show up."

She nods, her face unreadable.

I'd venture to guess I've said something that's not setting right. I'll fix it, but first—I motion to the shower over my shoulder. It's an ass thing to do, but I'm going to do it anyway. "We can talk. After you shower."

I can't talk to her smelling like sex and a man who's not me.

I'm trying to be adult here when everything in me is screaming to fuck her until she knows she only belongs to me.

She doesn't.

I can't claim her.

She's. Not. Mine.

I walk out of the bathroom, closing her bedroom door behind me, and pray she doesn't throw me out when she comes to her senses.

I needed that shower, not only for the practical application of getting clean. I didn't do it because Fin asked me to. I was relieved when he brought me to my bathroom. I was relieved when he didn't try to undress me. And I was triple relieved when he didn't try to take a shower with me.

All sanity may have left my body when I saw him on the porch and realized I reeked of sex and another man. It doesn't matter that we aren't in a committed relationship—I'd never be so cruel as to flaunt my sexual escapades in front of Fin, or any man I was occasionally fucking. Even Watt, whom I don't have any kind of a relationship with outside of our campus encounters, yet I'd never come to him smelling of another man.

See other people, but at least shower in between. I shudder.

Teeth brushed, my wet hair in a messy bun, yoga pants and a t-shirt donned, I find Fin in the kitchen. Cooking. The kitchen is nicely stocked, something I'm proud of. I can't afford to eat out, so I always have enough food for the week ahead. Though, today being Friday, supplies are limited to staples like bacon and eggs, which he's expertly fixing now.

"It smells good."

His head pops up, a genuine smile on his face as his eyes rake over me. "I hope you don't mind. I made myself at home. Thought food was a good place to start. I hope you haven't eaten."

"I haven't." I snag a piece of bacon on my way to the refrigerator. "And this is your house, Fin. You can do whatever you want."

After pouring a glass of orange juice, I turn to ask if he wants some, but freeze when I catch his eyes, already on me, his brow creased. "What'd I say?"

"You shouldn't give me such latitude, Pixie. I'll take it and then some."

I suck in a breath, not expecting the sexual tension that hits me full frontal. "Maybe I want you to. Maybe I *need* you to."

"Fuck." He drops the spatula and turns off the stove. "You don't know what you're asking for."

"No? I'm asking anyway." I brush my hand over his chest as he steps into me.

"What do you need, Marguerite?" His piercing green eyes drill into my soul.

"To know I didn't mess things up between us. I know we're not... Anything. But I—"

"You didn't." He cradles my cheek and the back of my neck with his big hand. "But I'd like us to talk about what we want. I consider you a friend." He presses his forehead to mine. "Shit, Margot, you're practically family." His breath wafts across my skin. "I thought I fucked up by coming here unannounced—"

"No." I pull back to see his face. "I starting crying the minute I saw you. I was so happy to see you—to see a…"

*"To see a… Finish that statement,"* he urges.

"To see a *friendly* face." Admitting that hurts more than it should.

His brow rises. *"Friendly face?"*

"Yeah, everything has changed. I mean… It's fine. It's just not what I expected." I scan the room. "The house feels lonely most of the time. It's so quiet without Joe and Sam, and even Jace, you and Matt here sometimes. This house was bursting with life last year. Now, it's a reminder of how alone I am—how much things have changed."

How desperate I am to finish school and start my life—to *have* a life.

*But what kind of life?*

"God, Margot. I hate that for you. I hate that their happiness has caused you to be unhappy."

"Don't, it's not like that." I wave it off. "I'm just having a pity party. Reality of what my life has become hit hard these past few weeks. It's fine. I'll be fine."

"Truth, Margot. Remember?"

How can I forget? Fin has a way of seeing me when others don't. And when he can't see all he wants, he insists I tell him the truth. But often, I can't give him that, so he only gets silence.

Like now.

"What about the guy?"

I cringe. "There's no guy."

One eyebrow tips. "Lie."

Jeez, this man. "Okay. There's a guy. But not in the way you're thinking."

Both of his eyebrows go up, and I laugh.

"Okay." I throw my hands up and step around him. "I don't know *what* you're thinking. There *is* a guy. We meet up every once in a while. It's not a thing. We don't date. We don't kiss. Clothes don't even come off. It's just sex at the bare minimum. A stress reliever. A distraction."

"A distraction from… Your life?" He steps toward me.

"Yeah."

"Your stress?"

"Yeah."

He moves closer. "Your loneliness?"

I bite my lips and give a curt nod.

He backs me to the kitchen table. "And you don't kiss him?"

I shake my head and offer a redundant, "No."

"Has he ever seen you fully naked?"

"Uh-uh."

He smiles. His lips press softly to mine, teasing gently. "We need to eat." He pulls away.

Okay? My head swims from the about face.

"You're going to need your strength." He smirks over his shoulder as he plates the scrambled eggs and bacon, which have probably gone cold.

Not that I care.

"Pixie?"

"Yeah?"

"I'm going to kiss the hell out of you and then get you naked."

Oh, no.

# *Twelve*

ONCE AGAIN, WE HAD SEX, LOTS OF IT, AND HER t-shirt stayed on the entire time. I don't know how she did it. I was determined to get her naked, skin to skin. Her bare breasts in my mouth, under my gaze, and the feel of them in my hands. I wanted to *see* all of her, worship all of her. Everything was going great. I was making progress, nearly there. Then bam, some jedi mind trickery, and the next thing I know, I'm buried inside her, coming like a rocket launcher.

Then she did it again. And again.

Jedi. Mind. Tricks.

*I'm* even sore from how much sex we had last night. I had a point to prove. I had a guy I needed to knock out of her memory. But I never got that damn shirt off her body.

I showered alone, unable to convince her to join me. She's hiding something. Something she doesn't want me to see. Or she's body conscious in a way I'm not picking up on. Margot is a sizzling ball of desire when she's turned on. She doesn't hold back. She's not shy, yet apparently, she is—about something. And I'm pretty sure her "sun sensitivity" can't be triggered by a bedroom lamp.... My Pixie is hiding something. I'm determined to figure it out.

Yet my brain turns off when she gets me hard.

Or she's a jedi. That's still a possibility.

I took her to dinner—a real date. I may not be able to commit to a boyfriend-girlfriend situation, but I want more than just sex. I enjoy her company. Her laugh. Her quiet ease I've only experienced when it's the two of us. I don't get the overly cheerful Margot she gives the world. I like to think I get the true Margo. The one who's working hard to achieve her goals, has demons she's determined to ignore or keep hidden, and takes on family responsibilities that shouldn't be hers. Sounds hauntingly familiar.

I like—really like—the Margot she is with me, more than I should and yet not nearly as much as I fear I could. I'm certain she could be *the one*, but I won't let myself go there. Our lives are too busy to even consider this being a *the one* kind of situation. If I dwell on it, I'll have to recognize how much I'm fucking this up by not wrapping up the deal, by even taking a chance on her slipping through my fingers.

So, yeah, not going there.

Now, we're at a UT football game, sitting on the fifty-yard line, close to the field in some pretty fucking impressive seats. One of the player's parents wasn't able to use their season tickets. Lucky us. Go Longhorns!

UT is my alma mater—my entire family's, actually. I haven't attended a game in years—but I watch them on TV religiously. I was on my feet cheering like a college freshman the second the band took the field. And forget about all the whooping when the team made their entrance. I was over-the-top excited. I was cheery Margot, for lack of a better description.

For the past few minutes, though, after a spectacular UT touchdown, Margot has become pensive and fidgety, her hands locked between her knees to keep them still. Her eyes are everywhere except on me, and I can't help but think it has to do with Watt Burns, whose eyes haven't left her since he made the last touchdown. If I were combustible, I'd be roasted Fin right about now as he throws his death glare my way every now and again.

I lean over, trying to figure out how he even found her in this sea of fans, and ask, "Are these, by chance, the wide receiver's parents' seats?"

Her head whips up so fast I fear she may strain a muscle. "Wha..." She swallows with effort and tries again. "How'd you know?"

Getting closer, eye to eye, I tell her a secret that's not much of a secret at all. "He can't stop staring at you—at us." I cock my head to the field, and her eyes dash that way before zipping back to me. "Is he your *there is no guy* guy?" I reference the guy she has sex with but not much else.

"I..." Her head falls to my shoulder. "I'm so sorry, Fin."

Fuck. I didn't really want to know that answer. Relief that she didn't lie mixes with jealousy I'm not proud of. He obviously wants more than just to be *some guy* to her. She has to see that, or maybe she does but she's not interested in more. Which is crazy. I've watched the sports shows. Everyone says Watt is as nice of a guy as they come. He's wicked fast and destined to play pro ball. What girl wouldn't want to lock that down?

Am I standing in her way? She lets me kiss her. I get her clothes off, at least the bottom half. Watt hasn't managed to do either. I don't even want to think about what she said the first time I made her come—no one else ever had.

Why am I different?

Do I *want* to be different?

Does that mean I'm committing to forever with her?

What if he hurts her?

What if *I* hurt her?

Jesus Christ, am I getting in over my head?

I capture her hand and squeeze. "I'm not sure I'm the one you should be apologizing to."

Her head pops up, worry dulling the sparkle in her brown eyes. "Why do you say that? He doesn't..." she trails off as her gaze lands on Watt.

On the sidelines, facing us instead of the field, his helmet held in one hand as he runs his hand through his disheveled hair, Watt gives a slight wave, his brows arching in question.

She smiles and waves back.

"Holy nutcrackers. I messed up." Biting her lip, she turns to me. "Do you want to go?"

"That's entirely up to you. But I will say, leaving might mess with his head even more. Plus, staying would give you an opportunity to talk to him afterwards to perhaps clear the air." My response is easy, calm, and entirely too evolved when, really, all I want is to have an inappropriate PDA moment, claiming her as mine, right here, in front of Watt and everyone.

But I can't do that.

She is not mine.

A fact that has been drilled home by coming here to find she'd just had sex with another guy, and now having my nose rubbed in it just proves how much she is *not* mine. But now I worry, maybe she wants to be.

And even scarier—maybe I want her to be too.

I can't believe I'm doing this—at *Fin's* suggestion. I thought coming tonight would be nice. A way to bond with Fin over more than just sex. Yet, here I am waiting for my somewhat regular hook-up to exit the locker room.

Fin made a phone call. Besides being a huge Longhorns supporter, his family owns MCI, the largest tech company in the United States. Of course he has contacts. Contacts that afford him access to the team and coaches. He probably could have gotten us box seats.

Do they even have box seating? That idea is so far out of my price range, I can't even answer that question. This is just another example of how far Fin is out of my league. I can't even afford to buy food at the game. Fin could buy the whole stadium if he so desired.

Fin nudges my shoulder. "I'll just say hello, and then let you two talk."

"Hmm." I nod, examining my tennis shoes. Does that mean he's leaving? Or he's just giving me space to undo my mess?

When I started sleeping with Watt last year, it was beyond casual. He was good with my rules. He just laughed and said *whatever you want.* I mean, what guy wouldn't want to have random sex with no strings? It wasn't until the end of the spring semester when he started asking for more. Coffee? Dinner? Drinks? A kiss? I laughed it off or distracted him with sex. That was the point, wasn't it?

No strings. No hassles. No relationship.

And it was good! I thought… Maybe I thought it was better than it was because I hadn't felt what *more* could be like with the right guy. Does that make Fin the right guy because he's definitely *more?*

"Margot?" Watt's voice has my head lifting and the sour pit in my stomach rumbling to life. His eyes dart to Fin at my side.

"Hey, Watt," I manage without too much difficulty. He smiles. I point to the man next to me. "This is Fin McIntyre. He's practically my friend Sam's brother-in-law. You remember Sam?"

Watt's smile grows like hearing Fin's connection to me as anything other than my boyfriend makes his day. "Yeah, sure. She's engaged to that big guy, Joe, right?"

"Yes. Joe is my brother," Fin jumps in, sticking his hand out. "Impressive game, Watt. I'm sure the pros have been knocking down your door."

"Thanks, Mr. McIntyre." When Watt shakes Fin's hand, I swear Watt's shoulders broaden before my eyes. "As for pro ball, I'm focusing on finishing school first."

"That's a smart plan." Fin touches my hand and motions behind him. "I'll just be up the ramp. It was nice to meet you, Watt. Have a great season."

"Yeah, thanks. Nice to meet you too." Watt moves closer but doesn't say anything.

My eyes keep drifting to Fin, trying to figure out what he's thinking. Is he really mad and just good at hiding it, or does he really not care that I'm talking to the guy I've had more sex with than him? Fin's being so adult about this, I don't know how to take it. My gut tells me he's mature and not an ass. But the insecure, broken parts of me think Fin just doesn't care—he's here for the sex—nothing more. That this has to be some kind of manipulation, but I know that's crap from my past, not Fin. I think.

I've had enough toxic men in my life.

"You okay?" Watt touches my hair near my cheek. It's intimate and caring. Not the Watt I'm used to. I'm used to the Watt that has testosterone steaming out his ears when he spots me on campus, raring to get his dick wet.

But that's not quite fair either. He's been asking to give me more, not trying to take from me. I'm the one holding the line on my rules.

"I'm good." I look up and catch the concern in his blue eyes. "Thanks for the tickets. I'm sorry if my being here with Fin upset you. I didn't think about it. I'm sorry if it messed with your head—your game."

"Nah, you made me play harder. Every touchdown was for you." His cocky smile is bright but short-lived.

"You can't mean that." He hardly knows me.

"I do mean it." He glances past me. "Is he the one?"

"The one?"

Watt steps into me. I back up, but he presses me to the wall. I flash a look to Fin, but his head is down, face tipped the other direction. Not interested or bothered in the least. I press my hand to Watt's chest, my attention back on him.

"The guy who flipped your switch." He bends down, whispering, "The one who taught your body to come like that?"

Heat rushes to my face and pools in my panties. Fin flips all kinds of buttons, some good, some amazing, and some downright terrifying. "I can't—"

"Yeah." Watt comes to his full stature, moving back. "That's him."

"But we're not..." Not what? Fucking like we can't get enough? Not an item? Not compatible except in the bedroom? Aren't in the same plane of existence?

"You're not?" He looks hopeful.

I don't want to give him hope, but I can't lie to him either. "No." Do I wish we were? *Yes, I do.*

"Then have coffee with me on Monday. Meet me at your favorite coffee shop before your first class."

I scrutinize him. "How do you know where my favorite coffee shop is?"

His bright smile is back. "I know things about you, Margot Dubois."

Color me shocked. "Like what?"

"Meet me on Monday and find out."

It's just coffee. It's harmless. He's harmless. He's not Bobby. Just because I'm meeting Watt for coffee doesn't mean we're dating. We can be friends. But do I want more with him? I keep telling myself I don't have time to date, but amazingly enough I have time to sit alone in my house—Fin's house—and let the loneliness nearly strangle me. Watt's here. He's asking. Fin's not. "Okay."

He kisses me on the cheek, saying, "I'll see you bright and early, say 7:30 am. Plenty of time to talk before class."

I move to answer, but he's already heading up the ramp, shaking hands with Fin before winking at me and disappearing around the corner.

On a sigh, I muster the strength to walk toward Fin. He's still here. Maybe it's a good sign.

Or he's just too polite to leave me stranded on a Saturday night on the UT campus.

# Thirteen

"OH MY GOD, FIN!" HER TIGHT PUSSY HAS ME IN a death grip as she tumbles over the edge again. I think that's number three. One more.

She thought I was leaving her. That I was so upset by the idea of her being with Watt—or any guy—that I'd up and leave her at the stadium and make her find her own way home. Like she doesn't know me at all. But I have a feeling it's not really about me, the type of man I am, but more about the type of men she's known in her past. Like that Bobby character. He's bad news. I'm happy she's not even in the same town as him for most of the year.

She clamps a hand on my wrist, trying to stop my sensual assault on her clit. "Please, I can't."

"Believe me, Pixie, you can." *And you will.* When she clenches around me again, my balls burn with the need to come, but not yet. I need a distraction. "Tell about your car. Why haven't you fixed the flat?"

"What?! You want to talk about my car... Now?" Her hands grip the sheets, her body rising and falling with each thrust of my hips. She gasps and moans, on the verge of coming again.

Fuck. I fall forward, braced on one hand above her head. "Tell me," I bite through clenched teeth.

She nods, her eyes on me, her hands burning a trail up my chest. "Even if I fix the tire, the car's not drivable. It died on me the day after I arrived from Dallas. I'll get it fixed. Just... Not now."

The determination in her eyes, mixed with want as she pulls me down for a kiss, nearly does me in. The need to come and the need to give Margot everything she doesn't think she needs is overpowering. She licks and bites my mouth like she's fucking starving for me. *The feeling is mutual, baby.*

Hunger and deprivation are our common language. Giving more than we receive our motto. Yet, I can't stop the raging pull inside me to give her everything and damn the consequences.

She shudders and calls *my* name. My. Fucking. Name. Begging me to come with her. "Don't make me do this alone," she cries. A tear slips from the corner of her eye. I kiss it away and do the only thing I can. I come with her. Spectacularly. Riding it out until there is nothing left but two souls begging for more.

In the early hours, I slip free of her hold and dress. My gaze keeps returning to her sleeping form. Peaceful is the only way to describe her in this moment. The morning light seeping through the curtains, rays dance across her face. My Pixie.

Sunshine is her color.

Bright is her soul.

Longing is her creed.

I can't give what she deserves—everything. Not yet. Maybe not ever.

I make a few phone calls, place a note on the pillow beside her— where I slept—and do what I chided her for doing: I leave without a goodbye.

It's the only way.

Clean.

Disentangled.

Necessary.

I sleep late, waking to an empty bed. Silence the only thing to wish me good morning. I know. Before I spot the note on his pillow, I know. He's gone. He left some time ago based on the coolness of the spot he slept on.

Ignoring the note, I slip out of bed.

Ignoring my lone car in the driveway, I make coffee.

Ignoring my desire to not read the last words Fin thought to leave me with, I read his note anyway.

*I had to go. I'm sorry.*
*Fin*

Yeah, I could have done without reading that. I squeeze it in my fist, balling it up, and toss it in the trash, where all unrealistic dreams go to die.

Locking up my hurt and disappointment, I take a long, hot shower. My body may prefer a bath, but lingering in a tub with nothing to do but think is not what my mind—or my bruised ego—needs.

*Thinking* something is true is nowhere as painful as *knowing* it's true.

I knew getting involved with Fin was a bad idea. Not because he's a bad guy, but because he's not. He's one of the good ones. The rare breed of man who's alpha and gentle. He sees past my happy persona I thought I'd perfected beyond scrutiny. He sees me. And I was found to be lacking. Not worthy of his time.

Shaking off my disappointment for wanting someone I knew I shouldn't and don't even have time for, I pull out my books. It's Sunday. My day for homework and planning out my week.

But before I start, I pick up his pillow and take one deep whiff of his clean, manly scent. His cologne lingers like the memories of his touch. I allow myself to wallow in self-pity for a minute.

A minute more.

One more.

Enough.

I strip the bed in army sergeant precision, emotions tucked away, disappointment not even in my vocabulary. I toss the sheets in the washing machine with detergent, slamming the lid harder than it deserves, and scald the last two nights off my bedding in hot/hot cycle. They may tatter and fall apart, but at least they won't smell like *him*.

Taking a look around, envisioning every surface he might have touched, I get out the cleaning supplies and remove any final trace of him, or Sam and Joe. Everyone who's left me for better things. It's extreme, but my anger is keeping the tears away, and my determination feeding my ability to move forward without crumbling.

This will not break me.

Hours later, as my stomach rumbles for food and my eyes blur from reading, the doorbell rings, followed by a sharp knock.

I open the door to a man in a suit, well groomed, and a smile plastered to his face. "Ms. Marguerite Dubois, I presume?"

"Yes." I glance around him. What could he possibly want? Then I spot it. A yellow sports car sitting in the driveway right next to my dilapidated Mustang.

"She's a beauty." He motions to my car. "I can see you have an affinity for yellow. That '65 is a classic."

"It is." I fight the embarrassment bubbling its way up. It's obvious this man has money, lots of it. I don't know what dealership he's from or the model of the car he thinks he's delivering, but it's way out of my price range—a universe apart.

He holds out a manilla envelope. "Mr. McIntyre insisted I deliver this in person. Today." He clears his throat and nods to the envelope when I don't reach for it.

I step back, my hand on the doorknob, ready to slam the door in his face. "I can't take that." I couldn't even afford insurance on that car, much less take on the car payments. "I can't afford that."

Mr. Suit steps forward. "It's fully paid for, insurance too." He waves the envelope. "It's all in here, along with the title and keys." His smile grows more forced. "Mr. McIntyre ensured everything was taken care of. There's even a prepaid maintenance plan and gas cards to cover a few years of fuel. He thought of everything." He looks over his shoulder to the waiting car at the curb.

For a split second I wonder if Fin is sitting out there watching. Seeing how his dutiful weekend romp accepts his lavish gift for her silence. A parting gift to take the edge off. But then I spot the Mercedes dealership name written on the door panel. Mercedes? Jeez, Fin, what are you doing?

"As I said before. I can't accept it." I move to shut the door, but his hand slams against it, forcing it open.

Unease mars his fake smile from a moment ago. "You can't refuse, Ms. Dubois."

Anger surges through me. If I were a man this conversation would be completely different. "Remove your hand from my door before I call the police." I may be little but my bark is mighty.

He pulls his hand back like the door just singed it. "Uh, I'm sorry about that. It's just… Mr. McIntyre—"

"You tell *Mr. McIntyre* I refused delivery. *I'm* not scared of him."

"I can't do that, ma'am." His tone is curt as if he'll bully me into taking this car.

I step forward, grip the doorjamb and rise to my tiptoes. "You will. Or I will burn it and tell him you never delivered it in the first place." I slam the door in his face, fighting back tears for being so rude to a man just trying to do his job. I quickly lock the door to ensure he's not desperate enough to try and force his way inside.

I can't believe Fin.

I will not placate his guilt with a consolation prize. Nor am I a charity case that needs his help.

I did not ask for it.

I do not need it.

I may live in his house rent-free, but that does not mean he has free rein to give me whatever he pleases.

# Fourteen

## October

"SHE BLOCKED YOU." VICTOR HANDS ME MY phone.

"Why do you say that?" It's been radio silence for a month. I knew I fucked up the minute I snuck out of her bed. The nervous phone call from the dealership, telling me she refused my gift, only confirmed it. Her ghosting me since, the nails in my coffin.

He leans over, showing me the text messages Margot hasn't replied to, and then scrolls up. "The messages before you made an ass of yourself show *delivered*. These new ones don't show anything. Which means, more than likely, she blocked you."

"So, she hasn't even *seen* my texts?" None of them? Not my apologies? Not my groveling? The ever-present ache in my chest—I'd see a doctor about it if I wasn't certain it's because of her—tightens its grip.

"Nor your phone calls and voicemails."

"Shit." She thinks I'm an ass and left it at that. No room for error. No room to barter or make amends. She's just gone. Like that. So easily dismissed. It feels like a slap in the face. Her intention, I'm sure. I closed the door behind me, and she locked and barricaded it.

Victor sits back down in the chair facing my desk, next to Michael. Their asshole faces gleam, enjoying my misery entirely too much.

"Today's her birthday." I glance out the window, my voice sounding hollow. I wonder if she'll throw away the flowers I'm having delivered today.

"Her twenty-first birthday," Michael adds salt to my reopened wound.

"I'm aware. But how do you know?" These two and their security checks. I'm sure they have a portfolio on everyone who comes in contact with the business or my family.

"I pay attention. Plus, Sam was saying she needed to call and wish Margot happy birthday when I left their apartment this morning," Michael fills in the gaps.

That's good news. I'm sure Margot appreciates the contact. They've grown further apart since Sam decided not to return to UT.

"As much as I love witnessing you dipshits fuck up your love lives, there's an incident you should know about." Victor lays a folder on my desk.

I pull it to me, flipping it open it, and frown. "When?"

"Two days ago. He's in police custody, but the forty-eight-hour hold is nearly up. They'll have to charge or release him." Victor stands, hands on his hips, eyes on the report in front of me.

"Can they charge him?"

"If the woman presses charges. It doesn't look like she will." His unease at that notion matches mine.

"Has there been any contact with Margot?"

Victor shakes his head. "Nope. None."

"Do you have a tracker on her?" Michael asks.

"Her phone. It's been there since Sam's father was murdered." Victor grins, loving this cloak and dagger stuff. "Precautionary at that point, but then I kept it going once we became aware of Bobby, Sebastian's friend and Margot's ex."

I hate to acknowledge Margot being even mildly interested in a guy like that, but I have to believe he didn't start out being an asshole. Maybe he was really good at hiding it.

"But Bobby hasn't been anywhere near Margot?" I already asked, but the knot in my chest has a matching one in my stomach after seeing the photos of the woman Bobby assaulted a few days ago—I have to be sure.

"No. He's made no attempt to contact Margot. With her in Austin, they won't accidentally run into each other. But I have an alert set if he gets within five miles of her when she's in town and thirty miles when she's in Austin, just in case he takes a road trip."

"Let me know if anything changes." I close the folder, placing it in my top drawer to read later. Victor gave me a copy for this very reason.

"You need to come out with us tonight." Michael stands, his eyes flashing to Victor before settling on me, waiting on an answer.

On my feet, I button my jacket and grab my laptop for my next meeting. "I'm not interested in going to that club." They know this, yet they still insist on asking, hoping one day I'll change my mind. I won't.

If I want to get laid, I'll do it the old-fashioned way. I'll pick up a stranger in a bar, not a sex club. Neither of which hold any appeal.

The only woman who can hold my attention is living in another city, celebrating her birthday with someone other than me.

I'm living the life.

I leave those two jackasses talking about their plans for the night and head to a meeting with my father, the CEO of MCI. He's been hinting about wanting to move up his transition plan for when he hands over the company reins to me. I set aside my worry about Margot and any dream I may have had of me being able to offer her *more*.

There is no *more* to give.

I'm clean out of space, no matter how much I'm tempted to make room. I don't see how it's possible to do so and juggle all my family and business commitments, which are one and the same. Starting a family of my own seems impossible. I can't even manage to date a woman long distance, much less commit to a wife and kids.

That future I dream of will have to wait.

Watt kisses my cheek as he steps inside. "Happy birthday, beautiful."

I try not to blush at his compliment, though I did dress up, wanting to look beautiful for myself as much as for him. "Thanks. You look kinda hot yourself."

His eyes darken, and he runs a hand through his hair. "If I can't touch you, Margot, you can't tell me I look *hot*. That's just cruel."

He's right. "I'm sorry." But he does look hot. Then again, he always does. Proved by all the women chasing him around campus.

Since our coffee date a month ago, we've de-escalated to platonic friends. Not friends with benefits. I didn't like the way I felt when Fin showed up at my door and I reeked like sex with Watt. The shift between Watt and me isn't because of Fin. He was the catalyst, opening my eyes to how my encounters with Watt had truly made me feel. I was using sex as an escape, which isn't really objectively bad, except it was for me personally. It didn't sit right after being with Fin. He opened my eyes to how incredible sex could be. And I didn't want to chase that ideal, knowing I'd never find it—not like I had with Fin. Plus, my rules were stupid, meant to protect my heart and keep me safe from people like Bobby who showed me how much being naked and vulnerable could hurt.

So, yeah, Watt and I are just friends.

"Who are the flowers from?" Watt points to the massive vase of yellow and pink roses that arrives just after lunch. They're beautiful. I may have rejected Fin's earlier gift, but I could never turn down flowers, especially in my favorite colors. He was paying attention—because I never told him—and that means something. I just don't know what.

Guilt eats at me for cutting him off so decidedly without even a *thank you but no thank you* for the car. But he's the one who left first. He's the one who closed the door on what *might have been* by sneaking out while I lay sleeping.

When I take too long to answer, Watt gives me a knowing smile and a gentle touch to the back of my hand. "Fin?"

Unable to speak his name, I simply nod.

"There have to be four dozen roses. It must have cost him a pretty penny. And look at these." He touches the tip of one of the roses with yellow at the heart and pink toward the tips of the petals. "Beautiful."

"Yes, very." I turn away before the pang in my chest brings tears to my eyes.

"Can I read the card?"

*I'd rather you didn't.* "Sure." I close my eyes and pray he doesn't read it out loud. But it must be too much to ask for, as in the next breath Fin's words leave Watt's lips, and it just seems wrong.

*Margot,*

*Happy 21ˢᵗ Birthday! May these flowers brighten your day like you always do mine.*

*Take time for yourself today. Do something you <u>want</u> to do instead of everything you <u>need</u> to do. This is your life. This is your time. Take it with <u>no regrets</u>.*

*Yours, Fin.*

*P.S. Forgive me, Pixie. Please.*

"Holy shit." Watt stares at the card long after he finishes reading the last line. His captivated eyes meet mine. "Will you?"

"Will I what?" I feign ignorance.

"Forgive him?" I'm surprised by the plea in Watt's eyes, like he's on Fin's side.

Was I wrong to not accept the car?

Was I wrong to cut all ties with him?

"I don't know." Fin always wants the truth from me. This is my truth as it stands today.

I don't know if I can forgive him.

And even if I can, I don't think I can forget.

After dinner that night, Watt leaves, and Fin's words play in my head on repeat. *Do something you want to do.*

Toying with my phone, I pull up his contact and click unblock, my finger lingering over his number. I hold my breath, waiting for a mass of messages to inundate my phone as if they've been held off just waiting for me to let them in. But none do. Silence is all I hear—all I should have expected.

*Do something you want to do.*

*Do something you want to do.*

*Do. Something. You. Want. To. Do.*

The phone is ringing before I even realized I'd actually clicked his number.

My heartrate increases with each ring and tick of the clock.

I've nearly given up when he answers, "Margot?" His voice is like honey, but it's his rush of air as if he was running to the phone that has me doubting my impulsivity.

"Bad time?"

"For you, Pixie, there is no bad timing."

Jinkies, I'd forgotten what a smooth talker he is. But it doesn't feel like a line. It feels like the truth.

I sigh and settle onto my back on my bed, eyes on the ceiling. "How are you?"

"Honestly?" His tone lowers, and I can picture him leaning back in his desk chair, eyes on the ceiling, just like me.

"Only the truth between us, right?" I embolden and bite my lip on bated breath until he speaks.

"Yeah. If we have nothing else, we have the truth."

*Nothing else...* I really shouldn't have called. "I think I should go—"

"No," he jumps on my words. "Please don't." He clears his throat. "I screwed up, Margot. I shouldn't have left the way I did. It was cowardice. I'm truly sorry. Can you forgive me?"

"I don't know," leaves me in a whisper with no conviction and an absence of hope.

"I've been miserable. You wouldn't respond to any of my phone calls or texts. I broke something between us, and it's eating away at me every day."

My eyes water, and I try to blink the tears away. "We have that in common, then." He makes a pained noise that sets my tears free and my chin quivering. "Thank you for the flowers and the note," I rush out before I can steady my voice.

"God, Pixie, please don't cry." The ache in his voice reaches though the phone and squeezes my heart.

My stuttered breath and sniffle convey he's not getting what he wants. Neither of us are getting what we want.

"Happy birthday, by the way. Did you do something just for you? Something you *wanted* to do?"

More tears fall as I nod and find my voice, "I did."

"What did you do that was just for you?" His voice is low with an edge like he's fighting his emotions too. "Will you tell me?"

"I called you."

"Fuck. Fuck. Fuck." Each curse gets stronger until he's practically yelling.

"Anyway." I sit up and walk down the hall. "I think this year's birthday celebration deserves some wine, don't you? I'm legal now, you know."

"Margot—"

"I just wanted to hear your voice. And say thank you for the flowers. They're beautiful."

"Pixie—"

"It's okay, Fin. I get it. I don't fit in your perfect life."

"That's not—"

"I have to go."

"Will you unblock me?" he rushes out.

"No." I end the call and block his number again. I'd delete him altogether if I could, to avoid temptation, but then he wouldn't be blocked anymore.

I pour a glass of wine and toast to myself, having my first legal drink of alcohol. I look around this place—his home. All I see is the absence of the people I love. The ones who grew to be my family, but are no longer in my life—not actively anyway. Sam called earlier to wish me happy birthday. It's the first time we've spoken since school started. She hasn't returned any of my calls. I'm starting to doubt this lifelong friendship idea. Maybe like Fin, it just wasn't meant to be.

I need to move out. I need to move on.

Watt offered me his spare bedroom. He has two roommates, but they never rented out the fourth room. Knowing my current situation and lack of funds, he offered up a trade: I cook and clean in place of rent.

Before I chicken out, I shoot off a text asking him how soon I can move in.

His reply is immediate and perfect.

**Watt:** *Hell yeah! Tomorrow. I'll come help you pack.*

I don't know what will happen with Watt, but the fact that he has room for me in his life and *wants* me there brings a smile to my face and loosens the knot in my stomach.

I finish off my glass of wine, pour another, and start packing.

# Fifteen

## ᴖ **November** ᴖ

**"D**O YOU WANT ME TO GO WITH YOU?" WATT asks for the millionth time.

I laugh and throw my pillow at his lounging form on my bed. "You can't. You have a game."

His blue eyes shine with the crooked smile that slides across his lips. "I'd miss it for you."

"No! You would get in so much trouble." I start packing my toiletries. When I moved in, Watt changed rooms with me so I could have the ensuite bathroom instead of sharing with the guys. How nice was that?

"Yeah, but it would be worth it to see the look on Fin's face when you show up with me on your arm." He kneels on the bed, his hands pressed together in front of his chest like he's praying. "Come on. Say *yes*. Don't you want to rub in how well you're doing, even a little?"

Am I doing well? I'm not sure cutting off the one person who made me feel more than anyone else ever has falls under the *doing well* header. "Nope."

I won't deny that moving in here has been one of the best decisions I've made in a long time. Watt and the guys fixed my car. They considered it a house project, only took a week to replace what needed to be replaced, and got it running again like it's only twenty years old instead of the decrepit age it really is. And cooking and cleaning is no big deal. They won't let me clean their rooms or bathroom, so it's just the shared living space that I maintain, besides my room and bath. And it's nice to cook for more than me, especially for three football players who appreciate every morsel put in front of them. So, yeah, this living arrangement is supercalifragilisticexpialidocious-sweet.

"Are you going?" Griffin sticks his head in my door, looking hopeful at Watt, then me.

"She won't let me," Watt pouts.

My gaze flips between the two of them as Griff, the team's quarterback and one of my roommates, plops down on my bed next to Watt.

"Seriously, Griff? You want your star receiver to leave you hanging?" He can't possibly be okay with that.

"No, but I think you need the back up as much as I do, and we've got other receivers."

Holy moly, these guys. My heart melts. "I'll be fine."

"She said no, huh?" A deep voice has me turning to find Evan, my other roommate and the team's center, at my door.

"You too? What, did I miss a house meeting or something?" I tuck my hair dryer in my suitcase and flip it closed, taking one last glance around to be sure I have everything before zipping it up.

"We talk." Evans scoots me aside with his body. "Are you done?" He motions to my case.

"Yeah. I think that's it, besides my dress I need to hang in the car." Before I can grab it, Watt bounds from the bed and nabs the dress I left hanging on my closet door.

Evan zips up my suitcase, and Griff holds out his keys. I look at his hand like he's offering me a snail. "What that's for?"

"You're not taking your car." Griff steps forward, his tone authoritative and commanding, further proof of why he's the team's captain.

"I'm not taking *your* car."

My three towering roommates line up facing me, outweighing me by hundreds of pounds, arms crossed, glaring down their noses at me. Yet, I'm not intimidated. It's actually quite sweet.

"You're not taking *your* car. It runs fine for intown driving, but not long distance. You need a reliable car. Mine is the newest. You'll take mine. I'll drive yours if I need to go somewhere these two aren't going." Griff dangles his keys.

Watt smirks. "Don't be stubborn, Pi—"

I glare at him. He *tried* calling me Pixie after he read Fin's card from my birthday flowers. I'm not having it.

"—Margot," he amends. "Be safe. If you won't let me go with you, then you need to drive a car we *know* will get you there and back safely."

What's a girl to do? I take their help even though I didn't ask for it. They have a fair point. I would be safer, and it's a relief not to worry about my car making it to Dallas and back without requiring duct tape and a prayer.

Car packed, hugs given to Griff and Evan, Watt wraps me in a lingering hug. "Promise you'll call when you get there and when you're heading home—at the least." He pulls back, meeting my eyes. "Call me if you need anything else, even just to talk."

"I will." I don't plan on staying long. One night. That's it.

When I pull out of the driveway in Griff's new Range Rover, I feel like I'm driving a tank, so high off the ground compared to my car. I smile, not letting my nerves show. *I can do this. I won't wreck Griff's sweet new ride.*

The three of them wave, standing in the street and watching me pull away, getting smaller in the rearview mirror until I turn the corner, exiting our subdivision.

Now I just have to put on my cheery persona, face my best friend who's moved on from our friendship—yet still wants me as her maid of honor—and her soon-to-be brother-in-law, Fin, who also moved on from our... Whatever it was we had. All the while being happy for Sam and Joe during their wedding shower, while also pretending none of that bothers me.

Yay! Good times.

I'm ready for this couple's shower to be over, and it's barely started. Margot arrived a while ago in a pale pink dress that reminds me of spring and the flowers I sent for her birthday. Other than fleeting glances, I haven't had a chance to say *hello*. She's busy talking to Sam, my mom, and two of my aunts across the room. Her effervescence, though beautiful, seems duller than the last time I saw her over two months ago. It's as if she's lost her glow—that inner light I love so much. The ache in my chest squeezes at the thought that I'm to blame.

After the shower, I plan to whisk her away for a chance to talk in person and clear the air. We have the wedding next month, and I'd rather not have this awkward silence between us. But that's only the surface reasoning I tell myself. Truly, I just want to see her again, hear her laugh, and feel the connection I fear I've irreparably damaged.

After a quick greeting with Joe and a beer hand-off, Dad pulls me into another business discussion, laying on detail upon detail that adds to the weight of what I'm already carrying. But I'd never tell him that.

"I'll set up a meeting with Uncle Gabe on Monday." I pat his back. "Don't worry, Dad. I'll take care of it."

"I know you will, son. You always do." Leaving me with that extra layer of expectation, he disappears to find Mom. He traveled a few days this week, having just arrived home this morning. He's in need of a little *bonding*. I don't want to know what that entails. They both prefer it when she travels with him. Mom couldn't this time because of Sam and Joe's wedding shower that's currently happening at their house.

Another beer later and missed opportunities to talk to Margot, and it's time for the guests of honor to open wedding shower gifts. With unease written all over her face, Sam sits next to Joe in the designated seats of honor Mom set out in view of all their guests as they open each gift. Margot, her maid of honor, dutifully sits next to her on the floor, pad and pen in hand ready to scribe. Of the two, I'm not sure which is less comfortable. I'd say it's a draw. These two are quite a pair, preferring a back seat to the limelight my family usually holds.

Matt and I take turns handing them gifts to open. The gifts Joe and Sam didn't want, but Mom insisted they have the full experience of getting married and part of that experience is letting guests dote on you with gifts. So, there they are, taking turns reading cards, opening gifts, and being sure Margot records the giver's name and item received.

The look on Joe's face when they receive place setting after place setting of their china pattern—he didn't even know they had—is priceless. And when he glares at me and Sam goes ape-shit crazy (in a good way) for buying them the same genius-level, counter-hogging coffeemaker I have, my life is complete.

Joe and I, deep in an under-our-breath discussion over my gift, forget our attention should be on the bride and the gift she's opening until she grabs our attention with a gasp, slams the box closed and makes a forty-yard dash out of the living room and up the stairs. Michael bounds after her seconds before Joe follows.

From there it's a slow build to chaos. The volume of questions and concern from guests increases with each passing second. I know I should stay to help calm the masses, but I need to check on Joe and Sam. Family first, chaos second.

At the top of the stairs, Michael blocks Jace and me from progressing further. "Give them a minute," Michael insists, his hand on my shoulder.

I scan past him to Joe, who's talking through the bathroom door.

"Please, baby, let me in." The pain in Joe's voice gets my attention more than the fact that Sam has locked him out.

As one of the numerous bodyguards makes his way up the stairs, I dart down to the study and find what I'm looking for in the top drawer of my dad's desk. I dash back up the stairs just in time.

"Stop!" I bellow, preventing Michael from kicking down the bathroom door, and force my way past the sentry. "Did it even cross your mind to pick the lock?" I ask Michael. "Aren't you the ex-FBI-military-extraordinaire?"

Michael pats his pockets. "Didn't come prepared to pick locks at a wedding shower."

Asshole. "Then it's a good thing one of us is prepared." I hand Joe the master key.

Relief softens his taut face as he moves to unlock the door. The stress and emotions radiating off him sends me on high alert. There is something really wrong here.

"Fin, I need you to stay back." The regret in Joe's voice does nothing to quell the impact of him verbally pushing me aside.

I'm the one who brought the damn key. I'm the one who's always there, getting his ass out of more trouble than I care to remember.

He says, "Michael, I need you to get that fucking package and ensure no one sees it."

"On it," Michael responds in full mission mode, jaw tense, ready to attack, as if inside those doors is a bad guy keeping Sam hostage.

There is way more going on here, and I intend to get to the bottom of it.

# Sixteen

ONE SECOND I AM WRITING DOWN WHO GAVE SAM and Joe what gift, and the next, I'm flat on my back, looking up at the ceiling, my eyes watering and pain radiating from my left cheek.

"Oh, shit. Margot?" Sebastian's concerned face comes into view. "You got tagged, didn't you?"

"Is that what happened?" I'm honestly a little fuzzy in the head.

His tapered brows soften when he smiles. "Yeah, Buttercup. She pegged you with her foot as she hastened her escape."

I try to get up, but a soft hand to my shoulder stops me. "Give yourself a second." He scans the room. "Do you know what happened? Why she ran?"

"No clue." My tears seep out the corner of my eyes as I realize how clueless I am. The second I saw Sam I knew something was off. We barely talk anymore, and by barely, I mean, we don't. But still, I can spot a faker a million miles off. Sam was faking her calm, her happiness. She and Joe seemed more settled before they started opening gifts, so I'm not sure what the trouble is, or maybe it's just the stress of the wedding and needing to socialize at an event that is solely focused on her—and Joe—but mainly her. It's a bride thing.

"Here, let's get you up and some ice on that cheek."

Sebastian helps me stand. Though I'm a little unsteady on my feet, he supports me with an arm around my waist. As we walk to the kitchen, I'm grateful for the assistance.

I've barely settled into a kitchen chair with a bag of ice on my cheek when Michael flies by, stops and comes back. "Hey, Doc." He walks toward us. "Joe needs you upstairs." Michael eyes me. "What happened?"

"Nothing," I reply to Michael and shoo Sebastian. "Go. I'm fine."

They stare at me, torn between leaving me and taking care of Sam or whatever's going on upstairs.

"Really. I'm fine, honest." Even if I wasn't, I would never tell them that.

Whatever they see in my eyes must be convincing as both turn and head back the way Michael came.

The kitchen is bustling with staff Mrs. McIntyre hired to work the shower. A few guests pass, even Fin's parents dart in and out of the kitchen. None pay me any mind. I have no idea what's happening, but I couldn't feel more useless. It's obvious I'm not needed. I could have skipped the whole shower, and I doubt anyone would have even noticed.

Yeah, it's a full-on pity party for one.

I walk to the main floor guestroom where I changed earlier. I drove straight here, afraid I'd be late if I went to my parents' house first. I quickly change back into the jeans and top, repack my bag, not even bothering to hang up the stupid dress I shouldn't have splurged on just for today—like anyone even noticed. Not even Fin, who never did take the time to say *hello*.

Yep, should have stayed in Austin.

If I skip the wedding, will they even notice?

Grabbing my bag and purse, I slip out a side door, texting Watt to leave me a ticket for tonight's game. I'll be back in plenty of time to make it.

**Watt:** *WTF? What happened?*

**Me:** *Don't know exactly. Shower's over. Heading back.*

**Watt:** *Are you okay?*

**Me:** *Not really.*

Dots bounce as I wait for his reply.

"Margot?"

I stop, seconds before walking into Victor's chest. He grips my shoulders, ensuring I don't stumble.

"Where are you going?" He eyes my bag.

"Home."

He scowls.

"Oh!" I grab the key from the side pocket in my purse, and hold it up to Victor. "Give this to Fin, would you?"

He takes it, studying it like he can figure out what it unlocks. "What is it?"

"The key to Fin's house." I step around the big guy. Victor would even intimidate my roommates. He's bigger than any of them.

My phone sounds with a new text. I'll check it once I'm in the car. I click the key fob to open the back. Only once I get there, a hand grabs my bag.

"Why are you giving him this key?" Victor places my suitcase in the back and closes it.

"I don't need it anymore." I round the car to the driver's side.

"Why not?"

I sigh and turn, obviously Victor's not going to let me leave until he gets what he wants. Crossing my arms, I give him my full attention. "Because I no longer live there." I open the door, toss my purse to the middle console and climb in.

"Since when?" Victor stands in my open door, not too close, but near enough where I can't close it until he allows me to.

"Since my birthday." I don't have to point that out. I could have just said a month ago, but no. I want him to tell Fin. So he knows I moved out after our phone call. I want him to feel the emptiness his rejection still inflicts.

"Whose car is this?" Victor eyes my ride as if he just now noticed I wasn't in my car. I'm nearly offended he assumes it couldn't possibly be mine.

"Not that it's any of your business, but I'll tell you to get you off my back." I want—need—to get the heck out of here.

He draws back as if I'd actually struck him. "It's not like that."

Right. Sure it's not. "It's my roommate's car." I motion to his body blocking my door. "Now, if you don't mind, I'd like to leave."

He steps back but doesn't release the door. "Don't leave, Margot. He'll want to talk to you."

That makes me laugh. "No, he won't." I look past him to the grand house Fin grew up in. I'm reminded all over again: *he doesn't have room for you in his life.* "He had the past two hours to talk to me and didn't. I'm not sticking around to make a liar out of you, Victor."

With that, he steps back. I close my door, lock it to make a point, start the car and drive off. If there was ever a day that made me feel more alone than today, I don't know when that was.

But then, I remember there are three great guys at home who like to spend time with me. Who go out of their way to make me feel cared for, seen, and appreciated. It might just be for my cooking, but at least that's something.

Hitting the highway, I call Watt.

When he answers, his friendly voice soothes my disappointment in today and in myself for believing things could have been different.

I glare at Michael again, hoping it will actually make him break this time. "I can't believe you're not going to tell me!" I completely lost my cool about five minutes ago.

The calm asshole I love like a brother nods his understanding. "It's not my secret to tell." He steps closer. "If it were, I promise I'd tell you." He at least has the balls to look pained by keeping me in the dark.

He's my best fucking friend—he and Victor. "There shouldn't be any secrets to fucking tell." We don't keep secrets from each other. I know more about him than I care to, and he with me.

The door clicks. I snap my gaze to my stricken brother, Joe. It's his goddamn secret! "What the fuck is going on?"

He holds up a hand, like that's going to keep me in my place. "Fin, I need to talk to Michael. Alone."

That guts me. My baby brother is sending me away so he can talk to *my* best friend. I'm the one who helps Joe with his problems, not *my* friends. Yes, they're his friends too, but I'm not feeling all that amiable at the moment. I remind Joe, "I can help."

He drops to the bed, exhaustion rolling off him like waves. "I know you can. And you will, but right now, I need you downstairs getting rid of all these people. Tell them Samantha is sick, thank them for coming, smooth over ruffled feathers, and get them the fuck out of the house. I'm gonna take Samantha home soon, and I'd rather not have to carry her through a house full of guests."

"And then we'll talk?"

He nods. "And then we'll talk. Tomorrow," he amends.

I want to fight him. I want to know now, not later. But I can plainly see he's at his end. He needs my help in places he can't be right now. I can do that. "Tomorrow, Brother."

"Tomorrow." He hugs me, his voice tight with emotion when he adds, "Thank you, Brother."

I have a task: apologize to the guests, usher them out, and clear the way for Joe to take Sam home. I can do that. It's clear. Achievable.

After fifteen minutes, I close the door on the last guest. Turning to my parents, who have their own questions poised to release, I hug them both. "I don't know anything. He just asked me to clear the house so he can take Sam home."

"You're a good brother, Fin." My mom pats my cheek before kissing it. "They're lucky to have you."

*Tell them that* is what I want to say. What I say instead is, "Thanks."

I leave Dad holding Mom on the couch and look for Victor, who's inexplicably absent. I find him in the driveway, watching the last guest drive off.

"You alright?" he asks when I stop beside him.

"Not even close."

His uncharacteristically kind eyes study me for a minute. "Michael texted. William is bringing the car around. Then Joe will bring Sam down to head home. Michael wants us at Joe's penthouse tomorrow for a meeting. He'll text us the time."

I blink a few times. "Who the fuck is William?"

Victor cracks. A big fucking smile softens his hard-as-nails demeanor. "Out of all of that, that's what you want to know?"

I shrug, it's the only thing in his statement that took me by surprise.

"He's Sam's bodyguard."

"And why does Sam need protection?"

"That's the question of the day." Victor faces me. "I imagine that's what tomorrow is about."

"You don't know?"

He smiles again, making me wary. He's going for comforting, but he's freaking me out. He doesn't smile this much. Ever. "I swear, if I knew, you'd know."

At least I'm not the only one being kept in the dark. I doubt Matt has any idea either. In fact, I don't even know where my middle brother is. He was here earlier. Then I remember, "Have you seen Margot?" Fuck. I totally forgot about her.

"She left."

"What? When?" I'm an idiot. I didn't get to say *hi* or tell her I wanted to talk, spend some time with her.

"About fifteen minutes ago." He hands me a key.

"What's this?"

"She told me to give you that. It's the key to your house."

"What—"

"She moved out, Brother. On her birthday. And if I were a guessing man, I'd guess it was after your sad sack phone call with her."

"She moved out?" Fuck. I didn't see that one coming. "Do you know where she's living?"

He holds up his phone and a cut, bare-chested guy with black hair and haunting blue eyes smirks back at me.

"Who the fuck is that?" I seize his phone.

"He's Griffin Quinn, quarterback for the Longhorns."

Shit, I knew that face looked familiar. "And why are you showing me Quinn?"

"He's her roommate."

My gaze slides to him. "The fuck?"

He grabs his phone back, shoving it into his pocket. "I don't know where she's living—yet. But I know with whom she's living. She drove his car here today. A new Range Rover. A sleek one too."

"Yeah, thanks. I could do without your car envy."

"I pulled the plates. That's how I found Griffin Quinn."

"Is she still in town? Can you track her?" I hate the desperation in my tone, but it can't be helped. This day is just getting worse and worse, and I know the only thing that will make it better is my Pixie.

"Negative. She's must have gotten a new phone, or she found the tracking software and disabled it."

"A new phone is more likely." I glance up; the sun is still high in the sky. It's only three o'clock. Early. Plenty of time to spend with Margot. If only she were still here. I meet Victor's expectant gaze. "So, we don't know where she lives. I can't call her because she's blocked me. And we can't track her any longer. Do I have that correct?"

"Yeah, I'm afraid you do, Brother."

"And I can't fly to Austin and find this Quinn fucker because we have to be at Joe's tomorrow to find out what shit show is going on with his life?"

"Yep."

Commotion to the side of the house halts our conversation until we see Joe's SUV leaving with Michael and William, I guess, in the front seat. Michael gives a curt nod as he passes. The back windows are too dark to confirm if Joe and Sam are in there, but I have no doubt they are.

"Fuck." It's the only word I have.

"Not to totally piss on your already soggy Cheerios, but Margot also had the beginnings of a bruise on her left cheek. I don't remember seeing it earlier. I have no idea how she got it or when."

"I assume you're talking about Margot?"

We spin around to find Sebastian standing behind us. He must have exited with Joe and Sam. "Yes, did you see her?"

"Yeah, I was coming down to check on her after Joe came and got Sam. But I couldn't find Margot anywhere."

"She left." I study the worry in his eyes. "What happened to her face?"

"Sam's foot hit her when she bolted. I was icing it until Michael came and got me. He said Joe needed me. I figured it had to do with Sam, so I went. I left Margot in the kitchen, planning on checking on her when I was done."

"But she's okay?" I have to know. I'm tempted as it is to fly to Austin anyway and fly back in time to meet up at Joe's. But I don't know when that is, and I don't even know if Margot is driving back today.

"She'll be fine. Maybe a little swelling and bruising. It knocked her silly for a moment more than anything else," Sebastian reassures me, digging his hands in his pockets and nodding to the curb. "I could use a drink. What about you guys?"

"I need more than just one drink. How 'bout my place? Macallan. Poker." I'm going to drink my Pixie out of my head or get shitfaced trying.

# *Seventeen*

## December

F I HAVE ONE GOAL TODAY, IT'S TO GET
Marguerite alone and make this right. It's been a month of hell. It
was bad enough when Watt was the only football player I had to
compete with. Now, she's not only living with him but two other
players: Griffin and Evan. They're the stars of the team, living under
one roof with my girl.

I have no idea if she's with Watt or Griffin—she drove his car to
the wedding shower, after all. Hell, for all I know it could be a regular
gangbang every night with all three of those assholes. My chest rumbles, and I stop seconds away from ruining my hair by digging my fingers in and giving a tight tug.

"The fuck?" Joe's voice reminds me I'm not alone.

I stop pacing and turn to face my brothers, knowing there will be
hell to pay for letting them see me at my wit's end.

"Did you just growl?" Matt's eyes are huge as he holds in a laugh.

"I—"

"Don't even try to deny it. I heard it too." Joe stops in front of me
and clasps my shoulder. "I'm sorry. I've been so wrapped up in my own
life, I didn't see how messed up you are over her."

*Her?* I shake my head, a denial on the tip of my tongue.

"Don't. Even." He slips on his tux jacket. "I'm the one getting married, but you're nervous as fuck."

"Are we talking about Margot?" Matt, my often-absent brother chips in with a knowing smirk. He just wanted to say her name and watch me wince. Asshole.

"We're not together," I clarify. "I fucked up. She won't talk to me."

"Then here's the perfect opportunity to change that." He holds up my jacket for me to slip into. "It's my wedding, Fin. The best fucking day of my life, and as much as I want it to be all about me and Samantha, you need to do what you need to and make amends." He pulls my jacket up my arms and over my shoulders and steps back.

I turn, facing them both. Listening.

"You told me once I was trying to logic my way into and out of my relationship with Samantha. Love isn't logical—"

"It's not lo—"

"It could be." Joe smiles at Matt and then me. "It *should* be."

Fuck. "When did you become the Mouseketeer of love?"

"When I found a woman worth being stupid over."

"Fuck." I *am* stupid over Margot. I've been a brainless idiot since we first slept together.

"Exactly." My youngest brother, bigger in stature and apparently love-mature, hugs Matt and me. "It's the best fucking thing ever." He kisses our cheeks and steps back. "Make it right, Fin." His questioning gaze lingers on Matt. "You need to find someone to knock the player out of you."

"Hey." Matt takes a step back, palms up. "I haven't *played* since the whole Lydia-Veronica incident."

Joe scowls, stepping forward. "Never speak those names again unless Samantha or Jace bring them up."

Matt's shoulders fall, his hands disappearing in his pockets. "I didn't mean anything. I'm sorry, Brother. I know I fucked up." He bobs his head. "Then... And now. Sorry."

"Over it." Joe grips the back of his neck. "Just stop being such a manwhore, huh?"

"I'm taking Jace's cue and turning over a new leaf," Matt assures us.

"*That* might be taking it too far. I didn't say celibate." Joe's speaking to Matt, but his eyes are on me. "You good, Brother?"

"I will be." I have to be. I have too much riding on my shoulders to be this fucked up over Margot. If I'm going to be this messed up, I might as well try it *with* her in my life rather than *without* her.

"I'm counting on it." He turns as there's a knock on the door. "Let's get me hitched."

Fiddling with the front of my dress, thankful Sam chose a style that works for me, I meet her eyes in the full-length mirror. She grins. "You look beautiful, stop messing with the dress. You can't see—"

"Thanks," I cut her off. "You look beautiful too." She does. She's radiating with joy and love. It's nearly sickening, but I'm so happy for her. Whatever was wrong before with Joe and Sam is resolved. She's been more communicative the past few weeks, filled me in on the whole emotional blackmail thing going on. It's hard to believe those kinds of things really happen. I mean, it's wild stuff. But then Sam's life has kinda been full of chaos since her father was murdered—which is also insane.

She lives a whole life separate from me I can't even begin to relate to. When you put it all together, it's understandable why she's been so distant. Who has the time to be a friend when your whole life is on the line from your dad's murderer, and then this crazy blackmail thing trying to get her to leave Joe? Jeez, who does that?

Apparently, Jace's ex does.

"Does he know?" Sam's soft whisper draws my eyes to her.

I glance at Fiona, Fin's mom, over Sam's shoulder. "No."

"But how—"

"Can we not?" I smile and move closer. "His mom is right there," I say through lips that barely move.

She just laughs. "Believe me, Fiona would be ecstatic to know you two were together. She's dying for her boys to get married and give her grandbabies."

That makes my brows lift. "Grandbabies?"

"Yeah, no. I need to finish school, start my career. Then, I'll consider giving her grandbabies." She snatches her phone off the vanity, a devious smile on her lips. "The idea of having Joseph's babies, though…"

She's totally sexting Joe right now. That makes me laugh, and she joins me.

"Margot, when are you going to come have lunch with me?" Fiona laces her arm with mine. "Sam, maybe the three of us could have lunch when you get back from your honeymoon, before school starts again for you both."

"I'd love that." Sam moves in for a hug. "Thank you for having such amazing boys."

Fiona swipes at her eyes. "Don't you dare make me cry." She squeezes Sam's hand. "You've made Joe the man he is today. His father and I started the groundwork, but you, my dear, made him the man he is by loving him like you do."

"Okay, no crying." Sam looks to the ceiling, blinking. "You promised."

Fiona fans her face. "You started it."

A rap on the door startles us enough to sidetrack their tears. "It's time," Michael's voice comes from the other side of the door.

"Oh my God." Sam looks stricken.

Now it's my turn to tear up. Because her only fear is being in front of all those people, their eyes trained on her. "Hey, you can do this. It's just a quick walk down the aisle. Jace won't let you fall. Then you'll be with Joe, and all will be good."

It's that simple.

She releases the breath she was holding. "You're right. The hard part was getting to this day. It's easy-peasy from here."

That makes me laugh. "Now you sound like me, Sammykins."

"Jinkies, Margot, I've missed you so much I'm starting to sound like you." She beams.

"Smarty-pants," I scold with no heat whatsoever. "I've missed you," I whisper, fighting back tears again.

"I promise I'll be a better friend." She leans in. "And I'm starting now. You need to let Fin in. He's the best. He won't let you down."

But he already has.

I nod and motion to the door. "Don't keep your man waiting."

"Or yours." She stills me with a look. "Open your heart, Margot. Let. Him. In."

*Wow!* All I can do is nod and pretend she didn't just knock me over by the fact that her words loosened the knot in my stomach instead of making it tighter as I'd expect to happen at the thought of seeing Fin.

We hold hands as we make our way to the front of the church. She kisses my cheek as I step up to the closed doors where I'll be walking down—solo—as her maid of honor and lone attendant. My nerves ratchet to a whole new level. What was I thinking, telling her walking down the aisle would be no big deal? I'm suddenly terrified.

"Hey," Sam's voice garners my attention. "You got this. You're beautiful. You're Margot the dark-slayer. You may be small, but you are mighty."

Joseph and Mary! This girl. "I am mighty," I whisper.

"I can't hear you, Marguerite." She smiles at her brother, Jace, who just appeared to escort her down the aisle. "Tell her she's got this."

His handsome face swings my way, his blue eyes sparkling with a warmth I don't remember seeing before. "Margot, you bring light wherever you go. Go light up that fucking room."

Wow, I didn't expect that from him. But I'll take it.

I nod and take a cleansing breath as the doors open, and music and cool air wafts over me.

Ready or not, here I come.

# Eighteen

**F**UCK. ME. THIS SONG. MARGOT IS DANCING WITH Matt, and I want to rip his head off. Her hips and shoulders sway, her body undulating like the sex goddess I *know* she is as Hailee Seinfeld reminds me I didn't know I was *starving* till I tasted my Pixie.

That's the damn truth. I knew I wanted a wife and kids, but I never felt this desperation until I laid eyes on Margot. It's been two years, and my desire for her only grows.

"Are you gonna just stand there and let your brother dance with your woman like that?"

I'd expect those words from Joe or even my dad, but never in a million years would I think my mother would utter such possessive words.

"Don't look so shocked, Finley. I've seen the way you look at her. I'm your mom, but I'm still a woman." She motions to Matt. "And don't think he doesn't know what he's doing. He's goading you into action." She unfurls my fingers, one at a time, from around the tumbler of whiskey I've been nursing but started strangling the minute Margot began dancing with my manwhore of a brother.

"I like her. She's good people." Her eyes lock on mine. "Don't misinterpret her effervescent personality as lacking depth and vulnerability. In fact, I'd say it means just the opposite."

She takes the glass she successfully pried from my grasp and sets it on a nearby table. "I need you to be careful with her, but not so careful that you don't budge from this spot."

"I—" I'm at a total loss of words. I didn't think anyone knew, and here I am finding out *everyone* knows.

"Go, before you force your brother to do something really stupid... Like kiss her."

"He wouldn't." I whip around to see him moving in. "Son of a bitch."

My mom chuckles. "Now, I take offense to *that*, Finley Granger."

"Oh, shit. Mom, I'm so sorry. It's—" She used my middle name. Fuck, I hate that name.

She pats my chest. "I'm only joking. I know you didn't mean it like that." She motions behind me. "Now, go get your girl and make me a grandmother already."

*Jesus, fuck.* "Mom."

"Don't *Mom* me. Go. I'm not getting any younger, and neither are you. You believe you don't have time for her in your life. Well, *make* time. You have my permission—if you needed it. Go. Be a little *less* responsible. Have a life, my sweet Finley."

She pushes me toward the dance floor and toward a future I'm closer and closer to grabbing and never letting go.

The tumultuous glare Fin is sporting is priceless, but it's the grip on the back of Matt's neck that has me concerned. "Brother," he grunts before pushing Matt aside.

Matt just laughs. "I was saving your place."

When Matt approached me a few songs ago, he whispered in my ear, "You ready to make my brother jealous?"

Making Fin jealous wasn't my intent, really. I just didn't want to be alone. Coming to a wedding *alone* just makes that fact so much worse.

Watt, Griff, and Evan all asked to come with me. One by one they approached me, asked to accompany me to Dallas and to the wedding, promising to stay by my side and fend off Fin, if I wanted them to. I don't know if they planned it. I never asked. I smiled, hugged, and turned each of them down, grateful for their support.

This—attending Sam and Joe's wedding alone—was an important step for me. To face my fear of seeing Finley again, and even Sam. She's worked to repair our friendship these past weeks. But still being face to face with Sam and Joe's love is not for the faint of heart. It takes courage to witness it and not turn to anger or crumble into a pool of tears for the want of it.

But Fin… I haven't spoken a word to him since my birthday, over two months ago. And before that, a total of over three months since the last time I spoke to him *in person*—the weekend he snuck out of my bed and tried to ease his guilt by buying me a car.

Granted, I'm the one who cut him off by moving and blocking his number. But he has to know it was necessary. Self-preservation. Just as I know if he really wanted to find me, talk to me, he has more than enough resources to do so.

"Are you not going to talk to me?" His low timbre sends chills down my back.

And reminds me of where we are. "I wasn't sure you wanted me to." *Weak.*

When the music changes into a slow song, he pulls me into his chest. "You should know better than that. I've never not wanted to talk to you."

I ignore the ache James Arthur produces in my chest as he sings "Quite Miss Home."

My smile is practiced, canned. I'm sure Fin hates it, but it's the best I can muster. "You did a good job of ignoring me at the shower."

His hand on my lower back fists before he brings me closer. "I was *not* ignoring you. I just couldn't find the time before you left."

*Right.* "Because talking business with your dad and brothers could never wait, given you see them at least five days a week if not more. Yeah, I don't see how you could *possibly* fit in a thirty-second *hello* with the girl you occasionally fuck."

*I did not just cuss.* Oh man, I need to stop pining over this guy. He'll never make room for me, no matter how much I want him to—especially because I'm even more afraid he actually might.

"Excuse me." I pull out of his hold and easily slip through the crowd. There are benefits to being small.

"Margot, wait." His large hand captures my delicate one. I suppose there are benefits to being tall and in command. People move out of his way.

Before we get into it, it's announced it's time for the bouquet and garter toss. Reluctantly, I let him guide me to the dance floor, where all dutiful single men and woman belong, so we can scratch each other's eyes out for a chance at catching a dream, a fantasy, of being the next to get married.

No, thank you. Hard pass.

"Don't look so miserable." Joe winks at me as he circles Sam around the dance floor before standing by her side as she turns her back to all of the maidens.

Kill me now.

Surprisingly, I'm not the only single gal here. I'm thankful for that, but I have no intention of vying for the bouquet. Any of these single ladies are welcome to it. Lined up, twenty or so feet behind Sam, I plan on stepping back to give everyone else room to run forward.

But as soon as the flowers leave Sam's hand and are airborne, a strong force pushes me forward. I stumble but right myself just as a mass of flowers flies toward my face. Out of instinct I reach up and nab it out of the air to avoid a full-face collision. Plus, they're flowers. And, well, I love them so. I couldn't possibly let them drop to the floor.

"Holy nutcrackers," leaves my mouth when I realized what I've done, then wince at my words. I should be acting happy, not put out that I caught the superstitious offering to the wedding gods.

Sam's whooping, clapping, and running toward me has me smiling, though. She's so happy. "I wanted you to catch it so bad."

*Obviously.* "Thanks?" What does one say to that?

After a few pictures with the bride and the *future bride*—who is apparently me according to tradition—because... Hello... I caught the bouquet, so it must be true! I have strict orders not to leave the dance floor, which offers a front row view of the garter toss.

Which, yes, if you're paying attention and under the influence of the wedding gods—who have a wicked sense of humor—Fin does, in fact, catch the garter.

A few not-as-awkward-as-I-assumed pictures with the bride and groom and the *next* bride and groom later, I find myself in Fin's arms on the dance floor. Only this time I'm not angry, and he's not seething with jealousy.

"I'm sorry, Pixie," he whispers into my hair, his cheek resting on the top of my head, my arms around his waist, his around me. We move slowly to the music, even when a fast song comes on, we don't change tempo. We stay in our corner, swaying in a small circle, like we just learned how to slow dance.

"What *exactly* are you sorry for?" My first instinct is to say, *that's okay.* But I don't want to be a pushover. I need to stand up to this man who is bigger than life and will have a boardroom cowering to his every whim in the not-so-distant future.

"For mucking this up. I did everything wrong." The rumble in his voice has my insides quaking—hoping.

Reluctantly, I pull away from his chest where my face was nicely nestled. "Not everything." My gaze catches his and sticks.

A soft caress to my cheek has me closing my eyes. "Come home with me, Marguerite. Let me do some more of those things I did right." His lips replace the tender touch of his thumb. "For everything else, you can teach me how to do it exactly the way you need."

I have no idea if he's only talking about sex, or sex and truly everything else. But for now, I'm concentrating on the sex part. "Yes, please."

His mouth descends on mine, and I forget about everyone else—everything else—except this moment and this man.

# *Nineteen*

CRASHING THROUGH MY PENTHOUSE DOOR, I barely manage to get it closed and locked before she jumps in my arms, her legs wrapping tightly around my waist, her mouth, devouring mine.

"Fuck, I've missed you." I squeeze her supple ass, grinding the steel rod confined in my tux pants against her.

"Missed you too." She pants against my lips. "It's been too long."

*Fuck.* That has me pausing on the way to my bedroom, my forehead resting on hers. "How long, Pixie?" I don't really want to hear how many guys she's been with since me, but I can't help wanting to know when the last time she has sex was.

"Since you, Finley." Her large, sad eyes break any semblance of control I had.

"Marguerite, you're going to have to forgive me." I resume the path to my bed.

"For what?" Her gentle hands bracket my face, all her weight held in my arms—and, God, I love it.

I love the fact that I can hold her with little effort. It makes me feel like I can protect her from anything. "It's been just as long for me." I brush my lips over hers. "I didn't want anyone else."

"Then what am I forgiving you for?"

"For this." I drop her on the bed rather unceremoniously, pull her to the edge, hiking her dress up as high as I can, and ripping off her panties. "Fuck." I still when her hand grazes my cock as she unzips my pants.

"You don't have to apologize for wanting me." Her harsh breaths match my own as I flick her heels off and kiss my way up her neck to her lips. "Fin." She arches, rubbing my cockhead across her opening. Then she shocks me by asking, "Can we not use a condom? I've been tested. I'm on the pill. I want to feel you." She gasps when she circles her hips against my steel begging-to-be-inside-her shaft.

I practically growl, "Same for the testing." I slough off my jacket, undo my tie as she pushes my pants down my hips. I slam into her so hard she cries out, but my grip on her shoulder keeps her from sliding up the bed. "This is what you'll need to forgive me for, Pixie." I pull out and do it again.

And again.

And again.

Only she's begging me, "More. Harder."

"Fuck." My girl is a dream. She's like that old commercial adage: She can *take a licking and keeps on ticking.*

The idea of licking her pussy has me revving up. My hips bang my cock home until she grips my neck and brings my mouth to hers, asking, "Are you gonna fill me up, Finley?"

Holy dirty girl, where did my little sweet Pixie go? "Is that what you want, Marguerite? Is that what you need?"

Her head tips back, and her wet heat grips me like a vise. "Yes, yes… Yes!" she cries as she comes.

Her pussy milks me, forces my release until I'm chanting her name over and over as I do what she asked—fill her up.

Spent, but nowhere near done, I drop to my knees and plunge two fingers inside her. Feeling her juices mingling with mine has visions of her pregnant with my baby dancing in my head and making my cock hard again.

Not a drop of fear inside me at the notion.

I descend on her clit, savoring her every moan and cry, her taste driving me crazy. When I bring her to the edge and back two more times, she's replete yet begging me to fill her again.

I told her she could teach me to give her what she needs.

She's doing a damn fine job.

On shaky legs, I grab my belongings and hastily dress in the living room, not bothering to use the hall bathroom. He found me last time. I need to make my escape before he wakes up. He's going to be so upset with me.

But it can't be helped.

After our second go, he tried to remove my dress. I made the excuse I need to go to the bathroom. I grabbed his tux shirt off the floor on my way, donning it after I cleaned up and removed my dress.

His frown at seeing me in his shirt instead of naked had me thinking fast and fighting the panic to escape. I distracted him with my mouth… On his cock. I could taste me all over him. When I commented on that fact, he grew instantly harder. I guess he liked the idea of that. It turned me on too.

I don't know if he could tell I'd never given a blow job before. If he did, he didn't say, and I worked doubly hard to hide that fact. Inexperience is not something I imagine Fin would be attracted to. He's a worldly guy. He'd like a woman who knows what she's doing in the bedroom.

Double standard aside, a guy might not want to know how a girl gains her experience, but I'm sure he'd take a seasoned, confident woman over a scarred wallflower any day. So, for Fin, I hide the wallflower and fake the confidence I need to suck his cock, making him groan in pleasure, fist my hair with need, and talk so dirty, I finger myself until we both come.

Wrapped in his arms, we fell asleep, content and spent.

Until I woke up to his hand on my bare breast. It took me a second to realize he'd slipped his hand under his shirt I was still wearing, his palm flush against my breast, his fingers cradling me like I'm something to cherish.

Fear and tears fought to the surface. I don't know which won. I guess both, as here I am, wiping at my wet cheeks, throwing his tux shirt on the couch, and zipping up my dress to make the walk of shame.

Though, thankfully, I don't actually have to walk or try to grab an Uber at this time of night… Err morning. I insisted on driving my car to MCI. I'm parked in the garage in one of his spaces. The penthouses have a private garage entrance and exit that is only for residents. So, there's no chance I'll run into anyone, except maybe Matt. But surely by now he's sound asleep like his brother.

Once I reach Griff's car, I take a solid breath and climb in. My thoughts on my roommate's generosity of lending me his car again are short-lived. But I force the guilt aside. Fin and I didn't make any promises. This is no different than the other times, except perhaps more desperate. And maybe that's why, for the first time ever, I wanted to forgo the condom, even though he didn't know it, he was giving me something no man ever has, himself, bare. But it's the feel of his hand on my breast—skin to skin—that rips me up inside, fueling the knowledge that I can never have a normal relationship with no barriers.

That thought has a new flood of tears falling.

When I arrive at my parents', I find my sister and younger brother gone. There's a note on my bed, telling me Dad went on a rampage. Jenny decided to take Zeke to her boyfriend's parents' home in Houston where they're going to spend Christmas. I was welcome to join them.

Instead, I drop my dress to the bed, grab a quick shower, change, and pack. Mom is working the entire Christmas break, including Christmas day and New Year's. Dad is always worse this time of year. I would stick it out if Jenny and Zeke were here, but without them, there's no point.

I'm not sure why I even come home anymore. Now that all the festivities around Sam's wedding are over, maybe it's time I make Austin my home. Or even Houston, where my sister is a nurse and living with her doctor boyfriend. I'll be surprised if she makes it through the holidays without calling with the news of her engagement. She's found her one. She's happy. Her life path is set.

I leave a note for Mom in her purse, where she's sure to find it and my dad won't. She'll be sad but understand why I can't stay. She needs to tell my dad to get sober or get out. He's not physically abusive. But he is verbally, especially to me. Maybe if we, their kids, take a stand, she'll do something about it. If I had my own place, I'd have Zeke come live with me. He has two years of high school left. I'm sure he'd hate to leave his friends, but he hates living with Dad more.

With that sad sack of thoughts weighing me down, I hit the road for home. Austin.

# Twenty

CAN'T BELIEVE SHE DID IT AGAIN. TECHNICALLY, she didn't do it the first time—she attempted to sneak out on me. I, on the other hand, *did* sneak out on her. Perhaps this is payback. Or her fear running amok.

She's hiding something. I'm one hundred percent certain now. She wouldn't let me remove her dress or my shirt she snuck on after using the bathroom. I wasn't going to push it, especially after she put her mouth on me.

Fuck. I groan and adjust my hardening length in my jeans. I'm not nearly as pissed as I am hurt and disappointed. I hoped last night was a turning point. I want to see where this leads. Obviously, she feels differently.

Or she got spooked. My gut tells me it's a little of both. I didn't make my intentions clear. I won't make that mistake again.

Pulling up to her parents' house, I notice the lights on the first floor are on. Maybe she's still up.

I lightly rap on the door, hoping to not wake her parents, if they aren't the ones awake already. Who am I kidding? I'm not above waking the whole damn neighborhood in search of my Pixie.

The door swings open to her father, who's looking haggard and hungover. He narrows his eyes at me, blinking a few times. I'm not sure if he's studying me or just trying to bring me into focus. I'd bet on the latter. "What the hell do you want?"

I offer my hand. "Mr. Dubois, I'm Fin McIntyre."

He only sneers at it with no intention of greeting me like a gentleman. "I know who you are."

I concentrate on remaining calm as I lower my hand to my side. "I'm looking for Margot. Is she here?"

He scoffs, hiccups, and then laughs, which only makes him hiccup again. "Last I heard, she was at Sam's wedding. I don't know where she is. Hell, she could be upstairs." He leans on the door, studying me this time, I'm certain. "You fucking my daughter, Mr. McIntyre?"

Jesus. This man. "I'd prefer if you didn't refer to your daughter in such a manner, Mr. Dubois. I care for Margot. I don't imagine she'd be too fond of your word choice either."

Another chuckle, hiccup, and an added nose rub. "I'll take that as a *yes*." He glances past me and then back. "She doesn't care for much of what I say nowadays."

I can't image why… He's a charmer. "May I check and see if she's here?" I'd ask him to call her, but I don't want to get into the whole *she blocked my number* discussion.

He moves back like he's going to let me in and then freezes. "Have you seen it?"

It's my turn to study him. "Seen what, sir?"

He nods. "Then that's a *no*." He shakes his head. "That's too bad. You're a good catch."

"I'm not following—"

"Tom, go back to bed." Mrs. Dubois comes into view. She's in scrubs. Based on the hour, I assume she's getting ready to leave for work. "I'll talk to Mr. McIntyre. You go on to bed."

He grumbles but wobbles away.

I stick out my hand. Perhaps I'll have better luck with her. "Mrs. Dubois, I'm Fin." No need to tell her my last name. She already knows it. Probably my first name too, but manners demand I introduce myself all the same.

Her hand is soft yet firm in mine. "It's nice to meet you, Fin." Her smile fades. "And before you ask, she's not here. I just found her note. She drove back to Austin."

Damn. I'm too late to catch her, and I'm wasting time here. "Thank you, Mrs. Dubois. I appreciate you letting me know." I step back. "Have a nice day at work."

I turn to leave, but her next words give me pause. "If you don't plan on treating her any better than Bobby, please leave her be. Don't go chasing what you have no intention of keeping. Or worse, what you don't plan on treating with respect."

Managing to keep my anger at bay, I face my sprite's mom and tell her the only truth I know. "I would never hurt Margot. And I will never disrespect her. I might have been an idiot at the beginning, but I've finally figured out what's important."

"That's good. That's real good." With a nod, she closes the door.

I have my phone to my ear before I reach my car, notifying my pilot that I will need the jet, after all.

I've got a girl to catch.

A future to figure out.

And a whole lot of commitments I'm going to have to delegate if I have any hope of succeeding at either.

I made the drive from Dallas in record time. I pull into Griff's space, turn the engine off, and press the opener to close the garage. Yawning, my head hits the headrest. I close my eyes. Maybe I'll just sleep here.

A knock on the driver's window has me startling with a yelp. "Holy nutcrackers, Evan, you scared me to death."

His smile just grows with his laugh. "You know you can say *shit*, right? It's not *that* bad of a word."

Not this argument again. My roommates are trying to get me to loosen up my language restrictions. I just prefer not to cuss. "I'll let you know when I decide to traipse down potty-mouth avenue."

That only makes him laugh harder. "Please don't ever change. You're funnier this way. All buttoned up, never showing any cleavage, and never cussing. It's original." I unlock my door, and he opens it. "I like you all the more for it."

"Thanks?" I screw my mouth up, not sure if he's giving me a compliment or making fun of my oddness. Honestly, I'm too tired to care. I cover my mouth when another yawn breaks loose. "I'm going to bed."

He grabs my bag from the back seat. "Why are you home, anyway? I thought you were staying through Christmas."

"I hate to mess up your wild Christmas plans, but I changed my mind. Home is *not* where the heart is." At least not *that* home.

"Uh, before you go in." He steps in front of me, holding the garage-entry door closed. "Forewarning, you have a visitor."

Frowning, I step back. "A visitor?" I note the time on my watch. "At this time of morning?"

"Yeah." His smile is sweet and reads of sympathy, but he's not saying any more. Opening the door, he motions inside.

I make it as far as the living room, my brain barely awake enough to even consider who might be waiting for me.

"Marguerite." His tone is knowing, but his use of my formal name leaves no room for misinterpretation. He's not happy.

"Finley, what are you doing here?" To say I'm surprised would be a lie, and yet a part of me is giddy that he actually came after me. Not just across town, but he followed me two hundred plus miles. Granted, he came by jet, given that he beat me here. Still. He came after me. That has to mean something.

His gaze slides to Evan before he moves into my space. "You left without saying goodbye."

The gravel in his voice has my body remembering what he can do to it. "I thought it was for the best." My reply is soft and reveals entirely too much.

He caresses my cheek. "You thought wrong. I'm here to remedy that."

For the moment, his closeness satiates my fear and guilt. I'm too tired to care like I should.

I force my focus to my roommate. "Evan, I assume you've met Fin."

"Yes, we've had coffee and a nice chat. I assume we'll be having a houseguest for a few days?"

I glance at Fin, who merely nods, his eyes fully on me. "Yes, it seems so." I don't miss the satisfied smile on Fin's face. He's entirely too pleased with himself.

"Well, I'm gonna grab some food and head to the gym." He thumbs over his shoulder. "Could I talk to you for just a quick sec, Margot?"

"Sure." I hand Fin my bag and purse. "Last room on the left." He takes my dismissal in stride and disappears down the hall.

Evan moves closer but doesn't speak until we hear my bedroom door close. "Holy fuck dogs, Fin is a scary motherfucker." But the humor in his voice tells me he's over the fear I'm sure Fin enjoyed instilling. "He loosened up, though, once he figured out I wasn't a threat to"—he waves his hand in front of me—"whatever it is you two have going on."

I narrow my eyes. "And how did he determine that, exactly?"

Evan's smile beams. "I told him I didn't want to fuck you."

A laugh bubbles free. "What?"

He shrugs. "I mean, you're hot and all. But—" he cringes. "You were with Watt, so that's like… I don't know… Sleeping with Watt. And, uh, no thank you."

I swat his arm. "Ow. Wow, you're really solid." I mean, like *really* solid, all muscle kind of solid.

His smile returns. "Hence the gym, baby." He flexes, totally hamming it up, then turns serious. "Anyway, what I wanted to know was if you want me to disappear for a few days. I'm sure I could bunk with one of the guys. A few are staying over the holidays, like me."

"No. This is your home. If anything, we should leave."

"So, you're a *we*, then?"

I sigh. "Honestly, I don't know. We have this *thing* that neither of us can seem to get past, but it's… Complicated." And hurtful. Scary.

Oh, and… Complicated. But it's also really good. Like now, he came for me. The heat in his eyes, and something I can't quite name, has me wanting to run to him and never let him leave.

"Okay, so no one is leaving." Evan brings me out of my head.

"No, in fact, I'll cook dinner. Say seven-ish?"

His boyish smile is back. His chocolate eyes, matching the color of his hair, narrow on me. "No sex in the kitchen. Remember. House rule."

"But the couch is okay?" I tease.

"Fuck no, the couch is not okay. We need to amend our rules. Sex only in our rooms. Places we don't share." He concentrates like he's making a mental note. "I'm gonna text the guys to make that amendment."

"Tell em I said *hi*. Oh, and sorry y'all can't have shower sex, since, you know, it's a shared space and all."

"You're evil, Margot. Pure, delicious evil. I'll be sure to tell them Fin is here too."

It's my turn to glare. "Don't make it sound like I need them. I don't want anyone cutting their break short for my drama."

He pulls me into a hug. "I promise." He tips my chin when he steps back. "But if you do need help with your *drama*, I'm here, okay?"

"Yeah, okay." I wave him off as I head to my room.

Now to deal with the oldest McIntyre, who won't be as easily handled as Evan and my roommates are.

No, Fin is a handful… And then some.

# Twenty-One

**N**EVER HAS A WOMAN WANTED ME SO MUCH YET been so desperate to avoid me, or the morning after, as much Margot. If I were an insecure man, I would have given up by now. Perhaps it's more my selfishness in wanting her despite the obstacles. I'm not easily deterred once a goal has been set. My girl will soon learn how stubborn I can be.

The sight of her room makes my pulse dance and a smile tip the corners of my mouth. I assume this is the master bedroom since she has an ensuite bath. Kudos to the guys for being so generous. I thought she'd have the same bedroom furniture she had in my house, but then I remember that was my furniture. She's not the type to take what doesn't belong to her, even if I would have gladly given it.

Her new furniture is a dark mahogany, a little more manly than I picture my sprite wanting. A king-sized bed sits against the back wall with matching nightstands on either side, a tall chest on the left wall, and a long dresser with a mirror above on the right.

But what makes me smile is the yellow bedding with pink flowers. It's so completely her: sunshine and bursting with life. It makes me want to fill her room with a never-ending stream of fresh flowers. I make a mental note to do just that.

I don't feel her until the door clicks and my senses heighten. I'm hit with the tension filling the space between us. I turn and frown at her uncertainty, eyeing me like she might reverse right back out the way she came.

"Don't even think about it, Pixie."

Moving forward, her twisted lips soften into a smile. "I'm sorry I left like I did." She lightly touches my hand as she passes. "You deserved better than that."

"I won't lie." My gaze follows her into her closet where she's removed her tennis shoes and socks. "I was disappointed to find you gone. I'd hoped we'd moved beyond disappearing acts."

She opens her mouth, but certain of her reply, I continue, "I skipped out on you first. It was cowardly of me. I'd say we're even—if there's even such a thing in relationships. I'd like to move on from here and respect each other enough not to do that again."

"Agreed." She turns, her back to me, slipping off her jeans. Her sleek legs and round rump have my cock getting ideas of its own.

"Why did you leave? What scared you?" I sit on the edge of her bed, her still in my sights, and toe off my shoes and socks. Waiting, not wanting to assume anything with this woman. She's going to have to tell me what she wants before I'll make a move.

Her back to me, she removes her shirt and then her bra. My breath catches at the sight of her nearly naked backside. My Pixie is a beauty. Slim, but not too much. Just enough curves to entice my hands and imagination. And that firm, round ass barely covered by her pink with yellow-flowered panties brings my cock to full attention.

*Sorry, it can't be helped. You're a vision.*

Silently, she reaches back to nab whatever's hanging on her closet door. Her face tilts toward me over her shoulder, but her eyes are cast down. As she rotates just enough to reach, I get a sweet peek at the side of her breast and a pale pink nipple.

"Jesus, fuck, Pixie. You're killing me." I run a hand over my jaw instead of my steel rod like I'm longing to do.

Her eyes flash to mine, but instead of want or a sliver of the seductress she is, all I see is sadness before her head turns and she slips the fabric over her head.

I press my palm to my chest and rub where it aches like a motherfucker.

*Who the fuck put that sadness there?*
*Please, God, don't let it have been me.*

"Margot?" The rasp of his voice has tears burning my eyes.

I tried. I thought maybe if I undressed and just turned around and showed him—got it over with—he wouldn't care, and we could move on. But I chickened out. I'm not brave like him. Like Sam. Like every other person in the world.

He said he's a coward for leaving my bed that morning. Well, I'm a coward every day of my life. I hide behind my personality. I've been doing it so long, I'm not even sure who the true Margot is. Am I that bubbly person? Or am I this person who just wants to fall to the floor and cry?

I swipe at a tear and go to him. Ignoring the concern on his face or the tears that continue to fall, I pull his head to my chest. He ensconces me in his warm embrace between his legs, his arms, around my back. His hold is just tight enough to feel the fierceness of his worry.

Kissing his head, I give him my truth. "I'm so tired, Finley. I don't want to talk about it… I can't… I'm not ready."

With no hesitation, he replies, "Okay," and pulls back enough to lift his gaze to mine. "What do you need, Marguerite?"

That's easy. "I need you to fill me up, let me fall asleep in your arms, and still be here when I wake up." A defiant tear falls.

He brushes it away with his lips. "My sweet girl, I got you."

His words warm me more than they should.

In a graceless dance, I help him undress. My need makes my fingers stupid and my breathing haggard the closer I get to feeling him inside me again. Finally naked, he slips off my panties and, without a word from me, he doesn't even attempt to remove my sleep shirt.

Sitting on the edge of the bed, he lifts me to straddle his lap. We both moan when his cock nestles between my folds. I dig my fingers into his hair and bend to kiss his mouth, but his hold on the back of my neck stops me from making contact.

"You're on top, Pixie, but I'm in control. Understand?"

I say, "Yes," when really, I want to thank him. I don't know how he knows what I need. But being at his mercy, the recipient of the pleasure he brings, is exactly what I need to knock the uncertainty away, to still the riotous thoughts, to find my center again. Even if it is a fake, bubbly persona… Or not.

"We're going to go slow." He bites and sucks my bottom lip. "You're going to want to go fast and hard." His fingers dig into my rear, gliding me against him. "But that's not what you need right now." He kisses and sucks my chin. "Trust me?"

*With my life.* "Yes, I trust you."

He seals my agreement with a deviously slow and succulent kiss. His hands move up my sides over my shirt, his thumbs finding my nipples. I shudder, and he pulls back. "I'm going to play with your nipples." He pinches them before I can freak out. "Over your top. Just your nipples."

I squirm in anticipation, but need to clarify, "Not under my top?"

"No. I understand that's a hard limit for you."

I'm that obvious—that easy to read? "But I wouldn't mind your hands on my back."

Surprise flits across his face before he hides it away. "Under your shirt?"

"Yeah. Just not in front."

"Anything else?"

I bite my lip and relish the way his eyes darken, the emerald nearly glowing. "I really want you to kiss me now."

His smile is lost in our kiss. Frenzied at first, but when our tongues meet, the dance changes.

I beg for more.

He coaxes me into savored kisses, needful caresses, and deep penetrating thrusts that fill me deliciously, endlessly, and tantalizingly slowly.

When my orgasm rips through me, he holds me so tight I believe I might be permanently attached to his chest.

When he lays me down and moves inside me and over me with such tenderness and care, my eyes water in awe of this beautiful man who will rule an empire, but for the moment, he's all mine—ruling me.

When I come again with him tumbling after, I think I see eternity in his eyes that never leave mine and promise things I can't accept, and he could never give.

Yet, wrapped in his arms, I fall asleep. Satiated. Thankful. And blissfully happy.

# Twenty-Two

THE SUN TICKLES MY NOSE AND URGES ME FROM sleep. A moment of panic is quelled when his grip on me tightens like he knows exactly what I'm feeling.

"I'm still here, Pixie." His lips graze my neck as he draws circles across my stomach. "I promise you'll know when I leave." He grinds into my backside, pulling me tighter.

It doesn't feel like he wants to leave anytime soon. No matter how much I want him to stay, I know he can't. My life is here. His life is in Dallas. His priorities don't include me. We're just having a fling. It can't be more. It *won't* be more. I can't allow it. He was good about knowing I have a secret, but knowing and seeing the evidence are two completely different things. But he's not asking for more, so I don't need to even consider how I'd manage *more* with school and the increasing demands of becoming a doctor—if I was willing to try.

"Did you sleep?" A glance at the clock tells me I need to get up. I'm not sure what we have to make for dinner. I may need to run to the store.

"I did." He leans on his arm when I roll over. "I woke up only a few minutes before you." His eyes are bright and content and soothe my wayward thoughts.

"I may need to go to the store. I promised Evan I'd make dinner. He'll join us. I hope you don't mind." I watch for any sign of disappointment or irritation but find neither.

"I don't mind. I'd like to get to know at least one of the guys you're living with."

"You know Watt." Probably reiterating the fact I live with my ex-lover is not the best move.

He gently bites my shoulder. "Don't remind me."

"We just friends, Fin. Nothing more."

His head pops up. "Really?" The relief on his face is a surprise, but the fact he let me see it in the first place is the real revelation. "No sex?"

His vulnerability in this moment is a little overwhelming. I didn't expect him to care—not this much. I palm his cheek and keep his gaze. "I told you I haven't been with anyone since you. I didn't lie. Watt's become a good friend—all the guys have. They look out for me. They fixed my car. Watt gave me his room so I'd have a bathroom to myself. I don't even pay rent. I cook and clean. That's our deal. But I know I'm getting the better end of the bargain."

Fin's forehead meets mine. "Don't sell yourself short, Marguerite. You're a catch in any sense. They're lucky to have you around. Watching out for you gives them something they need. As much as I hate that it's three guys, it's nice to know you're not alone here. That they have your back."

The emotion in his voice is palpable. I can't get sucked into the fantasy he sets loose in my head. "I should get up. See what I need to get at the store." He lets me slip out of his hold, but I can feel his reluctance linger on my skin as I grab some clothes and shut the bathroom door.

I freeze, leaning against the door, chiding myself for wanting more with Fin even though he's not asking—not offering.

A soft knock has me jumping.

"I'll drive you to the store," his muffled voice comes through the door.

I crack it open, his near naked form before me in boxer briefs. "You'd go shopping with me?"

His smile is light and teasing. "You think I don't shop?"

My brows shoot up. "Do you?"

He shrugs. "Sometimes. But I do have someone who does most of the shopping for me."

Figures. Isn't that what most rich people do?

"Doesn't mean I can't come with you."

"True. Give me, like, ten minutes."

His mouth opens, but instead of saying what he's thinking, he nods and steps back.

I open the door farther. "What were you going to say?"

Fisting the shirt he picked up off the floor, his look is pensive. His gaze meets mine and then the ground as he runs his hand through his hair.

I step toward him. "Just say it, Finley." I suck in a breath when my hand meets the solid planes of his chest. "I don't want you to hold back from me." That's rich, considering the secret I'm holding back from him—but not just him. Everyone.

Is this where he tells me he's leaving?

He caresses my chin. "I don't want you to shower. I want you to smell like me." He brushes a kiss across my jaw to whisper across my lips, "Don't wash my cum from your body."

Holy nutcrackers. "That's... Wow."

He smiles sheepishly. "Crass, I know."

I grab his hand as he turns to dress. "Hot."

His eyes linger on our hands before roaming across my sleep shirt, catching on my lips, and stilling on my gaze. "You make me want things, Marguerite," he whispers like regret and yearning all wrapped up in an unfamiliar package.

The ever-present want and fear when I think of a future that can never be war in my stomach. "Don't. What I have could never be enough."

"Don't sell yourself short, Pixie." He squeezes my hand before releasing it and turning away. "You have more than enough of what I need."

I linger on his impressive form as he pulls on his jeans. But when he turns to look at me again, I turn away, disappearing behind the bathroom door before he can witness the fall of my shoulders and hope slide from my face.

Regret follows me as I jump in the shower and do exactly what he asked me not to.

I wash all evidence of him off my body.

Where he lingers, water can't penetrate.

It can't wipe him from my mind.

It can't cleanse him from my soul.

And it can't save my riotous heart from falling.

We didn't go to the store. While we were sleeping, Evan stocked the kitchen with enough food to feed everyone for a week, and the exact ingredients Margot needed to make homemade spaghetti sauce—his favorite, according to Margot.

He wasn't home when I left her to dress. He left a note saying he'd be gone the rest of the afternoon but home in time for dinner. Lucky me.

"Does that happen often?" I continue to chop up the vegetables she handed me a bit ago.

"What? The groceries?"

"Yes. He just decides what you're making for dinner?"

She shrugs and scoops enough meat mixture to make another meatball. Yeah, she knows how to make homemade meatballs too. If I didn't think she was perfect before…

"When I moved in, I gave them a list of what I could cook, but offered to learn anything they wanted. Instead, they came back asking me for a list of the ingredients for each dish so they'd know what to buy when they went grocery shopping." Her smile is whimsical as she hand-rolls more balls before placing them on a cookie sheet. "Honestly, they do most of the shopping. I can't afford to feed the three of them, and thankfully, they don't expect me to. But I do buy what I can, and, of course, I have some food I like that they couldn't care less about."

"Like?" I'm enjoying our easy conversation as we work side by side.

124

"Oh, just little things like yogurt, the kind of crackers and cereal I like. They're not big on raw vegetables, but I sneak them into their salads, and, amazingly, they eat them. Now, cooked veggies, they'll eat. There's actually not much they won't eat. Most of the time, I think they're just so happy to have home-cooked meals instead of fast food or taking turns ordering takeout. They train so much. After school, practice, and working out, they're too tired to come home and figure out dinner. Anyway," she moves to wash her hands, "it's nice to cook for them. It's nice to feel appreciated—needed."

That's exactly what I was trying to tell her earlier about them taking care of her—looking out for her. I'm sure they feel the same way she does about cooking for them.

Everybody likes to be needed. Wants to feel what they do matters, even if it's only to one person.

I finish my chopping and rinse my hands as she places the tray of meatballs in the oven. "Can I ask you something?"

She eyes me with uncertainty before she decides. "Sure."

"Would you tell me about your dad?"

She starts on the sauce. "He was such a great dad when I was younger. He was present. So funny. But then… Things happened. Bills piled up, and he started drinking. Inevitably, he lost his job. Now he can't find anyone to hire him, and if he does, it doesn't last long. He's angry at himself, but takes it out on the world—on his family." She turns, and the fondness in her soft brown eyes makes my chest ache. "Sometimes, I still get a glimpse of the man he was, but it's been so long. I'm not even sure he's still in there. He had a blow up yesterday, that's why Jenny and Zeke left for Houston. We're all tired of it, and Mom won't put her foot down. Plus, she works twelve-hour shifts in the NICU and usually picks up extra hours. By the time she gets home, she doesn't have the energy to deal with Dad, much less force him into rehab."

"Would he go if y'all suggested it?"

"He would use the excuse: *we can't afford it.* Which is true. We can't."

"You mean *they* can't afford it?" She or her siblings should not be saddled with paying for their father to get sober.

"Same difference. None of us can afford it."

"And if money were no object? Would he go?"

"I really don't know, Fin. I want to say yes, but I truly have no idea what he would do if he could afford it. People get sober all over the world without going to a treatment facility. I think if he really wanted to get sober, he'd find a way or at least try. But being drunk, broke, and out of work doesn't hurt as much as not drinking, I suppose."

"He could do it for his family. That should be a big enough reason." My anger at his selfishness is hard to keep at bay. But I try. For her.

Her hurt is unmistakable. "In a perfect world, it would be enough. But it's not."

# Twenty-Three

"**H**EY, MARGOT. YOUR PHONE IS RINGING IN your room." Evan sticks his head around the corner, fresh from a shower. He got home a while ago, sticking to his room. He thinks we want privacy, but this is his home too. He shouldn't feel like he has to hide out.

"Thanks." I pass his towel-clad, wet-from-the-shower stature. "You're gonna dress for dinner, right?"

He thinks about it. "I guess I can put on some shorts. I wouldn't want to make a certain someone jealous."

That makes me laugh. "Please don't."

"Okay, no shorts then." He laughs as he enters his room.

Grabbing my phone off my dresser, I don't recognize the number but listen to the voicemail.

When *his* voice comes on, a chill rips through me. "Call me. This number. Don't make me call you again, Mar. You won't like the consequences."

*Mar.* I always hated when he called me that. Though, after the way he treated me, I hate everything about him. But I still fear him more than I hate him.

Closing my bedroom door, I call him back.

"Good girl, Mar. It's good to know you can still take orders." Bobby's audible leer fills me with disgust. I wish I'd never met him, never given him the time of day. Desperate-for-attention and Bobby don't mix. I found that out the hard way.

"Don't call me that."

"What? *Mar*? But it's so fitting. Don't you think? You look like this perfect package. But then get you undressed, and the fantasy dies. You're *Marred*-got. Hence the nickname. Fitting. Perfect. Unlike you."

I was raised not to hate people, not to even use that word. But there is no other way to describe how I feel about Bobby. I H-A-T-E him. Pure and simple. "What do you want?" I need to move this along, regretting every second I waste on him.

"I heard who you're dating," his rasp softens like he's trying to get all buddy-buddy.

"I'm not dating anyone."

"Okay then. *Fucking*. What does it matter? Fin McIntyre has enough money to do whatever he wants with you. And I'm sure he does. You always were a little dirty, huh, Mar? You like it hard and heartless."

*No.* He can't know about Fin. This is not good. I can't have Fin dragged into my past with Bobby. "That's because you don't have a heart. You wouldn't know the difference."

"Touché." He clears his throat. "Here's what I do know. You're going to get your new boy-toy to give you ten grand—that you're going to gladly hand over to me—or I'm going to tell him all about how fucked up you are."

I don't care what he threatens. I'm not asking Fin for money. "What makes you think he doesn't already know?"

"Because he's still around. You must be pulling that keep-my-shirt-on routine. Am I right?" He's so cocky.

"You can tell him whatever you want. There's no way I'm going to ask him for money—not for you. Not for me. Not for anybody."

"Two weeks, Mar. You've got two weeks." He hangs up before I can beat him to the punch.

I don't want Fin to know my secret, but I sure as heck don't want Bobby thinking he can blackmail me either. If he gets a taste of Fin's money, it would never stop. Bobby enjoys humiliating me too much. I'm sure he plans on telling Fin no matter what. But even if he didn't, he'd make life hell for Fin, showing up at MCI, spewing lies about me or Fin. I can't have Bobby do that to Fin. I never thought things with Fin were a forever type of situation. I guess this is the sign I needed to end things where we stand.

I won't feed into the fear. I will fight Bobby. I will win. But most importantly, I will protect Fin and his family from my ass of an ex.

Dinner is incredible. Margot's meatballs have to be the best I've ever tasted. Seriously. The. Best. Evan's head barely comes up from his plate until it's half-empty. Like he had to soothe the starving beast in him before he could even consider casual conversation.

But my girl hasn't been the same since she came back from her room, either answering or making a phone call. With Evan here, I don't want to ask, but it's obvious whatever occurred has taken the wind out of her sails.

"Man, Margot, I'm sorry for whatever brought you home from Dallas early, but I'm happy to not have to go two more weeks without your cooking." Evan shoves a whole meatball in his mouth and smiles at her like she hung the moon.

I can relate.

But his compliment only grants him a soft, "I'm glad you like it," from Margot.

Something is definitely off.

Evan meets my gaze, his quizzical brow silently asking a question I have no answer to. I give a soft shrug while Margot studies her food.

"That's a hot car you're driving." Evan chooses what he thinks is a safe topic but may end up being catastrophic.

"Thanks. You're welcome to take a look at it."

"The color is… Familiar." He glances at Margot, who's checked out of our conversation. "Don't you think, Margot?"

Her head pops up. "I'm sorry. What?"

"Fin's car. Have you seen it?" he asks.

"Uh, no." Her eyes lock on me as she continues to speak to him, "What about it?" Her head tilts as she studies me for a reaction I have no intention of giving her.

"It's yellow. Like your Mustang. Coincidence, don't you think?" Evan is digging my grave. He just doesn't know it.

Her eyes widen. "Really?"

"Evan, I wanted to thank you, Watt, and Griffin for fixing Margot's car." A course correction is needed.

"Yeah, well,"—he leans back, wiping his mouth—"we did what we could. It's good for driving around town, but it needs more work than our knowledge affords us."

Margot smiles at him. "You all did more than enough. Really."

"We were happy to do it. It was fun, all of us working together, like a house project or something."

I eye Evan, silently asking for his help when I dare suggest, "I have a guy who could fix whatever else is wrong—"

"No," Margot jumps in. "I don't need your help or your money."

Her last word has me narrowing my focus on her. I didn't specifically mention *money*, yet she felt it necessary to clarify. "You'd almost be doing me a favor. I wouldn't have to worry about you driving a great but dilapidated car." I point to Evan. "Your roommates wouldn't need to worry about you or lend you their cars when you drive home."

"*This* is my home." Her voice rises to a surprising level I've not heard from her before.

I simply nod. There's not much I could say that she'll be open to. I pick up my plate and glass. "Thanks for an exceptional dinner." I step away before I push harder than she's willing to let me.

When she doesn't follow, I take it as a good sign and start cleaning up the kitchen. A few minutes pass before Evan places the remaining plates on the counter.

"She went to her room."

So it wasn't a good sign after all. Yeah, this is not going as planned.

"I need a favor." I continue to clean as I talk, "I have a feeling I'll be leaving soon. When I do, I'm going to leave you my keys for Margot. She'll fight you. She'll fight me. But she needs a reliable car. I can have my guy here tomorrow to pick up her Mustang. Maybe if she doesn't have a choice, she'll drive my i8."

He scratches the back of his head. "Man, I don't want to piss her off. But I agree. Her car has seen better days. It's a classic, but sometimes classics are meant to be admired and not driven. This is about her safety."

"Agreed. So, will you help?"

"Yeah." He jumps in, helping me clean. "How will you get home?"

"I'll take a cab to the airport." I don't tell him it's a private airport. I don't need to flaunt my money. I may love expensive cars, but I don't talk about them unless someone brings it up and specifically asks me a question.

"I could drive you."

"I appreciate that. Let's see how it plays out." I have a feeling it will be in the middle of the night or in a few minutes. It all depends on her and whatever's crawled into that brain of hers and flipped a switch on the interior view I finally got a sight of this morning. She let me in. She may not have told me her secret, but she acknowledged there is *something* she's hiding. I felt her opening up in a critical way she never has before.

I just pray her closure is temporary.

# Twenty-Four

I PACE THE FLOOR OF MY ROOM, COUNTING THE seconds, the breaths, the heartbeats since I left Fin in the kitchen, escaping to the stillness of my room. Stillness? There's nothing still about me or how I'm about to explode with doubt and nerves.

I can do this.

I *have* to do this.

*Why, again?*

Oh, let me list the reasons: I can't let Bobby use Fin; I can't tell Fin my secret. He'd leave for sure. Which brings me to the truth: I'm too flawed for a man like Fin. I'm too flawed for an asshole like Bobby. There's no middle ground. There is no ground at all. Just paper-thin sheets of lies too flimsy to even hold a lightweight like me.

"Pixie."

His sultry voice infiltrated with concern has me squeezing my eyes shut, wishing I could bury my head in the sand and pretend he can't see me. Pretend I don't exist.

See no evil. Hear no evil. Speak no evil. But it's not evil I'm peddling. It's lies.

And I'm the master of deception.

Sleight of hand connoisseur.

Distraction's mistress.

Fin's arms wrap around me, and I sink into him. "Tell me what's going on." His lips brush my ear.

132

Faking a calm I don't feel, I give him the only truth I can. "I need two things from you."

"Anything." His lack of hesitation makes this only harder.

"Promise, whatever I ask of you, you will simply do and not ask why."

"I have one condition, then, whatever you ask is yours." He turns me in his arms. "I need you to promise me…" His green-eyed stare pins me in place, in his arms, which is never a bad place to be. The realization of how much I'm going to miss it—miss him, has me closing my eyes and turning my face away as I try to stop my tears. I will miss him more than I have a right to.

"Promise." He leans in, capturing my face in his hand as he brushes his lips across the other cheek.

Give and take. He's a negotiator at heart. A businessman who knows how to cut a deal. But I'm not stupid either. "Whatever you ask of me can't negate or impact what I ask of you."

"Understood." He walks me backwards a few steps. "Promise me, Pixie. Whatever I ask of you, you will do as long as it doesn't interfere with what you ask of me."

I hold up my finger. "And it doesn't require I reveal things I'm not ready to reveal."

His mouth quirks on one side. He's trying not to smile, and I desperately want to see his panty-dropping smile right now. "Agreed." With the flat of his hand on my chest, he pushes, and I fall onto the bed. Yet I'm not alone. He follows me over, bracing my landing, his face mere inches from mine. "Promise me."

"I promise," comes out much easier than I anticipate.

He nods just once. "I promise too." He softly moves my hair away from my ear so he can trace the curve too tenderly for words. "What do you want, my Pixie?"

"I want you to make love to me." The crack in my voice is not to be helped. This will be the last time he touches me. I'm not so broken I can't fathom the importance of savoring his every last touch.

He closes his eyes for a brief moment, his head resting on mine. "You don't need me to promise in order to ask *that* of me." His eyes open, and he brushes his lips across mine. "Granted. What else?"

I shake my head until I decide, "I'll tell you afterwards."

"Afterwards? Am I on a time limit here?" He chuckles. "I'm not sure if that's an incentive to make it quick or draw it out to avoid the inevitable."

I lose my fingers in his lush, dark hair. All the brothers have such great hair. Same hair. Same eyes. Same confidence. And yet they are as different as they are similar. "I'm in no hurry. The timetable is yours for the taking or the savoring."

"Savoring." He licks across my lips. "I'm all about savoring you, Marguerite." A soft press of his lips, a quick lick of his tongue teases mine. "And in order to do that I need you naked."

A raised brow from me has him amending, "As naked as you are comfortable with."

I wish I could give him all of me.

I've no doubt feeling him skin to skin would take what Fin gives to a whole new level.

He'll have to settle for half of me naked, while I know he's already captured me in my entirety.

Every inch.

Every morsel.

Every beat of my heart belongs to him.

It's too bad he can never know.

"Finley," she begs.

The need in her voice is powerful. I feel like a god when I'm with her, and I fear this may be the last time. The ache in her voice, the tears in her eyes, and the intensity of her touch—it feels like goodbye.

And damn if the ache in my chest doesn't make it that much harder to breathe. Or the need in my steel cock that much more desperate to pour my seed into her, filling her up, reminding her body whom she belongs to.

My calm has left me. Exiting on every thrust, on every moan, on every sizzle of pleasure that races through my body as she comes around my cock. Again. And again.

She said I had no timeline. I've taken full advantage. This is our third go-around, and I just might be able to eke a fourth out of us.

I'm not giving up.

No matter what she requires of me, I will not give up on us.

I will find a way.

"Please." She pinches my nipple.

I hiss in a breath followed by, "Fuck," and give her what she needs. I suck a little too hard on that spot below her ear that makes her squeeze my cock, then whisper in her ear when I start to rub her clit, "Come for me, Pixie."

And fuck if she doesn't, like she was waiting for permission that she never needs from me. Her entire body trembles with uncontrolled spasms, her eyes screwed shut, her mewl echoing in my ears.

I'll never forget the sight or the sound of my Pixie coming undone in my arms. Never.

The vision, the memory locked in my brain is enough to tip me over the edge and seize her so tightly, I fear she may break.

She doesn't. Thank God.

I collapse beside her. Her panting rivals my own.

"Please don't ask anything of me that requires me to move. Not yet," I beg of her. Obviously not beyond it and definitely not capable of a fourth round anytime soon. Even if she sucked my cock—*oh, fuck. It twitched.* I can't.

Her giggle has me turning her way.

She motions with her chin. "How are you hard again?"

No shame left in me, I admit, "I was thinking of your mouth."

"Holy nutcrackers, Finley. You're a stud." She means it as a compliment, but all I can think about are all the women she thinks I want instead of her.

"Only for you, Marguerite. Only for you." I throw my arm over my head and close my eyes. I just need a quick power nap.

But she curls into me, her head on my chest, and her body flush against mine has me wanting to hold her forever and yet wanting to rip the Band-Aid off all at the same time.

"Pixie, tell me the second promise you want from me. It's time you tell me what you need."

The moisture on my chest conveys all I need to know, but still I hold out for her words. Words that will rip my flesh off along with the Band-Aid as she painfully pulls it free.

"I need you to leave." She buries her cries in my shoulder.

I pull her tight, willing what's left of my strength into her.

"You can't come back here." She sniffles and sits up, wiping at her face with her sleeves. "You have to forget"—she motions between us—"about this."

"I'm not forgetting you, Marguerite." I sit up, swing my legs over the side, put my elbows on my knees, and cradle my head. She's crazy if she thinks I can forget how things are between us. She's rocked my world. My calm, predictable existence seems so bleak when she's not in it. When her light isn't shining in my vicinity, the gray seems that much darker. I'm not even sure I can breathe without my Pixie.

"I could never forget you either, Finley."

*Yet you're asking me to leave.*

Movement has me peeking around my shoulder just in time to see her roll out of bed and stop at the window. She pulls the curtain back and rests her forehead on the glass. "Tell me what promise you need from me."

Unable to locate my underwear, I pull my jeans on, finger the key fob in my pocket and lay it on the dresser. "Let me fix your Mustang and leave you the BMW i8 in exchange."

Her sigh fogs the window. "Okay. I'm not happy about it, but..." Her tear-reddened eyes lock on me. "A promise is a promise."

I step closer, brushing a tear from her cheek. "One more thing. I need you to unblock my number." I pin her with a glare when she tries to protest. "Stop. I won't call you. I won't beg. But I need to know I can reach you if I *need* to." I pull her into me. Her fight has all but left her body. "If something comes up. If I need to know you're okay, you're safe, or if an emergency arises." I kiss her head. "I need this, Margot. Don't deny me. Please."

"Okay." She squeezes me tight for a minute before she slips out of my arms and into the bathroom. No falter in her steps. No looking back. No regrets.

When I hear the click of the lock, I know that's my cue.

It's time to leave.

She thinks it's forever.

It's not.

# Twenty-Five

## ⚊ New Years Eve ⚊

ONCE A WEEK, SINCE I WALKED OUT OF HER HOUSE in Austin, I text Margot. I said I wouldn't, but I can't help the need to test the waters and ensure the pathway is still open. Desperate? Perhaps. Sorry? Not in the least.

**Me:** *Happy New Years, Pixie.*

And because I can't help it...

**Me:** *Miss you.*

Text dots dance on the screen, letting me know she's still receiving my texts in addition to the *delivered* status. I've never paid attention to the status of a text message before my girl. Now I live and breathe for that damn status to appear after I hit send.

It's ridiculous, yet it provides a modicum of peace. A nine-letter representation of hope: *Delivered.*

**Pixie:** *Happy NY to you too. Please, don't miss me.*

It's a knife to the chest, her request not to miss her, and no hint if she misses me as well. I down the rest of my prized Macallan. The drink

I used to savor has no taste. The burn and the numbness it brings are all it has to offer me now.

Spending Christmas alone, no special someone in my life, never bothered me before. But this year, given Joe and Sam were on their honeymoon, Matt is in a funk, and my Pixie is God knows where with God knows who, the absence of that kind of love in my life blares at deafening levels. I stayed at my parents' long enough to wish them *Merry Christmas*, eat, and hightail it home where I could indulgently mope in private.

The days since have not passed in better fashion or usefulness. The only productivity I can muster is work-related and even then, it's putting out fires or tasks that cannot possibly wait or be delegated.

*Jesus, I'm a sad sack.*

I skip the refill of whiskey, deciding water would be a safer bet. At least until the guys get here for poker.

A quick knock on my door has me turning just in time to see Victor pass through the entryway and step toward the bar. "You look better today."

"Do I?" Nothing has changed, so I'm not sure how that's possible.

"Nah, you still look like someone took your favorite pussy away."

That actually makes me laugh. In a sense it's true. Only it was Margot who took herself away. I slouch on the couch and close my eyes. Maybe I could sleep for a few hours and wake up to a new me. Because this guy is driving me crazy. I was so confident the day I left her, believing I could win her back. But I haven't a clue how. She pushed me away for reasons I can't fathom. She has secrets she's not willing to part with. Other than kidnapping her, I'm not sure how I can force myself into her life when she so seamlessly pushed me out of it.

"I may be able to help with that." He sits across from my slumped position on the couch. My dead stare must give away my confusion as he clarifies, "The ban on your favorite pussy."

Again, dead air between us. I'm not much for company these days.

"Bobby is the one who called her that day." He holds up his hand. "I know. You didn't want me to invade her privacy. But fuck, man. You look like shit and act like ass." He savors a sip of whiskey.

I envy his small hum of appreciation. I know it's good. I just can't taste it anymore. But his last words pique my interest. "Do you know why Bobby called Margot?"

"No. But I do know he called her just a few days ago. Two weeks after the last time, almost to the minute. It's as if he had a reminder on his phone: *Call Margot, be an ass.*"

I crack a smile.

"Ah, I saw that." He points at me while holding the tumbler of dark goodness in his hand. "We managed to clone his phone today. If he texts or calls her again, we'll know."

"But you still can't track her?"

"No. Not unless you want me to go to Austin and get it done. Or… You could ask Evan to do it."

There are some lines I'm not willing to cross. "She trusts him. He's a good guy and not pretending to be her friend so he can get in her pants. I need him on my side and still in her good graces. I'm not willing to compromise their friendship."

"We'll have to rely on Bobby's tracker and watching his activity, then. But even if she comes to town, we have no way of knowing if he's near her."

"I'll ask Evan if he can at least let me know if she leaves town." I can't imagine he'd have a problem with that, especially if I let him know about Bobby.

"I'm hungry. When's food coming?" He gets up and heads to the kitchen.

"A couple of hours yet. Snack on some fruit."

"Alright, grandma. I won't ruin my appetite." He tosses me an apple as he sits back down with two apples and a bunch of grapes. "What are the chances you'll come with us later?"

He knows the answer. I don't know why he keeps asking. "What are the chances you'll skip going?"

"None."

"Same." No way in hell I'm going to a sex club when the only woman I want is two hundred miles away, hiding secrets like the CIA, and determined to keep me out like Fort Knox.

"Come on, Margot. You're only a few hours away. Drive your shiny new car down here so I can see it," Jenny begs.

"It's not my car, Jenny. Fin is only lending it to me while mine is being fixed," I remind her for the hundredth time, and, like every other time, she'll completely ignore me. She likes her fantasy of Fin and me together. She's done nothing but taunt me with him since the first day we met in Austin, years ago, when I came to visit her while I was still in high school. Even then, she tried to get me to go home with him. Not like he was asking. Not like I would ever make a move, especially not on Joe's brother. That's some convoluted mess I never had any intention of getting mixed up in.

Yet, here I am. Driving Fin's car, texting him occasionally, even though he said he wouldn't reach out to me except in the case he *needed* to. I guess he needs to on a weekly basis. And I soak up every last drop of his attention, even if it's in the form of a borrowed car and occasional text messages. It's something.

It's all I have.

"Can I bring Evan? We had plans to hang out tonight." Neither of us are much for the party scene. My sister's will be silliness mixed with board games and probably charades or something of the like. Far from the typical drunken college New Year's Eve kegger Evan and I want to avoid.

"Yes! Get your ass in the car now! Plan on staying a few days, will you? We didn't get to see you for Christmas. Even Zeke missed seeing you."

Yeah, about Zeke. We need to figure out what to do with him and returning to my parents' house. Mom's been threatening to drive to Houston to get him if we don't bring him home soon. But she's not willing to kick Dad out to ensure his home environment is as safe as possible. Granted, Dad isn't a violent drunk, but he is a mean one. Verbal assaults can leave scars just a deep as physical ones.

"I'm sorry I missed Christmas." She knows I just wasn't up to it. Fin leaving took more of me than I bargained for. I told him to leave, but when he did, the hole in my chest became a cavernous pit. Nothing can ease it. Nothing can fill it. Nothing can camouflage the gaping hole in my life. It's just there.

I should give it a name. Set a place at the table for it. It's a part of my life now. I need to get used to it.

"I know. Go. Now. See you soon." She hangs up before I can protest or give her an affirmative answer.

Of course I'm going. Even if Evan doesn't come.

But he does.

He's all smiles and chatter the entire way there. His excitement is nearly contagious. Nearly. My face cracks with a smile, and I have to feel my lips to be sure I'm not bleeding. It's been two weeks since Fin took my smile, my hope, my now-unattainable future with him.

Two weeks.

"You're going to have to stop moping at some point," Evan says as we approach Jenny's apartment she shares with her boyfriend.

"Who says?"

"Life. History is full of broken hearts that mend. Unrealized dreams that morph into other dreams. Disappointments that turn into blessings." He squeezes my hand. "This too will pass, Margot."

"I wish it would pass already."

His smile is sweet but mocking. "No, you don't. You're wanting to hold on to the past. What never was. What might never be. You have to give it up to find out what *can* be."

I groan. I know he's right, but still… "Who died and made you the Dalai Lama?"

I thought he'd laugh, but he doesn't. "Experience made me wise. Pain made me strong. Disappointment made me resilient."

Well, jinkies, I hadn't expected such deep thoughts from him, or his willingness to be so open. Maybe he's on to something.

It's time to stop being sad.

Stop feeling sorry for myself.

Time to figure out what I want and what I'm willing to do to get it.

# Twenty-Six

## ᐱᴸ March ᐁᴸ

JENNY CALLED THIS MORNING. MOM IS devastated. She was leaving for work and found Dad passed out in the driveway. She couldn't wake him, nor get him into the house. She had to miss work. Not just because he's a drunk fool, but because he was blocking her car. The only way she could get out of the driveway was to run him over. And though she's rightly upset, she's not murderous. I guess that's something.

"What's wrong?" Watt enters my bedroom, gym bag over his shoulder, hair wet from his shower.

"Jenny called." I continue to throw a couple days' worth of clothes in my smallest roller bag. "We're staging an intervention."

He moves closer, his hand grazing my arm. "Your dad?"

"Uh huh." I don't trust my voice won't crack from the effort to keep my emotions in check. I don't know why I care anymore, why my dad's pain continues to haunt me.

*Because it's your fault.*

I disappear into my bathroom, close my eyes and take a deep breath.

"Hey." Watt follows and wraps me in a hug. "It'll be okay. It might be tough at first. But trying to help your dad get sober can't be a bad thing."

I nod against his chest. He's right. But that's not really why I'm

144

upset. To face my dad is to face my part in his addiction. *I'm* the reason he seeks escape. It *is* all my fault.

Watt cradles my face, urging me to look him in the eye. "You don't give up on the ones you love," he says with vehemence.

I'm sure some tough-love counselors would tell him otherwise. Sometimes you have to walk away to make your point. But I suppose my siblings and I have all done that already, and it hasn't made a lick of difference. He's as drunk as ever. Maybe even worse.

Watt leaves me to finish packing, but when I enter the living room, he is standing there with a different bag slung over his shoulder. I frown, narrowing my eyes on him. What's he up to?

"I'm going with you," he says like it's a done deal.

"No. I can't ask you to do that."

"You're not asking, and neither am I. You need a friend. I'm going." He takes my bag and heads to the garage where Fin's car is parked.

Even though I didn't park my Mustang in the garage before, the guys wouldn't let me park the i8 outside. The car costs more than this house, they reasoned, which is true. *Probably.* I didn't really want to know for sure, so I didn't research it. That knowledge would only make me anxious to drive something *that* expensive.

He drives most of the way, but when we stop just outside the Dallas city limits, we switch. "Listen, as much as I appreciate you coming with me, I'm not sure seeing you will help my dad's attitude toward us confronting him. He might even say some things I'd rather not subject you to. So, maybe you could drop me off and then go see a movie, get something to eat, or whatever. Give us a few hours to see this through."

His stare is considerate as I glance at him from the driver's seat. "I can see having a stranger there might make him defensive. I'll agree as long as you promise to call me if things go south. I'll stay close."

"Okay." I breathe a sigh of relief not to have to worry about Watt. What he'll see, and what Dad will do or say. It's one less thing to stress over.

When Watt drops me off, I wait until he leaves before entering the house. Tension radiates off the walls, so thick and stifling it's hard to breathe—or maybe it's guilt keeping me from getting a full breath.

"Ah, so I see all my ungrateful children have returned to gang up on me," my father's voice booms from the den.

My shoulders fall on a puff of air. This is not going to be fun.

"We're not here to gang up on you, Daddy," Jenny starts, but he's not paying her any mind.

His eyes are locked on me. "You're the reason I'm like this."

I nod, hating the defeat that consumes me. "I know." I do.

"Well, at least we agree on that," he hisses.

"Tom—" Mom tries to interject, but this is my battle.

I step closer. My voice might not be strong, but my back is straight. "Would you rather I had died?" I often wondered—felt—that was the way he wished it had gone, but until now I've never given voice to the words.

"No! God, no," Mom cries. Her fierce rejection softens the edges of my guilt a little. I know *she* doesn't regret what they did for me.

But my father… Well, he regrets it all. I have no doubt.

"Oh, come on, Daniella. Be honest. Things would have been so different if we hadn't ruined ourselves going into debt saving her." Dad's words hurt more than any strike ever could.

Mom is on her feet, my brother rising to her side. His face is pale, but he's willing to protect her if it comes to that. My mom lays into Dad, "You are a pitiful excuse for a man, Tom Dubois. If it wasn't for our beautiful children, I would wish I'd never met you."

He flares back, his eyes wide with disbelief before something like realization enters them and tears begin welling up. Her words hit their mark.

I almost feel sorry for him. Almost.

Pounding on the door gives us pause. When no one makes a move to answer it, I do, moving like a zombie out of the den, past the formal sitting area to the entry. Stunned.

I swing open the door.

My shock at Dad's admission allows the man on the doorstep to wrap his hand around my neck and squeeze.

It's been months of the same old, same old. I text Margot occasionally and receive a few updates from Evan. Bobby's been in contact with her, but we haven't been able to trace it as he's not been using his cell phone when he calls her. He hardly texts anyone, except his steady fuck he meets up with a few times a week.

I've kept my head down and focused on work—the usual. Except, I'm making plans. I'm giving her the space she needs, but I'm not giving up. Once she graduates in a few months, I'm there, at her door, beginning her to take a chance on us—on me.

Pitiful? Maybe. But I've learned a thing or two from watching Joe with Sam. The direct course is always the better choice. I'm going to lay it all out there, put it all on the line. Show Margot I can make her a priority. I've got it all planned.

Just two more months till her graduation. Then, depending on her next steps, I'll be there with my proposal, or my backup proposal, or the backup, backup proposal. I've got a solution to whatever direction she decides to take regarding her schooling or career.

I'm the fixer, and I'm ready to *fix* us.

A rap on my office door has me looking into a stern-faced Victor when he opens the door without waiting for my reply. My glare at him for interrupting my winning-Margot-over thoughts doesn't even faze him.

He motions over his shoulder seconds before Watt follows him inside. "Security called me when Mr. Burns requested to see you."

"Really?" Standing, I eye Watt with his hands buried in his pockets. His mess of blond hair, blue eyes, and impressive size remind me why I hate the idea of him ever having a piece of my girl. Dismissing him for a moment, my attention slides to my best friend. "And you couldn't give me a heads-up as you went to retrieve him?"

I don't even need his answer. I know why. He likes to keep me on my toes, reminding me that I'm not nearly as in control as I like to think. "Remember who signs your paycheck, Brother," I mumble as I pass him, holding my hand out to Watt.

Victor just laughs.

Watt shakes my hand, his eyes bouncing between Victor and me. "I'm sorry to barge in like this, but I didn't have your number."

I wave toward the seating area. "Sit. Tell me what brings you here, in person." I don't point out that he could have looked up the MCI corporate number and asked for me. Granted he would have gotten Angela, my PA, and not me directly. But he would have, eventually. Angela would never turn anyone away, especially if they knew Margot.

Watt sits on the edge of the couch. "Evan told me about his deal to contact you if Margot left town."

I flash to Victor, already fidgeting with his phone. Turning my focus back to Watt, I confirm my suspicion. "She's left town?"

He nods. In that one gesture I'm filled with joy over the idea of seeing her again with an overshadowing worry over Bobby's intentions.

"She's here," he confirms. "They're doing an intervention for her dad. I dropped her off at her parents' house and came straight here. I don't know this Bobby character, but he seems like bad news."

Watt's evident worry makes me like him even more. "He is. Believe me. I appreciate you coming here to let me know."

In my peripheral vision, I catch Victor walking toward my private bathroom, his phone to his ear. Him seeking quiet but not leaving my office for privacy tells me I need to get ready to leave.

Pushing the intercom on my phone, I tell Angela, "Cancel the rest of my day. Emergencies only." Even if nothing is going on with Bobby, I need to check on my Pixie. I've no doubt her family drama will take its toll.

"Of course." Angela knows the score. If I hear from her today, it will be a true emergency, and she tried in every way to handle it before reaching out to me.

Victor steps out of the bathroom, his pensive features ratcheting up my concern. "He's there."

"How the hell did he get there so fast? How did he even know Margot was in town?"

"I don't know, Brother." He heads for the door. "Let's find out."

I grab my cell, my jacket, and motion to Watt. "Come on."

Watt lives up to his nickname as he steps to my side. "What's going on?"

We meet Victor at the express elevator to the garage.

I call Margot. It rings before going to voicemail. "Fuck." I scrub my face and call again.

"What?" Watt's tone equals my stress. "Tell me what the fuck is happening."

Victor fills him in. As we step in the elevator, I call her sister, Jenny. It goes directly to voicemail.

By the time we reach Victor's car, I've left voicemails for her entire family. Even her asshole of a dad.

With Victor behind the wheel, we hit the road at a speed that should alarm me. Instead, I find it relaxing, knowing we will get there as fast as humanly possible. Victor has sweet skills behind the wheel. He also has friends in the police department, whom he just called as a heads-up in case things are as bad as we fear they might be by the time we get there.

My heart racing, I try Margot again. Voicemail. "Fuck!"

"What does he want?" Watt asks from the backseat.

"We don't know." I meet Victor's glance. "Whatever it is, it can't be good."

# Twenty-Seven

BOBBY SMASHES ME AGAINST THE ENTRY WALL.

"What did I tell you, Mar?" His face is inches from mine, his voice, low and menacing. "The price doubles for every week you ignore me. You owe me a pretty penny now. Would have been so much easier on you if you'd just given me the ten grand I asked for."

I smack and pull at his wrist, trying to loosen his grip. "I hate you," I manage around his stranglehold on my neck. I punch him as hard as I can on the cheek.

Stunned, he shakes his head for too brief a time, then pulls me off the wall and slams my head against it again. "Back at ya." He leans down, his nose in my hair as he breaths in. "I thought I was gonna to have to take a trip to Austin to get my hands on you. But lo and behold, I spotted a yellow-ass sports car zipping past our favorite hangout. When I realized it was you driving, timing couldn't have been more perfect."

*Perfect?* More likely damned.

He pulls back, his grip tightening, bringing me with him. His eyes are crazy, full of hate as he flexes, ready to slam me against the wall again. But before he can, I knee him in the groin, followed by another punch. As he bends over and sucks in air, his grip loosens. I'm able to twist out of this hold and dart away. But I only make it a few steps. He wrenches me back by my hair. My scream has my brother and sister running in from the other side of the house. Their eyes bulge when they spot us.

"Call 911—" I yell seconds before his fist makes contact with my chin. My ears ring, and my vision spins as I collapse to the ground.

"You're a no-good bitch, Mar. So full of secrets and deceit." Bobby reaches for my leg. I kick, but I'm no match in my dazed state. He easily grabs my ankle and starts dragging me out the front door.

"Leave her alone—" is all I hear before my brother, Zeke, flies over my body and tackles Bobby to the ground. They roll, landing in the grass. Zeke gets in one good punch before Bobby manages to get to his feet.

I sway as I stand, my head reeling, my vision spotty. The panic I felt initially morphs into rage and hate for a man who has done nothing but cause me pain.

"You little shit." Bobby charges Zeke, knocks him down and starts pounding on him.

"No!" I run at Bobby with every fiber of my being, knocking him off Zeke, who's lying limp on the grass. But I can't stop fighting to check on my younger brother. I just have to pray he's okay.

"I'm going to kill you, Bobby." Tears burn my eyes as I continue to scream, scratch, and pound on him with all my might.

Another punch to my face makes me lose consciousness for a moment or two. Long enough for the situation to have changed.

My dad is on the grass, a bat in his hand, swinging at Bobby like he's swinging for the fences—going for a homerun.

Jenny is cradling Zeke on the grass.

My mom has the phone to her ear and is screaming at my dad, "Kill him. He hurt my baby!"

I stagger to my feet, dizziness plaguing my vision. I don't know if Mom is talking about me or Zeke. Either way, I have to stop this before anyone else gets hurt, or anyone besides Bobby goes to jail. A quick scan of the yard leaves me with no weapon options besides myself—my body.

Watching Daddy as closely as possible and still keeping my focus on Bobby, I take a few running steps and leap at his side, clinging to him like a spider monkey. He stumbles and gasps for air I knocked out of him. Before he can recover and start wailing on me, I smash my head into his temple. The pain is excruciating. My hold weakens, and my vision flickers.

Bobby groans, blood flowing down the side of his head, angry words spewing from his horrible mouth.

The last thing I see is the green grass as he throws me off him, spiraling toward it at an alarming rate.

"Jesus, fuck," leaves me as I leap from the car, yelling, "Call 911," and hurdle the white picket fence of the Dubois front yard. I make it to Margot's dad in three strides, ripping the fence rail out of his hands that are as bloody as Bobby's face. Relief floods me at the sight of this asshole, unconscious and subdued by a man more than twice his age.

Mrs. Dubois' sobs get my attention as she points behind me. Turning, I see the aftermath of what looks like a massacre, only it's Zeke and Margot, bloodied and laid out.

I catch sight of Victor and Watt running our way. "Police were already called," Victor informs.

"Make sure he doesn't get up." I point to Bobby, knowing Victor will make sure he's down for the count.

I rush to Margot, hovering over her, afraid to make a wrong move. Her limp form is only feet from her prone brother and sobbing sister, who's trying to comfort both of them. Zeke is moaning, which I hope is a good sign. But my sprite is silent and still—way too fucking still. I can't move her. What if she has a neck injury?

Falling on my knees beside her, bending low to see if she's breathing, I nearly cry in thanks when I hear and feel her breath on my ear. I quickly move to her neck, finding her pulse is strong and steady. But fuck, what do I know? She's the one who wants to be the doctor.

*Jesus, Pixie, wake up so you can tell me what to do.*

"Margot." My voice cracks as I struggle with where to touch her.

Her forehead is bleeding, her cheek and jaw are red and swelling, and bruises smudge her throat. "Did he choke her?" I look around, but no one answers.

I try again, louder, "Did Bobby choke her out?"

Watt and Victor's heads pop up. Victor repeats my question to Margot's parents.

But it's Jenny's soft voice that gets my attention. "We don't know. He was hurting her by the time Zeke and I found them at the front door. She screamed at me to call the police. So, I did." Her glazed eyes fall to her brother's still unconscious face. "I think Zeke ran to help her. But I didn't see all of it. My parents didn't see anything until she was already on the lawn, fighting Bobby, and Zeke was lying here, like this."

Each word is like a punch to my gut.

A strong hand grips my shoulder. "She's got a pretty good knot on her head." Victor squats beside me. "I'm sure that's why she's not awake." He checks her pulse. "The cops are here. The ambulances are about a minute out. You go with her. Watt and I will stay here and meet up with you at the hospital."

All I can do is nod.

My eyes don't leave her form as the EMTs work on her, and I speak to the cops, telling them all I know. Then I follow as they load her in the first ambulance. Victor promises to bring her parents as soon as the police let them go.

I stop, glancing at her brother. "What about Zeke? Can he come with us too?"

One of the officers who knows Victor is at my side in seconds. "Mr. McIntyre, Jenny will go with Zeke in the other ambulance. We'll meet y'all there as soon as we wrap up here." He hands me his card. "I've called ahead. They know you're coming and to keep you informed on Zeke and Margot's conditions."

I nearly laugh. If they think they can keep me away from my girl's side, they have no idea who they're dealing with.

# Twenty-Eight

THE SOUND OF HIS VOICE REACHES INTO MY subconscious. I hear his words as if they're coming from inside me. That's impossible. Yet... The rumble of his frequency vibrates in my bones, urging me upward. From wherever I am. I focus on his tone more than what he says. The more I try, the harder it is to hold on.

A deluge of memories hits me.

*Bobby choking me.*

*Bobby punching me.*

*Me hitting and kicking Bobby.*

*Zeke fighting.*

*My dad with a bat.*

The reel of slow-motion images screeches to a halt with a stabbing pain to my head.

I flinch and moan, but I make no sound that I can hear or any movement I can detect. It's like I'm not connected to by body, not fully. Pain. I definitely feel pain. Everywhere.

A soft touch to where I know my cheek to be draws me closer.

A squeeze on what I'm sure is my hand sends me flying forward.

His voice, brighter, unfiltered, still deep, but understandable, no longer muffled.

"Come on, Margot. Wake up. You can do it, baby."

"Baby?" I say, but I hear nothing. "You..." I stop, hearing a raspy voice that sounds nothing like mine. Did someone else speak at the same time, saying the *same* word?

154

"That's it, baby. Come back to me." Another touch on my cheek before warmth envelops me. It feels like he's pressed against me. No pain. That's good. "Try again, Margot. What are you trying to say?"

"You... D... Don't... Call me that." That raspy voice is definitely mine. What happened to it? I sound like a cheese grater if a cheese grater could talk.

A puff of air hits my face as he chuckles. "I've called you *baby* before." When he presses his lips to mine, I'm certain I feel it. They're my lips, and I'm attached to them. Thank God.

"Pixie," I insist, though I'm pretty sure it sounds more than a weak reply.

Another chuckle. "That's right. You're my Pixie." A gentle caress along my jaw. "Now open your eyes, Pixie. Let me see those big, soft brown eyes I love so much."

*Love?* Did he hit his head too?

"Can't." I take a deep breath, but it hurts like needle pricks.

"Why can't you?" The bed dips, and I'm certain he is sitting here with me.

"Hurts."

A muffled exchange I can't make out happens a few feet away.

"What hurts, Margot?" Another brush of my cheek.

"Everything."

Another muffled conversation. Then his voice is closer. "The lights are off. It's dark in the room. Can you try to open your eyes for me?"

I swallow and lick my lips, feeling like I'm closer to being me again. I lift my hand to shield my eyes but hit something—him. "Sorry."

He captures my hand, and when I feel warmth that prickles my palm, I know he's holding my hand to his face, his scruff tickling my hand. "It's okay. I'm nearly in bed with you. I've been so worried. We all have."

"We?"

"Yeah. Your mom, Dad, Jenny, Zeke—"

"Zeke!" I scratch out, remembering Bobby hurt Zeke when he

tried to protect me. I try to sit up, my eyes popping open. The sight of Fin's worried face, the pain in my head, and his grip on my shoulders stills me.

"Shh, baby. Zeke is fine. He's in the room across the hall giving everyone hell because they won't let him see you."

"He's okay?" I won't be able to live with myself if Bobby hurt him all because he was trying to help me.

"Yes. He's bruised and has a mean black eye, but he said you saved him."

"He was trying to save me." The crack in my voice has me closing my eyes.

Fin's soft lips touch mine again. "Don't leave me."

"I'm so tired, Finley." But I have to know. "What happened to Bobby? My dad?" I'd never get over the guilt if my dad went to jail for hurting Bobby.

"Bobby's under arrest and being treated at another hospital. He won't be hurting you or your family again. I promise."

I nod as my eyes close.

"So many are here to be sure you're okay."

"Who?" I open my eyes and blink away tears.

"Me, for one."

That makes me smile. "Obviously."

His eyebrow rises and falls. "Obviously. Then there's Sam, Joe, Matt, Victor, Michael, Jace, Sebastian, and Watt."

"That's everyone." I can't believe they're all here.

"Evan and Griffin wanted to come, but we told them to enjoy their spring break. I didn't think you'd want them to cancel their plans."

"No. Good call."

"So, about that pain?" He searches my eyes.

"Can I go home?"

His brows furrow. "You just woke up after being attacked."

"This bed is uncomfortable. I'd really like to leave." I look around the hospital room. "How long have I been here?"

"About six hours. You've been coming in and out of consciousness for a while now. Where do you want to go?"

"Where *can* I go?"

His smile is panty-dropping. "Anywhere. Your choice. But let me be clear, Pixie. Wherever you go, I go."

I like the sound of that. "In that case, I'd like to go to your place. If that's alright."

"That's my first choice, but your mom might fight you on that."

I start to shake my head and stop when the throbbing worsens. "She's got Zeke to worry about. What happened to my dad?"

Somberness overtakes his smile. "He's waiting to see you. He's in a bad way. Talking nonsense. He agreed to go to rehab, but he's waiting to see you first."

"But he's not in trouble with the police?"

"No. It was self-defense. He was protecting his family. But I did remove the fence post from his hand before the police got there."

Fence post? "I thought it was a bat."

"He ripped it right off the fence and beat the crap out of Bobby." He's impressed.

"I never thought I'd see a day where my dad protected me."

"I think seeing you and Zeke hurt reminded him of his fatherly responsibilities. Sobered him up, so to speak."

"If I see him, promise me you'll take me home after?"

His smile is back. "I promise, Marguerite." He palms his phone. "I'll text Sebastian, get the paperwork rolling."

"Sebastian?"

"Yeah, he's your doctor. I called him on the way to the hospital. It's nice to have friends who are doctors." His smile brightens. "That will be you one day."

I want to sink into the bed and disappear.

"What? What's wrong?" He moves back to my side.

"I—I'm not sure I want to be a doctor anymore." I bite my lip and wait for his disapproval.

He runs his fingertips across my cheek that doesn't hurt. "Whatever you want, Margot. I just want you to be happy. You've got a brilliant brain and a giving heart—use them in whatever way makes you happy and fulfilled."

"Really?" There's not an ounce of disappointment.

"Really."

"Girly." My dad's voice draws my attention as he slowly enters the room.

Fin starts to move off. "I'll just give you two some privacy—"

"No!" I panic and grab his hand. I don't want to be left alone with my dad, not when I'm feeling like this. I just don't have it in me to take one more hit today. Maybe he won't be such a jerk with Fin here.

Fin returns to my side. "Whatever you want, Pixie." He eyes my dad questioningly and then settles back with me, holding my hand securely, his other resting on my thigh. He gently squeezes both.

Feeling Fin's comfort, I reluctantly sweep my gaze to my dad, who holds up his hands. "I'd prefer he stay too." His eyes lock on Fin. "He'll make sure I'm not an ass to you."

That's the best thing my dad has said to me in years—maybe ever.

I feel like an interloper witnessing something so raw and personal. All I can do is hold my girl's hand while her father admits his darkest thoughts. Or what I assume to be the darkest, because, damn, they are *horrible*.

All I want to do is kick him out of the room, out of her life, and erase his existence from her memory bank. Instead, I focus on her, silently offering support and whatever strength she can eke out of me being by her side.

His hand shakes as he reaches for her free hand. I'm not sure if the shaking is from withdrawal or emotional distress.

She pulls away before he can make contact. Her grip on me tightens.

He repeats what he tried to say while he sobs in the chair next to her bed. More composed, fully intelligible this time. It doesn't make his words any easier to hear, though. "I'm so sorry, girly. I didn't mean what I said. I don't really wish you had died. I just—"

What the fuck?

"I don't believe you. Your actions show otherwise." Margot's voice is tight, unforgiving. I don't blame her in the least.

He nods, wipes at more tears as they fall. "I know you don't. You have no reason to. But I promise I will get sober. Stay sober. I will do whatever it takes to make things right between us."

She shakes her head. "Don't do this for me. Don't tie your sobriety to our relationship. You need to find a reason to do this for yourself. Something to hold on to when things get tough." Tears run freely down her cheeks, and my chest constricts. "You think things are bad now? Just wait. When you're strung out, dying for a drink, you'll be blaming me again." She points to her chest. "I didn't do this to you. You are weak and pathetic. You blamed me when I was eight years old. For all I know, it's your faulty genes that did this to me. *I* should be blaming *you* for what happened. But I don't." Her voice softens. "I blame you for after. Making me feel like I was broken, no good. You were ashamed of me and didn't miss a single opportunity to be sure everyone within hearing distance knew it. I blame you for that.

"I blame you for letting Mom carry the financial load all these years. I blame you for being a sucky father to Jenny and Zeke. What kind of an example have you been for Zeke? Do you want him to grow up spewing hate at his wife and kids? Because that's all he knows. He doesn't know what love looks like. None of us do." She points at him, her face flushed with anger. "I. Blame. You."

He stands. His fingers twitch, and he moves to touch her again, then pulls back, sinking his hands in his pockets. "I hear you, Marguerite. I can't disagree with anything you've said. And I'm willing to listen anytime you need to unload on me. I deserve it and much more. But know this." He scrunches up his mouth when his chin quivers. "When I saw that boy hurting you, I was ready to kill him." He points at me. "I would have if Fin hadn't stopped me. He was hurting my little girl, who never did anything to the world other than try to be the happiest, most agreeable person in the room. I know that's not the real you, Margot. You don't have to pretend you're happy all the time. Maybe Fin can help you see that."

His gaze meets mine. "Don't break her heart."

Fuck you, asshole. You wished my Pixie dead? *"I don't plan on it."*

He shakes his head. "Yeah, well, I never *planned* on being an asshole of a husband and father. Shit happens. Do better than I did. Treat her like you don't deserve her—then maybe someday you will."

On those parting words, he walks out.

My Pixie looks as stunned as I am.

"Wow," she whispers.

"Wow is right." That was a mic drop moment if ever there was one.

# Twenty-Nine

I BARELY REMEMBER MY OTHER DAD. THE ONE HE WAS before I broke everything. Before he became the callous and angry man he is now. His words spin on repeat in my head. Not just those he said today, but those from before. The mix is confusing and fills me with anger, but also sadness, guilt, and regret.

None of those feelings am I too happy about, but I'm not sure I can don my happy-go-lucky persona today. The day my past comes up to beat the crap out of me and my brother, forcing my dad to face his addiction, and me... I have to face my fears. Especially with Fin standing in his bedroom doorway, watching me like I might fall apart in tears or explode in anger—each equally likely to happen.

"I don't know what to do, Pixie." He stops before me. His fingers graze the side of my face that's not banged up. "Tell me what you need. How I can help." His sorrowful green eyes have me melting into him.

My head on his chest, I mumble, "It unsettles me that you're unsettled."

He rubs my back and kisses my head so tenderly. "I know. I want to take charge. Get you fed, showered, in bed, and then hold you until we both find our footing."

I look up, my millionth tear for the day slipping free. "That sounds nice."

He nods. "It does." He leans down, barely touching his nose to mine. "But you've had a rough day. I don't want to push. I don't want to stress you out by taking over, by asking you to do something you're not ready for."

161

"I have no doubt I'm not ready for anything you're willing to offer me, Finley."

"I know that too." He pulls me into him.

Wrapped in his arms, his head resting on mine in a place that doesn't hurt, we just hold each other and breathe until we're in sync and my heart-rate matches his. As much as I want him to be my rock, it's comforting knowing he's a little undone by all of this and needs my comfort too.

It gives me hope. Maybe we're not so mismatched for each other. Perhaps I can give him something he needs. I already know he can give me everything I need, and then some.

Fin motions to his bathroom. "Why don't you shower or take a bath while I make us something to eat?"

"Sounds like a good plan."

He drops my suitcase on the chaise lounge near the bed. Turning, his uneasy gaze meets mine. "I want to shower with you, but I know that's one of the things you're not ready for. But if you need help, I don't want to leave you stranded." His hands clench and unclench before he slides them inside his pockets.

"Can you help me with my shoes and maybe my pants? I'm not sure my head can handle bending."

"Of course." Relief floods his entire demeanor. He wants to help. I gave him an achievable task that lets him and doesn't compromise my insecurities.

Easy peasy.

Barefoot and naked from the waist down—yes, he was nice enough to remove my panties for me too—I'm left to my own devices.

Showered, I stand naked in his bathroom drying off, ignoring the aches and pains. I trace the bruises on my neck, the swelling and bruising on my jaw and cheek where Bobby punched me, and the bump, cut, and bruise on my forehead where I head-butted him. Perhaps not my smartest move. I wonder if it'll scar.

What's one more? Though, this one will be harder to hide, unless I wear bangs for the rest of my life.

My woman steps out of the bathroom, her eyes meeting mine as she blindly reaches back and flips off the light. "Hi."

"Hey. Feel better?"

"Yeah. It's amazing what a shower can do." She touches her hair. "I can't wait until I can wash my hair in two days."

Though she had bumps on her head, it's the stitches on her forehead that made Sebastian give her that order. "If it's really bothering you, I could wash it in the sink."

"In the sink?" She glances to my bathroom and frowns.

I pull back the covers on the bed. "The *kitchen* sink. You'd lie on the counter on your back, with extra towels under your neck for cushion and support, and tip it back with your hair in the sink. We'd cover up your forehead, but I think we could make it work."

Her smile has heat blooming in my chest. "You're so smart."

I chuckle. "I watched my mom do it to one of my cousins when we were kids. I don't see why it wouldn't work for you. My counter is long enough." I'd have one of those salon sinks installed if that's what she needs. It's not the same as showering with her. But the idea of getting my hands on her hair does something to me.

"Maybe tomorrow."

"Tomorrow, then." I fluff up the pillows on the side closest to the bathroom. "Here, get comfortable, and I'll be right back with food."

I don't stay to watch her climb in my bed. The thought of it gives my cock ideas—the sight of it would make me rock solid. And that's the last thing she needs right now.

Returning with tray in hand, I toe the door closed, just in case one of my brothers or Sam decides to drop by unannounced and wake her up. We're not the best with boundaries. I totally get why Joe used to get all wound up when I'd use my key to his place. I've learned over the years to call ahead, knock, and make plenty of noise in their entryway if I do use my key. Those two go at it like they're going for a world record, everywhere, anytime, and walking in on them doing the nasty is not on my list of things I ever want to witness.

Sex is an intimate act, hopefully done with someone you care about. I don't have any desire to see my brothers or friends have sex. Hence why I'll never join Victor, Michael, or Matt at the club they like to frequent. Yes, there are private rooms, but the three of them have no problem sharing women—at the same time. Not something I want to think about, much less witness or participate in.

"Why are you frowning?" Margot tilts her head, creasing her brow and then flinches from the discomfort.

"I know that hurt." There's no way in hell I'm answering her last question.

"Yeah, everything hurts."

"I have meds that'll help." I set down the tray of food, place a kitchen towel over her chest and hand her a bowl of potato soup. "I wasn't sure how your jaw is feeling, but I figured something easy to chew would be a better choice."

She eyes the soup as she takes it from me, smiling. "This is perfect. Potato soup is one of my faves."

I set a glass of water close at hand on the nightstand next to her and a napkin on her lap, then pull a chair from the sitting area close to her side of the bed.

"You're not going to join me?" She looks to other side of the bed, which would actually be hers if I hadn't given her my side.

"I thought I'd sit here. I wasn't sure if you'd want me in bed with you."

Her eyes go wide. "You're not planning on staying in here with me?" The disappointment in her voice nearly has me jumping for joy. "I thought—"

"Pixie." I lean over her, carefully kissing her temple. "I'm not leaving you alone. I simply didn't want to assume anything." Pulling back so we're eye to eye, I hint at what I really need us to discuss as soon as she's feeling up to it. "The last time we saw each other, you asked me to leave and to *forget about you.*"

Her eyes glisten, and her chin starts to wobble.

I press my mouth to hers to still her tears if only for the briefest of moments. "Eat, Margot. We'll talk later."

She nods and takes a tentative bite, not because it's too hot but because her jaw *is* sore. I don't imagine she's had to endure too many punches to the face. If I have any say, she never will again. I avert my gaze as I've no doubt my murderous thoughts are flashing across my eyes. When I can breathe through the need to kill Bobby for hurting her and her family, I look up to find her already watching me.

"Does it hurt too much to eat? I could mash up the potatoes."

She shakes her head.

"What is it then?" Her silence and her intense stare have me putting down my soup and moving to her side. "Tell me."

"I'm sorry." She hands me her bowl, and I set it on the nightstand next to mine. "I didn't want to push you away." Her pain is evident. I move closer, slipping her hand in mine and kissing the back of it, running my lips over her soft skin.

"Why did you?"

"Bobby wanted me to get money from you."

I pull back, surprised. I didn't expect that.

She moves with me, tightening her grip on my hand. "I wouldn't. I would never ask for or take your money. Never." Tears fall as her adamancy grows. "He called while you were in Austin. I told him I wouldn't do it. I sent you home. And rejected his calls, except for the few times I was stupid enough to answer without checking the screen first."

"Why didn't you block *his* number?" I didn't intend to get into this now, but the fact she didn't block his number but blocked mine hurts.

"I considered it. I felt it was better to tolerate his calls and listen to his voicemails to ensure he wasn't going to do something more heinous than blackmail me. I couldn't handle it if he tried to get to you or anyone else I care for."

"He was blackmailing you?"

"He tried. Is it blackmail if I don't take the bait?"

"But you took the bait. You broke up with me."

Her eyes widen, and she leans back. "We weren't a couple. I didn't *break up* with you. I *removed* you from the equation. He lost his bargaining chip when he couldn't threaten me with losing you."

"I don't understand. How could him threatening you make you lose me? What aren't you telling me?" I brush a hand over my face. "And to be clear, I *wanted*—I *want*—a relationship with you. I have for a long time. That's why I was there, why I followed you to Austin. If I didn't want more, Margot, I would have let you leave and let that be it."

"He was going to tell you my secret," the shame in her whisper makes me want to kill him all over again.

"*He* knows your secret?" I don't even try to hide my anger.

"We were boyfriend and girlfriend," she implores. "He was my first. I thought I could trust him. But… I was wrong. When he found out… He dumped me." She turns away from me. "He was so angry and hateful. So cruel. Forget I said anything."

God, I'm an ass. "Margot."

I reach for her hand, but she rolls to her side and sinks down, pulling the covers up. "I'd like to sleep now."

"Would you like me to stay? We don't have to talk."

"No. I'd like to be alone. Please."

I get her to take her meds and then leave her alone. I don't want to, but it's obvious that's what she wants.

I won't force my presence on her. She's had enough of that today.

# Thirty

MY SLEEP IS RESTLESS AT BEST. IF I SLEPT FOR more than a few minutes at a time, it sure doesn't feel like it. I roll to my back, thankful Fin's comfortable mattress hugs and conforms to my body in all the right ways. Nearly as well as he fits me, despite our size difference. It's amazing that's even possible.

"It's about time you woke up."

"What—"

"You've been tossing and turning for the past thirty minutes or so. I thought you'd never wake up." Sam leans forward in the same chair Fin occupied before he left me to rest—before I all but made him leave.

"You've been here a while?" I turn to face her, not sure my head can handle an upright position just yet.

"A while. We visited with Fin for a bit. But I wanted to sit with you even if you were sleeping. Just in case you needed anything."

"We?"

"Me and Joseph." She lays her hand on my arm. "He's upset. More than he was at the hospital."

"Why is Joe upset?" I edge up a little. Maybe if I take it a little at a time, my head won't start pounding when I get up to use the restroom, which I need to do shortly.

"Not Joe, silly. Fin."

"Oh." I reach for my glass of water, but my hand is not the steadiest. Sam helps me sit up enough to drink without making a mess.

She eyes me when I've had all I want. "He, uh, kinda found out Bobby knows about my secret."

"Kinda found out?" Her smirk is too perceptive.

"Okay. He *knows*, and he wasn't all that pleased an asshole like Bobby would know, and he doesn't."

"He has a point."

"Yes, but Bobby wasn't an asshole when he found out. My secret caused him to become an asshole. I don't want to see that happen with Fin. I'm not sure I could bear to see the kind, gentle alpha turn into an alphahole."

She shakes her head, laughing. "You're delusional, Margot. Your situation will not have the same effect on Fin. Bobby was already an asshole. He did a good job of hiding it. He's a self-centered, arrogant, superficial prick. Fin is none of those things, plus he loves you. Bobby is incapable of loving anyone but himself. I don't even know why Sebastian was friends with him. It makes me worry about Bash's character—"

"*Love?* Who... No. It's not possible." My heart races, and I'm finding my next breath harder to take as I fan my face. "He doesn't. He can't."

Sighing, she sits on the edge of the bed. "You're the one who pointed out that Joseph loved me before I saw it, before I was in the right frame of mind to even except it. Trust me, Fin has been in love with you for years. Granted, he may not have known it until recently, but I'd say he's well aware of his feelings for you now."

"Since when?"

Sam taps her chin as she considers my question. "I'd say since the wedding for sure, but probably since the happy hour you two slept together."

"How did you—did he tell you that we—" I'm fully sitting now; my pounding head will have to wait, my racing heart and thoughts taking precedence at the moment.

"No. He didn't. He wouldn't. He's too much of a gentleman.

As much as those guys give each other a hard time, they respect the women they sleep with—they don't share details. None. Not even Fin and Joseph, who are as close to being twins as they come."

That makes me smile. "They kind of are, aren't they? Except Joseph is a little move cavemanish. Fin is more reserved, calm."

"You wouldn't say that if you saw him at the hospital. He was ready to rip off doors and heads to get updates, to get you into a room instead of staying in the ER, and he wasn't going to let any other doctor treat you except Bash, unless Bash agreed you needed care he couldn't provide. Fin is every bit the caveman Joseph is. He just hides it better. Under his suits and calm exterior is a roaring Neanderthal who just wants to protect you, provide for you, and claim you for himself."

She's right. I've seen it around the edges, but he does a good job of hiding it. Maybe as well as I hide being all happy, Fin hides the need to claim and conquer. "And Bobby knows something about me Fin doesn't."

"Yep. That's the kicker."

"I need to tell him," I whisper.

"You need to tell him." She gives me a soft hug. "You won't regret it. I promise."

"Give her time to recover." Joe finishes his tumbler of whiskey.

I'm envious he can taste it, though I'm certain he doesn't appreciate its subtleties. But I'm mostly envious that he and Sam have made it past their rocky start, overcome tremendous hurdles, and are now on the other side, married and nauseatingly happy.

They're able to make his demanding job and her being in school full-time work. She'll graduate this May—like my Pixie. Only Sam will probably be done. She's not going on to get a masters or a doctorate like Margot will be. *Maybe.* She said earlier she's not so sure anymore. I don't know what's changed her mind, made her doubt her dreams she's been working so hard for. That's a discussion we still need to have.

There are so many. I'll add it to the list.

"If I'm going to make this work with Margot, I need help. I'm overloaded at work as it is, add in Dad wanting to retire and hand off the reins earlier than any of us anticipated—especially me. I thought I'd have time to start a family of my own before taking over, but now—"

"We make it work." Joe stands beside me as I gaze out over downtown Dallas. "We hire. We delegate. We reorganize, whatever we need to do to distribute the workload more evenly." He faces me. His green eyes reflect the lights outside. "You've always carried too much on your shoulders. Part of that is Dad's fault. Part of that is yours for always saying *yes*. You have to learn to say *no*. We won't think less of you, and we sure as hell won't love you less. *We* make it work. You and Margot aren't in this alone." He clasps my shoulder. "Isn't that what you drilled into me last November? We're stronger together than we are apart." He pulls me in for a hug, tight and powerful. "You've been my savior my entire life. *Let* me help you now, Brother. Let us *all* help you."

The knot of emotions in my throat has me patting his back a little too hard and nodding my acquiescence.

We pull away, both glancing at my bedroom, wanting our better halves to come join us.

"I'll talk to Dad and Matt. We'll touch base in a week or so. Until then, don't come to the office. Take care of your girl. If you don't, I'll let Samantha kick your ass."

"Like she could." I chuckle.

He raises an eyebrow, his face falling serious. "She just might. She nearly toppled Michael the other day. She's gotten good at all that martial arts stuff. Real good. *I'm* scared to tell the woman *no*."

That makes me laugh even harder. "You're a foot taller and outweigh her by at least a hundred pounds. You're not serious."

He shrugs. "I can't take it when she's sad. If it made her happy to beat the crap out of me, I'd let her just to see the pride of accomplishment on her face. A moment's happiness with my Sweetness is worth a lifetime of pain."

Damn. That's deep, and serious, and a bit screwed up, but I know what he means. Her belief in herself is worth any amount of pain it might cause him. She's come a long way, but he'd die to see her reach the top. Whatever the *top* is for them.

"You're a good man, Joe." I pat his back. "I'm proud of the man you've become. And I'd be honored to follow in your footsteps as I try to be the same for Margot."

He sets his glass in the sink. "Don't you know, Brother?" His eyes dash to mine. "You already are that man. I try every day to be just like you." His eyes shine as he passes. "Every fucking day, Fin."

# Thirty-One

**A**FTER JOE CAME IN FOR A QUICK HELLO AND A hug, he and Sam left. I go to the bathroom and brush my teeth. My tummy rumbling and in need of more water, I venture out of the bedroom. The house is quiet, peaceful, and still. Like time may have stopped, and we're stuck in a time dilation—just off-kilter to the outside world that's ticking by.

My smile at my silliness falters when I spot Fin sitting on the couch. He's not moving. He's not drinking. If he didn't blink, I'd believe my time dilation theory was true.

I step closer, afraid to break his trance, but needing to feel our connection. "What are you doing?"

He doesn't jump. His eyes slowly drag up my bare legs to his t-shirt I'm wearing. The corner of his mouth tips, and his eyes are bright by the time they reach mine. "Thinking." He holds his hand out, beckoning me forward.

I oblige. "About?"

I reach him seconds before he says, "You."

I still. "Me? That can't be good."

His smile grows, his eyes so tender. "Thinking of you, my Pixie, is always good."

I surprise him when I straddle his lap. I'm rarely forward except when we're about to have sex, or having sex. Then I'm downright vixen-like. But this is not that or false bravado. This is just me, needing to be close to *him*.

172

His hands grip my thighs. "You okay? Did you get any sleep?"

"A little. I was restless. It could be the medicine, the stress of the day." I rest my forearms on his shoulders, lining up my face to his. "But I think it's the fact that I needed you there beside me, and instead of asking—I sent you away."

His eyes close, and his fingers flex.

"I'm sorry, Finley. I keep pushing you away, when, really, all I want to do is pull you closer."

His arms are around me in a heartbeat. Firmly but gently, he hauls me all the way against him. "I need you to stop doing that."

I nod, our eyes locked in their own embrace. "You have to help me. I don't know how to be what you need."

"Baby." His anguish is unmistakable. "You have always been what I need. I don't need, nor want you to be anything other than what you are in this moment."

"Even if it's not *bubbly Margot*."

"Especially when you're *not* bubbly Margot. Can I tell you a secret?" The gravel in his voice makes me squirm in his lap. As if he can read me, his hands squeeze my ass. "Fuck, you're not wearing any panties," he hisses.

I ignore his kneading fingers and the building want. "Tell me your secret, Finley."

"I've always seen past bubbly Margot. I know she's a part of you. Unlike your father, I don't think that's a false you, it's just not all of who you are. I see the woman beneath. She's the one I want, not the one you give the world. I want my Pixie, in all her bright, shiny, dark, breakable, self-conscious ways." He caresses my cheek. "I see you, Marguerite, and I love you."

I suck in a breath. Holy... "You love me?" How?

"Yes. I love you. I have for a while now. We have things to work out, but I'm not giving up on us."

"But you don't even know—"

"I don't need to—"

"—my secret."

Both hands cradle my face. "I love you, Pixie. I don't need to know your secret to love you. Your secret is *not* who you are. It might be a *part* of you, but it's not *you*."

"But… You might not want me after you know… After you see—"

"I will. I always will."

"But you can't—"

"I can. I will. My love is not conditional. Even if you tell me you could never love me, it does not stop me from loving you. I give my love freely. Unconditionally. Without limits. I won't be perfect. I will screw up. I'll say the wrong thing—do the wrong thing, but that does not change my love for you."

"Fin." My cry is desperate and pleading. He's crushing me from the inside, breaking walls I've worked so hard to fortify. "I can't—" *get a breath.*

"Breathe, Margot. Jesus, fuck. Take a breath." He holds my arms in the air, my ribs expand, and I get a solid breath in. "Good. Again." He breathes with me. In. Out. In. Out. Slow and steady. "Better."

He releases my arms, and I wrap them around him, laying my un-bruised cheek on his shoulder. "I'm afraid, Finley," I whisper into his neck.

"I know." His rubs my back. "I'm scared too. But I'm more afraid of never having a future with you than I am of *making* a future with you."

"Do you know what I love about you?"

He freezes.

All I can do is smile against his shoulder as I continue, "Your honesty. Your ability to say your truth. You've always been honest with me. Even when you snuck out of my bed—it was honest. You didn't lie. And I appreciate that so much. Promise me that will never change. We will always have truth between us."

He hugs me. "I promise."

"I promise too." I sit back. "I know I still need to tell you my secret, and I will. I just need a minute to feel steady on my feet. Today was a whirlwind of events, emotions, and change. I just—"

"I'm not rushing you. Take all the time you need. But understand this: we're Margot and Fin now. We are a unit. We're one. There's no more pushing me out, sneaking out. Hold back your secret, but don't hold back anything else. Deal?"

"Deal." I kiss his cheek and shake on it, holding his hand. "One more thing…"

"What's that?"

"I love you too, Finley."

My pulse rages as my brown-eyed Pixie floors me. "Could you say that again?"

She moves in closer, holding my face. Her breath skating across my lips only makes me want to seal our deal with a kiss. But I need her words more than I need the next beat of my heart.

"I love you, Finley… Uh… McIntyre." She frowns. "What's your middle name?"

I capture the back of her head, keeping her close, her lips nearly mine. "I tell you what. When you tell me your secret, I'll tell you my middle name."

"You know I could look it up, right? You McIntyre brothers are famous. Too famous for your middle name not to be all over the internet. I know I've seen it. I just don't remember."

"But you won't. Just like I won't ask questions or find out your secret before you're ready to tell me." The awe on her face reminds me of the world she needs to get used to if she's going to be with me.

"You could do that, couldn't you? Find out everything about me?"

"I could. But I won't, Pixie." A quick press of my lips to hers is not nearly enough, but it soothes me until I can get more. "I need you to *give* your secret to me, to carry, to heal with you."

She shakes her head and bites her lips as her eyes fill with tears.

"It can't be healed, Fin." Her chin wobbles, and each word is tight with emotion. "Don't think you can fix me, because you can't. I'm flawed. It can't be erased."

God, my girl. "You're killing me, Marguerite. I don't mean physically. I don't care what perceived physical flaw you're hiding. I'm talking about the scars you carry on the inside. The ones that make you doubt your worth. Make you think you have to be the happiest person in the room. You don't, baby. You just have to be you. And when you're ready, you give me your secret. Let me love you and carry it until you believe enough to stop hiding."

"Holy nutcrackers," she whispers. "You're like every dream I ever had except way better, way hotter, way sexier, way sweeter in every way."

"Sweet?" I chuckle. "No one has ever called me sweet."

"But you are." She leans back, drying her face. "You are sweet to me. You may give the world buttoned-up-in-control Fin, but you are tender and thoughtful with me. Your calm crumbles for me." She placates me with a heated kiss that ends too abruptly. "I like you sweet and undone. Give the world what you want, but give me everything else."

"Jesus, fuck, I don't think I could love you more." I suck her lips, licking and cajoling her to open for me.

She breaks our kiss. "Same." And comes back for more, letting me in, our tongues warring, not for control but for maximum reward.

She cries out.

"Shit." I pull back—I'd accidentally gripped the injured side of her jaw. She's still hurt and in no shape for this. "I'm sorry. I forgot. We shouldn't—"

"Oh, yes we should." She kisses the hand I quickly removed from her face. Her light brown eyes glisten with want. "Make me forget about today."

"I don't want to hurt you, Marguerite." The idea of causing her pain is unacceptable, but easing her pain, irresistible.

She eases back on my lap, resting on my knees. "You won't." She tugs at my workout pants. "Help me."

I place her hands on my shoulders. "Hold on." I lift up enough to work my pants and underwear down as far as I can with her on my legs, then pull her close so I can kick them off the rest of the way.

She giggles nearly the entire time, and it's perfection.

Holding her cheek, I tell her what I've often thought but never shared, "Your laugh is like lightning in a bottle. Surprising, unexpected, and worth waiting for."

"I…" she stutters over her reply.

"Shh, come here, Pixie." I kiss her softly. "You're horrible at taking compliments." I kiss a little harder but carefully, remembering her injuries. "I'm going to love you slow and easy, baby."

"Please."

God, the way she begs is seductively innocent.

She frames my face and locks her mouth to mine.

And her need is intoxicating.

Deft fingers relieve me of my shirt, reminding me that while hers stays on, I can still play with her nipples and touch the warm, silky-smooth skin of her back.

Someday, I'll get to experience every inch of her and know I've earned her full vulnerability.

But not until she's ready.

When that day comes, I will relish her trust and show her she has nothing to fear.

Until then, I'm going to love my Pixie better than she's ever dreamt, and more fully than I've ever anticipated.

Sinking into her sweet pussy, we cry out as one, move as one, love as one.

# *Thirty-Two*

## April

"**O**H MY GOD, I'M SO LATE!" I RUSH TO THE bathroom and scrub my face, putting toothpaste on my toothbrush and shoving it in my mouth. I don't even have time for a shower. That will make him happy knowing I'll smell like him and carry his *gift* on my underwear all day.

"You cussed." Fin stands in the doorway, his brows up, his eyes wide with amusement. "You don't cuss."

I smile around my toothbrush, catching a glob of toothpaste foam in my hand before it drops on my sleep shirt. "A'm rate!"

He chuckles and crosses his arms over his impressive chest. He's gotten even bigger since moving in with me and the boys. He works out with them every day when we're in town, which is nearly all the time. It's a challenge to see who can lift the most weight. Amazingly, he wins most of the time. I don't know how he does it. He's on a level all his own. It's good for Watt, Evan, and Griffin to have stiff competition. They've never been this focused before.

There was an adjustment period where all that testosterone flying around had to settle, but it wasn't as awkward as I thought it would be.

Fin's a good influence on them outside of the gym too. He's great with numbers and, of course, business, tutoring them when they ask— which is often.

UT's McCombs School of Business even asked Fin to do a

two-week lecture series for graduating seniors. The content is up to him, but mainly a *how to succeed in business* type of thing.

He's loving it. It's like the breath of fresh air he needed to find room for a personal life when his career was his whole life.

"You're late?" he asks, trying to stifle more laughs as he interprets my I-have-a-toothbrush-in-my-mouth talk.

"Yesh!" I finish brushing, spit and rinse and spit again. "You're making me late." I pat my face and hands dry and start to tame my hair into a messy bun.

His gaze meets mine in the mirror as he stands behind me. "I'm not the one who pushed this lovely ass into my morning wood." His hands squeeze said *rear*, and he kisses my neck. "Though, I'm happy you did."

I turn, stopping his fingers from dipping lower, starting something I don't have time to finish. "I love you, Finley, but I have to go."

In the closet, I slip on panties and a bra, grab the first clothes I see and dress.

"No shower?" He smirks from the bed when I glance over my shoulder.

"No time."

"Hmm, that's too bad."

I giggle and know he's full on smiling now without even looking. "Yeah, I'm sure you're broken up about me smelling like you all day."

"Broken up? *No.* Turned on? *Yes.*"

"You're always turned on."

"Because you're sexy as fuck." The insistence of his statement gives me pause, has my heart racing, wishing I could skip class today.

I'm too close to graduation to miss class for sex. I mean, I just had two spectacular orgasms. How greedy does a girl need to be?

"Your lunch is in your pack, and coffee is on the island," he interrupts my sex fantasy of him doing me on his desk.

I slip on my tennis shoes and stand before him. "You made me lunch?"

He pats his knee, prompting me to lift my unlaced shoe to his thigh. "You said you have a busy day today. I wanted to be sure you ate. You didn't feel well yesterday when you skipped lunch."

I switch feet and watch him tie my other shoe. "How did I get so lucky?" These past seven weeks or so have been amazing having him here with me and the guys.

Setting my foot on the floor, he pulls me between his legs. "I like to think I'm the lucky one."

"Maybe we both are." I actually mean it. He makes me *feel* like I'm worthy of him feeling lucky to be with me. I'm starting to believe it's true.

He smiles on a nod. "That's my girl." He kisses me breathless before releasing me. "Stop by the house when you're done. I wouldn't mind a repeat of this morning without our roommates overhearing us."

Oh, loud sex. I wouldn't mind that. "Deal."

"Have a great day, Pixie."

"Have a good day at the office, Mr. McIntyre." And by *office*, I mean his old house in Austin. He works there during the day, but lives here with us.

When Fin sprang the idea of working remotely in Austin until I graduate, I couldn't bring myself to leave my roommates. They took me in at a difficult time. And having only a few months of school left, it didn't seem right to leave them when they'd come to rely on my cooking. Plus, they've become my family, and I wanted Fin to get to know them.

It's worked out for all of us.

They get to watch a man who's killing it in life, who's an amazing human being, and who loves me enough to sacrifice for my goals.

I… Well, you see what I get out of it—him.

Fin gets to remember what it's like to have fewer responsibilities, though nothing has changed, really. He's just learned to prioritize, delegate, and say *no* to his family and overburdened workload.

Life is good.

"She still hasn't told you yet?" Joe stayed on the line after our conference call with Matt and our dad.

"I think she's waiting for graduation." She's been under a lot of pressure, trying to decide if she wants to pursue becoming a doctor, a nurse, or maybe even a teacher. Her Bachelor of Science degree could be used toward many vocations without any further schooling.

"Are you okay with waiting? I'm not sure I could stand Samantha keeping such a big secret from me."

"What would you have me do? Tie her down and make her tell me?" *Show* me?

Do I want see my girl naked? *Yes.* Do I want to shower with my girl? *Absolutely.* But it has to be when she's ready. It doesn't matter if it's been two months since we admitted our feelings to one another. It has to be on her terms.

He laughs. "Hardly."

"I promised her time. That's what I'm giving her."

"That sounds like a plan to me. Anything more I can do to help you out?" He may be my little brother, but he's been my biggest supporter in my working from Austin arrangement.

Dad was skeptical, at best.

Matt just laughed and called me *pussy-whipped.*

He has no idea. Joe and I shared a look and told him, "Just wait." It'll happen to him soon enough, and when it does, Joe and I will be there to remind him how amazing it is to be *pussy-whipped.*

All men should be so lucky to have found their soulmates, their other half who makes it all worthwhile, challenges their idea of the future, and dares them to be vulnerable and open to receiving the most amazing gifts only a true love can give.

Yeah, I'm PW'd, and I'm damn proud.

"There is one thing you could do for me." I remember my discussion with Margot about her Mustang. "We won't be back in town before graduation, unless something comes up in the next few weeks. Would you mind getting Zeke her Mustang?"

"Her brother? Seriously?" His shock is apparent. "You convinced her to keep the i8?"

I laugh. "I didn't. The i8 did. She loves the feel of it. The way it handles. The way it makes her feel. She's the one who asked if she could keep it and suggested her car go to her brother now that it's all fixed up and roadworthy again."

"Damn, I never saw that coming."

"Me neither. But I did buy the car for her. I just never thought she'd accept it."

"You know that kid is gonna wreck that sweet Mustang. He'll be racing it all over town."

"Fuck, I didn't think of that." I can't have him killing himself in the car I may have suped-up too much for his own good.

"Don't worry. I'll scare him straight. I'll take him to the junkyard where all race-car-driver-wannabees' egos go to die."

We get a good laugh out of that until we hear, "Shit, I wanna go."

"What the fuck?" Joe growls.

"Matt! You little fuck," I chastise.

Obviously, I'm going to have to stop having personal conversations over conference calls, assuming everyone else hung up—even when it's a call with my family.

"Y'all don't tell me shit. I had to hang on to get the deets," Matt justifies his sneaky ways.

"You could have told me you wanted to stay on. I just assumed you didn't care." He doesn't show interest in our lives often.

"*Ouch.* Fuck, Fin. You could've used a little lube with that prodding remark," he quips.

"Touché."

Unusually serious, Matt adds, "I'm happy for you, Fin. Margot's great."

"Thanks."

"And, Joe, I want to go with you when you deliver the Mustang... Aaand, I want to help scare the shit out of Zeke. He's been without a father figure in his life. We need to show him being cool doesn't mean taking a chance with your life or another's."

"Wow, Matt. That's rather deep of you. I'll call them and make plans for this weekend," Joe advises. "I'll let you know."

"Sounds good," Matt replies to Joe. "Hey, Fin. When is her dad getting out of rehab?"

"A few more weeks. Just in time for her graduation." Her dad has done really well in rehab, according to her mom and brother. Margot isn't ready to visit him yet, but she's not against him coming to her graduation.

"Speaking of that," Joe pipes in. "Are you still thinking of hiring him?"

"Yep. I told him as long as he stays clean, I'll pay off his debts and give him a job he can be proud of." He doesn't need to know I already paid off the family debt and the mortgage. Danielle, Margot's mom, called me crying when she found out.

I hadn't intended on her finding out so soon. I also didn't ask for details on *who* they owed. Victor knows, but I told him I don't want to know until after Margot shares her secret, as I have a feeling it's tied to their debts. I promised her I wouldn't go fishing for information, and I haven't. Having Victor do it was the only way to lessen their load and Margot's guilt.

"That's big of you," Joe comments.

"You'd do no less for Sam."

"True. Good point. With that in mind, we'll keep an eye on Tom. Though, I'm positive you'll have Victor or one of his men ensuring he stays on point."

"For now, one of Victor's guys is going to be his sponsor. Tom is open to the idea and has already met... Fuck, I forgot his name. Anyway, it will be good to have his sponsor at the office. They'll go to

AA meetings down the street from MCI. It seems like the best plan for success. Now, if he can just stay clean and make amends with Margot, all would be perfect."

"Some things aren't possible," my youngest brother reminds me. "Samantha and Jace know that better than anyone." Sam and Jace's estranged mother has yet to bounce back from losing their dad.

Sam seems to be handling it better than Jace. But then again, she had to when they both abandoned her after Daniel's murder. I surmise it's Jace's guilt that keeps him holding on to hope regarding their mom's recovery.

"Fuck. How'd we get so lucky with Mom and Dad?" Matt asks.

"I don't know, but we need to hug them a little harder the next time we see them." It's a good reminder how privileged our lives have been, both financially and in the supportive parent department.

"I'm gonna call Mom now. Bye, fuckers." Matt hangs up. Or we *think* he hangs up. You never know with him.

"Love you, Brother," Joe beats me to it.

"Love you, Brother. Thanks for the support. Tell Sam to hug you a little longer this evening for me."

He laughs. "Alright, but when it turns sexual, that hug is no longer from you."

"Pussy," I tease.

"Only for her." He reconfirms his solid line that he's proud to be pussy-whipped by his woman.

"Yep, only for our girls."

# Thirty-Three

## May

I ZIP UP THE DRESS FIN LEFT FOR ME ON OUR BED. It's a black, sleeveless, form-fitting midi with a halter neckline. It's perfect. Not because it's beautiful, which it is, but because of the high neck and the note that was laid on top of it.

Margot,

I'm so proud of you. You've worked hard for this day. I hope it is everything you dreamt it would be. I wanted to get you something special to wear for your graduation. When I saw this dress, I was certain it would give you the coverage you desire. I support your choice to hide from the world, but there is no hiding from me. I see you and love every inch. Even the parts I haven't seen, I still love.

Yours always,
Fin

185

I fight the tears wanting to fall. Though I'm wearing waterproof mascara, I'd prefer not to ruin the rest of my makeup or don a red nose and puffy eyes before my graduation ceremony. I have no doubt there will be tears—but I'd like to defer crying till afterwards. *You hear that, tears? Wait!*

"Holy shit." Watt is the first to spot me when I emerge from the hall to find all my guys waiting, dressed to the nines in perfect-fitting black suits. It'll be a miracle if one of them doesn't split the seams of their pants or jacket before they walk across the stage. I'm not sure football players were made to wear suits, but I have to say, they look quite handsome.

"Margot, wow," comes from Evan.

Griff just whistles, scanning me from top to bottom.

But it's Fin who holds my attention, his head cocked to the side, his chin low, his emerald-green eyes savoring me like I'm his next meal. I can appreciate the sentiment as he's looking quite delish in his black suit, white shirt, and black tie.

"Thank you for the dress. It's incredible." I stop my hand as I instinctively palm the spot between my breasts.

His gaze jumps to my hand before he steps into me, joining our hands between us. "I concur with the guys. You're stunning." He slips his hand in his pocket. "There's just one thing missing."

"Oh, no, what—" My thought disappears as he drops to one knee. "You… Oh, God!"

Holding my hand, our gazes lock. "Marguerite, I think I've loved you the moment I spotted you. We didn't have the smoothest start, but all good things are worth working for. And I promise I will work every day to be the man you deserve, the man worthy of your future, and your heart. Marry me, Pixie. Be mine forever."

"Fuck," slips free before I can stifle it. I slap my hand over my mouth, mumbling, "Oh, shit."

The room erupts in laughter and a lot more cussing in support of my slip-ups.

Fin shakes his head, humor lighting up his features. "You're going to have to be more specific. I need a *yes*… Or, God forbid, a *no*."

"Yes, Finley. Oh, my fucking God, yes!"

More laughter, more exclamations in support of my potty mouth.

Fin stands and wraps me in a hug. "I never thought proposing would get my Pixie cussing. What is the world coming to?"

"Maybe it's the real me." I shake my head, not giving two shits about my makeup as I bury my face in his chest. "I love you so much."

His lips find mine as he whispers, "I love you too, baby."

"Ring, dude!" Watt exuberantly exclaims.

Fin breaks our kiss. "Fuck. I'm mucking this up."

"No. No, you're not. It's perfect. *You're* perfect." I press my hand to his chest.

His gaze flits to me before he opens the ring box. "If you don't like it, we can get whatever you like. I just thought this seemed to fit you." My confident man is hesitant.

"You're killing us! Show her!" Griff urges from the sidelines.

I dip my head to catch Fin's eyes again. "I'll love it because you picked it out. That's all that matters, Finley." I nod to the box. "Show me the pretty."

His smile is soft and innocent. I wonder if that's how he looked as a child. "If you don't—"

"Open. Open. Open." The guys start chanting.

He chuckles, "Maybe I should have done this in private."

"Nuh-uh, this is perfect." I squeeze his hand. "Show me, handsome."

"Okay." The box opens with a *pop*.

"Oh. My. God." I flash from the ring to his face and back. "Oh, my God," I whisper. "Finley."

He pulls the ring from the box and slips it on my hand.

"Oh, my God! Finley." On my left ring finger sits the most incredible yellow diamond engagement ring with a pavé diamond band. It's huge. It's beautiful. "It's yellow." My voice cracks. I'm about to lose my composure, it's so perfectly me.

"Shh, Pixie. Don't cry. You said you didn't want to cry today." He kisses my mouth, my cheeks, and holds my hand between us. "You like it?"

"Are you crazy? It's yellow. It's sunshine and spring on my finger. It's perfect." Tears fly free on their own accord.

He swipes every tear dry. "I'm glad you like it. It just screamed Pixie when I saw it."

"It matches my car." I start to cry harder.

"Baby." He envelopes me in his strong embrace. "Cry all you want. I've got tissues to spare." He hands me one so I can dab my eyes.

After that it's congratulations with whoops, hollers, and hugs all around from each of the guys. They even hug Fin, whose eyes are a little misty, which only makes me start to cry again.

On the way to the colosseum, we talk to his parents, Joe, and Sam, who's also graduating today from SMU in Dallas. It's sad we can't share this day together. But it's par for the course for our friendship. Joe is her best friend now, and I have Fin. We still want our girl time, but our rocks—our men—are who we want to share everything with.

I didn't truly get it until I stopped fighting Fin long enough for him to show me the way. And it's been an enlightening journey, full of healing, love, and—wouldn't you know?—amazing, knock-your-socks-off sex.

"You look happy." Watt stands with me as we wait to file into the auditorium. Alphabetically, he's the closest to me with me being *Dubois* and him *Burns*. Griff is near the middle since his last name is *Quinn*. And Evan *Scott* is with the mass of other S names.

Fin and my family disappeared a while ago to find their seats. Everyone made it. My sister came in from Houston with her fiancé. Mom, Dad, and Zeke drove in from Dallas. My dad has been out of rehab for less than a week. I'm sure it must be overwhelming being thrown into a social celebration this large right off the bat. Fin and I discussed no alcohol today. It's the least we can do to show our support.

"Margot?"

"I'm sorry." I flip my hand around my head. "I was lost in thought about my dad and stuff."

"He looks good. So much better than the last time I saw him."

"Yeah, he does. Mom says it's like he's a new person. Or at least the old person she fell in love with."

"That's good, right?"

"It's great."

He tips my chin. "But?"

I shrug. "It's just… Hard to trust."

"I get it. I haven't been in your shoes, but the only advice I have is to take it one day at a time. Nobody's perfect. He's gonna screw up. Have hard days. Hopefully, he'll be able to get right back up. That's all any of us can do, right? Fuck up and move on."

"Yep." I'm sidetracked like a squirrel when my ring catches the light. I can't believe I'm engaged.

"Are you gonna tell him?"

My head snaps up. "What?" Watt can't know. There's no way he knows my secret.

"Look." He moves closer, his head down so only I can hear. "I know there's something you've been hiding. I don't need to know what it is. But you would never let me touch you… You know."

I stare at him in horror. He just chucks my chin. "He loves you, *Pixie*."

I swat at his chest for using Fin's lovename for me.

"Nothing is going to scare him away. If you're going to marry the man, have babies with him, you need to tell him."

My stomach churns at the notion. But he's not wrong. "I know."

He kisses my cheek. "I promise. It'll be better than you think. You got this." He squeezes my hand. "*Though she be but little, she is fierce.*"

I laugh, my smile settling my nerves. "A jock who quotes Shakespeare? That's a rarity."

"Not as rare as you think. We're not all knuckleheads."

"No, you definitely aren't. I'm going to miss you and the guys. It'll be weird not having four guys to cook and clean for."

"Believe me, we're going to miss your cooking something fierce." His eyes soften. "But I'm going to miss *you* most of all, Margot. Promise you and Fin will come visit, even if it's not for a game."

"Absolutely. We wouldn't miss it for the world. You just let us know when and where, and we'll be there."

"Line up everyone!" One of the coordinators flashes Watt a look, knowing he's out of line.

"I guess I gotta go find my *rightful* place." He leans in and kisses my cheek, just barely missing the corner of my mouth. "I'll see ya when I see ya, Margot," he reminds me of our farewell after our... Well, sexcapades.

Squeezing his hand, I rise up on my tippy toes and kiss his cheek. "I'll see ya when I see ya, Watt."

It's silly, really. I'll be seeing him later. But it's a mark of times past, times that will never be again. We're all moving forward. Me with Fin, and the guys—all three were drafted into the NFL.

Our futures are just beginning, but first we have to say goodbye to the past.

# Thirty-Four

**W**ATCHING MARGOT GRADUATE WAS MORE moving than I'd anticipated. My heart even panged for the three fuckers we live with. They've become good friends. They'll never replace Victor and Michael, but it's been great having a reprieve from my normal routine while living in Austin with Margot.

But our time is coming to an end. We've got the summer to figure out what we're doing. Or really, she has the summer to figure it out. Wherever she goes, I go. She passed the MCAT with flying colors. She doubted it. I didn't. She's got a fantastic brain in that head of hers. Now, it's up to her what she wants to do.

I'm all in either way.

When my Pixie finds me in the crowd, the emotions shining in her eyes have me wanting to steal her away until nothing but joy remains. But she and I will have to brave the next few hours as there are surprises yet to come.

Pulling her into my side, I kiss her temple. "You ready?"

Her smile is contagious and eases my worry. "Absolutely."

We meet everyone outside under the guise of taking pictures under some trees. But when she steps out and catches sight of Sam and Joe, she nearly collapses. Thank God I have a good grip on her. "Fin? What did you do?"

I chuckle. "I didn't do anything, Pixie. When my little brother couldn't keep his mouth shut about me proposing today, Sam insisted they fly out to be here."

191

"Margot!" Sam moves towards us quickly with my youngest brother in tow.

"Sammykins, what are you doing here? You're supposed to be graduating today!"

Sam waves her off. "Oh, please. You know I'm not big on all the center-of-attention stuff. I'm more than happy to miss walking across the stage to be here for your big day and your bigger big day." She holds out her hand. "Let me see it."

The light shining off my girl as she shows off her ring puffs my chest out in pride. I feel like I made that fucking ring just for her with my bare hands.

"Congratulations, Brother." Joe pulls me into a hug. "I'm proud of you."

The girls squealing about being sisters-in-law pulls our attention. We both just laugh, shaking our heads and watching the show.

The joy just keeps spreading as her parents, siblings, and my parents find us, and then the shocker of all shockers, Matt taps me on the shoulder. "Congratulations, Brother. I'm really happy for you."

I pull him into a hug, getting a little choked up. "It means a lot, you coming, Brother." I'm sure I hug him longer than he's comfortable with, but I give him credit for not pulling away first.

Victor and Michael are next. More hugs and congratulations.

"Fuck, is anyone holding down the fort at home?"

My dad pats my shoulder. "We've got it handled. You're off the next three weeks. Don't even think about MCI. You hear me?"

The lump in my throat threatens to choke me out. "Yes, sir. I hear you."

"Three weeks?" Margot's bigger-than-usual eyes find me in the mass of our friends and family.

I hug her close. "It was supposed to be a surprise. I'm taking you to Joe and Sam's island."

"You're not serious?"

Turning us away from the crowd, I step a few paces with her in my arms. "I'm dead serious. It can either be a nice vacation. Or—"

"Or?" My Pixie's eyes start to water.

I fear the waterworks are only going to get worse either in joy or my being an insensitive asshole for suggesting, "Or a wedding and honeymoon."

She smacks my chest so hard I startle at her strength. "Get out of here!"

I'm really trying not to laugh, but she's so damn cute. "I'm serious, Pixie. I don't want to wait, but if you want the big wedding in a church and all the buildup, we can do that. But if you don't, this is the perfect opportunity to have a destination wedding and honeymoon all in one."

"Yes!" she shrieks and starts jumping up and down in my arms. "Holy fuck, Fin. Yes!"

Silence is all I hear behind me before the roar of laughter begins.

"Baby, as much as I love your newfound loose tongue, we may need to work on the volume and locale of such outbursts." I'm barely keeping it together. All I want to do is join my brother and friends in their cackling.

"Oh, no," she whispers, her eyes filling with tears. "I'm so sorry."

"Hey." I bend and grab her around the ass, lifting her so we're face to face. "I'm only kidding, Pixie. Really." I kiss her wobbly chin. "Please don't cry, baby. I might just join you for making you lose your joy."

"Lose my joy?" She presses her forehead to mine. "Don't you know, Fin? You are my joy."

"Fuck, Pixie. The things you say." I hold her tighter for as long as she'll let me, trying to gain my composure. "I need you, baby."

She smiles and kisses me softly. "I know, but I don't think we can dump our friends and family who have come all this way to celebrate with us. We need to give them an hour of our time at least." She smirks and wiggles her brow.

"I know you're kidding, but I'm not sure I can last an hour without being inside you."

"TMI, Brother." Joe comes up beside us and pats my back. "Make it an hour and a half, and then the four of us can sneak out. Deal?"

"Deal."

"Good. Now." He looks to Margot. "Did I hear correctly? Are we having a wedding on our island?"

My Pixie's grin is earth-warming. "Yes. Yes, we are. Can we do it? Can we make it work?"

Joe looks at me and smiles. "She has no idea, does she?"

"None," I reply instantaneously.

"What?" Margot questions.

"We're McIntyres. We can get anything done when we put our minds to it."

"And money," Matt adds.

"Oh," Margot exclaims.

"Yeah, a little of that too," I agree.

"So, yes to a wedding?" Sam slips under Joe's arm.

"Yeah, Sweetness. You alright with sharing our honeymoon spot with Fin and Margot?"

He probably should have asked her that before suggesting it to me.

"Of course." Sam flits her gaze between me and Margot. "We get to come, right? I mean not for the honeymoon. But for the wedding."

"Everyone is invited." I look to my dad, and he just winks on a solid nod. He'll make it happen. He'll have MCI covered so we can all slip out for the wedding. "But after the wedding, everyone has to leave. No spectators at our honeymoon."

"Sounds like a plan."

Margot and Sam start squealing, and wedding plans start flying when they're joined by mine and Margot's moms.

This should be interesting.

"Let's go eat and talk game plan." I grab my girl and start heading for her i8 that matches her engagement ring.

We've got food to eat, good times to be had, and then better times after I get my Pixie home. Alone.

# Thirty-Five

'M EXHAUSTED. I DON'T THINK I'VE CRIED THIS
much, except maybe the time I woke up and found Fin had slipped
away without a goodbye. Or maybe when I told him to leave after
Bobby threatened me and my relationship with Fin. I cried for a solid
week that time.

"You're awful quiet, Pixie. Are you okay?"

His husky tone has me rolling my neck and taking in his profile
and muscular forearms. He removed his jacket and tie and rolled up his
sleeves some time ago. The sight of him never grows old. He steals my
breath nearly every time I see him, or when I find his eyes already on
me. Like now.

"I'm just tired. Coming down from the adrenaline high. It's been a
crazy day. I thought I was just graduating today, but it turns out I got
engaged, planned a wedding that's taking place in less than a week, and
had the most amazing evening with family and friends who dropped everything to come celebrate with us." My voice cracks for the umpteenth
time today.

"Pixie." Warmth and worry resonate in that single word.

I pat his hand. "I know. I don't know how I could possibly have
any tears left." I point to a fast food place. "Can we stop and get a soda?
Maybe it'll help me perk up."

"You don't need to perk up. You need rest. Your stomach still bothering you?"

"No. It seems to have calmed down. It's just stress of finals and figuring out what I want to be when I grow up. Plus, I've never had an iron stomach."

He links our hands. "I think a cup of hot tea and bed is what you need."

"Hmm." Though that does sound good, what I really need is some strong coffee and confidence.

Inside the house, I slip off my shoes and ask Fin to unzip my dress. "I'm just going to get comfortable and take my makeup off."

"Get ready for bed, Pixie. I'll make tea."

"Coffee, please. That French vanilla kind Sam likes so much." I can't figure out that damn machine Fin loves so much to make anything other than straight coffee. He's an expert at it.

I don't look back to confirm that he's giving me the eye, trying to figure out why I want coffee. I don't typically drink caffeine after dinner. It's not even seven pm, but I'm wiped out. I really could fall asleep for the night.

After hanging up my dress and stowing my heels, I take a quick shower and throw on sleep shorts and a t-shirt. Fin is just coming in the bedroom as I exit the bathroom.

"Better?" He sets a steaming mug of *something* on my nightstand.

I take a deep whiff and know he made me coffee, despite his reservations. "Thank you, and I do feel better. I don't mind dressing up, but it's nice to be in comfy clothes."

"I love you dolled up *and* just like this." He kisses my neck and squeezes my sides before sliding down to cup my ass. "I'm going to grab a quick shower."

"Sounds good." I pick up the steaming mug and blow across the top.

He pauses at the bathroom door. "You sure you're okay?"

"I'm sure, Finley." I motion with my chin. "Go. I'm going to enjoy my coffee my fiancé made me."

He smiles sheepishly, completely uncharacteristic for my confident man. "I like the sound of that."

"Then I better say it a lot as we don't have much time before it turns into *husband*."

"Fuck," he growls. "You just made me hard."

I giggle and blush like a schoolgirl, but manage to say, "Don't waste it in the shower."

His progress halts, and he slowly turns. "Did you just tell me not to jerk off in the shower?"

More blushing. "Maybe."

He shakes his head and laughs with a lightheartedness I can feel long after he drops his clothes and steps into the shower.

I'm lost in thought on the couch in our bedroom for so long, it seems like he's dressed and at my side in minutes. I've only managed a few sips of my coffee. He kneels down before me, takes my mug and drinks, savoring a few mouthfuls. His brows rise. "I forget how good that is."

"It really is. You make a mean cup of coffee, my *fiancé*."

That gets me a panty-dropping smile. He hands it back to me, and between the two of us, we finish it in no time. Then he sits next to me, pulling my feet onto his lap. He immediately gets to work massaging the arch of my right foot.

My moan is not to be stopped. He knows how much I love a good foot massage. Is there actually such a thing as a bad one?

"Tell me what's going on, Pixie. I can feel your churning thoughts from here. For the last hour, actually."

"I'm ready to tell you."

His stills, and one brow arches. I'm not even sure he's aware. "Tell me…?"

"All of it."

"All of it," he confirms.

"Yes."

He considers me for a minute before he nods and simply says, "Okay."

As much as I know there is nothing she can say that will change the way I feel for her, I'm leery of what this conversation holds. She's kept herself hidden from the world, yet remained right in the center with her chipper attitude and Susie Sunshine demeanor. I know my girl's pain runs deep. My fear is someone *hurt* her, and that could only mean I'd have to kill the bastard responsible. Not the best way to start off a marriage—me in prison.

She fidgets on the couch, moving so she's facing me, her back against the armrest. I keep up my foot massage. I need the contact, and perhaps it will soothe the worry that mars her beautiful face.

"Before you start, I just want to remind you that I love you unconditionally. Nothing you say will change that. Understand?" My tone is harsher than intended, but I need her to know I'm seriously not doubting my love for her in any way—and neither should she.

A sweet smile softens her worry. "Thank you, Fiancé." She winks.

I'm relieved she can tease. "You're welcome, Fiancée."

After taking a few cleansing breaths, she jumps in. "I was always small for my age. Much smaller than my mom and sister." She motions to me. "As you know." Her gaze flits to my hands on her feet and stays. "It's like I grew to a certain point and just stopped. It wasn't until after I turned seven that the reason became more apparent. I started playing soccer, or I *tried* to play soccer. But I couldn't keep up. I'd get out of breath, lose steam quickly. Sometimes I'd get dizzy and have to sit down before I fainted. Then it started happening at recess or during PE, basically anytime my body was stressed physically, I'd have trouble catching my breath and start to feel lightheaded.

"My mom, being a nurse, knew it wasn't normal. I didn't have asthma, which was their first thought. I did have a heart murmur, which I'd had since birth, but many kids do. It's not really an issue unless other symptoms arise."

"And you started to get sick?" I interject as flashes of everything I know about the heart zips through my brain.

"Yeah. I got pretty sick. Barely having the energy to get out of bed some days. I started missing school. My parents missed work. Then one day, I passed out at school when I stood up from my desk. It had nothing to do with exertion that time."

I trail my hand up her leg, needing more contact, needing to confirm she's here, in my sights, next to me, and my hand is, in fact, touching her. But still my heart races. What if she has a heart defect that can't be fixed—that shortens her life? What the hell will I do without her?

Her eyes flash to mine as if she senses my worry. "It's fine, Fin. I'm fine *now*." She sits up, cupping my face. Her smile is welcome and desperately needed. "The look on your face, babe. I'm fine. I promise."

Unable to stand the distance, I pull her into my lap and hold her tightly. My breath is ragged, and my eyes sting. "You can't leave me. I just got you back."

She gasps, her hold on me tightening. "You're stuck with me, Finley Whateveryourmiddlenameis McIntyre." Her wobbly voice has me peering into her eyes. She smiles through her tears, gifting me with a chaste kiss. "My heart is strong and beats every day for you," she breathes across my lips.

"Then tell me quickly. I don't think I can stand the suspense. What the hell happened? What was wrong?"

We both swipe at our eyes as she sits back on my knees. Her hand then presses to her chest, a move I've seen her do so often over the years. Many people do, but for her this move has more meaning—a deeper context.

"I was born with a heart defect. I had a hole in the upper chamber of my heart. Sometimes it heals on its own, or medicine can alleviate the symptoms, but mine required open heart surgery when I was eight."

*Fuck.* My grip on her thighs tightens as I work to remain stoic. I don't care about her fucking scar, but she does. I can't let her think my emotions are about her having one, but the fact that she had to endure so much, especially as a kid…

She fingers the center of her chest between her breasts. "My scar runs from here"—she points to the midline of her chest a few inches below where her collarbones meet—"and runs to here." She trails her fingers down about eight inches. Her hands drop to mine. "It didn't really bother me as a kid—the way it looked—not at first."

Her head falls, and I link our hands, waiting until she's ready to continue. "My dad starting drinking, heavily. When he was drunk, he could be cruel. He made me cover it up. Said he didn't want to see my *damage*. That nobody wanted to see something *so disgusting*."

I catch a tear as it falls. Her are eyes on me, but she's not really seeing me. "Kids at school could be mean." The corner of her mouth lifts. "I had to redo the second grade and was lucky enough to be put in Sam's class. She defended me. Helped me stand up for myself. But I started wearing clothes that would hide my scar. I never wore swimsuits except at Sam's when we knew no one else was around." Her smile grows. "Jace was actually pretty cool about it. If he invited friends over, he'd throw me a t-shirt, not because he thought I needed to hide it, but because he knew I did."

Her eyes lock on me. "He and Sam have had a hard time, but he has always been really great to me, like a protective older brother. He never let anyone mess with me, and he never made me feel like I had anything to be ashamed of."

"Fuck, Pixie, you don't have anything to be ashamed of."

"Yeah." She nods, but I can see she doesn't believe it.

"Tell me about Bobby. Does he have something to do with all of this?"

When she starts to cry, it takes everything in me not to call Victor and tell him to take Bobby out. Not really. But it's tempting. And he *could*.

# Thirty-Six

I T WAS RIDICULOUS FOR ME TO EVEN THINK I COULD make it through this without crying. But the shame and regret involving Bobby are hard to admit.

"He wasn't an ass at first. He was really sweet, attentive. He... Uh... Was my first. He didn't know anything about my scar—that didn't come till later."

Fin tenses below me. Who wants to hear about past lovers? I never want to hear about his, that's for sure. I've no doubt they're all tall, modelesque types.

"I thought I could trust him. I was wrong. Once he saw my scar, he didn't care how I got it. He just wanted to get away from me. He said it made him *sick to see it*. I was *evil and manipulative for hiding it from him.* He wanted a *normal girlfriend.*"

"He's a dead motherfucker," Fin all but growls, his jaw clenched.

That should frighten me, but it doesn't. I know I'm completely safe with Fin, and the fact that I doubted him says more about my insecurities than about the type of man he is. "I don't think he'll be bothering me anytime soon. I'm sure he'll be in jail for at least the next few years for attacking me, Zeke, and Dad."

Fin laces his fingers in my hair, bringing me closer until we're nose to nose. "He'll never touch you or those you love again."

I run my hands up his shoulders and into his hair. "I know. You won't let anyone hurt me."

"Damn straight."

201

We stay locked in our embrace until we've both calmed. "Anything else you want to know?"

"Watt. Does he know?"

"No. He suspects *something*. But our sexual relationship was different. I learned from Bobby not to be that vulnerable again."

Fin lets out a punch of air. "Any other guys?" His question is forced like he doesn't really want to know, but can't help asking.

"I've only been with three guys, Fin. You are number three."

"I wasn't asking about numbers. I want to know if anyone else has hurt you." He searches my eyes like he's looking for more secrets.

I caress his jaw with my thumb. "That's all. I don't have any other secrets." When he still doesn't say anything thing, I try another tactic. "I don't suppose you want to tell me how many women you've slept with."

His jaw ticks. "Hardly." He furrows his brow. "Do you really want to know?"

"No." I touch his brow. "I was just trying to lighten the mood. I don't need to know unless there's something you want to share."

He lets out a punch of air. "I'm not even sure, really. It's more than Joe but less than Matt."

I laugh. They are such guys. "I definitely don't want to know how you know that."

Shrugging, he pulls me closer. "We're tight. We're brothers. We don't share details, but we don't have any secrets either." He grimaces. "Most of the time. Joe kept some pretty big secrets when it came to protecting Sam, but I don't blame him. As for Matt, he's going through something. The whole thing with Lydia and Veronica blackmailing Sam, and his unwitting participation, has really messed with his head. But the fact that he showed today and plans to come for the wedding is a good sign."

"I think Matt will be fine. And Joe and Sam seem good now."

"They are." He takes a breath before continuing, "I need to tell you something."

The seriousness in his voice gives me pause. "Okay."

"I swear to you, I didn't dig. I don't know any details. But I paid off your parents' debt," he rushes out either in relief or fear of my retribution.

Wow. My heart pangs. "All of it?" I know it was substantial. I tried to help over the years, but my mom wouldn't hear of it. Dad, well, that was not a topic I cared to discuss with him. There hadn't been much I wanted to talk to him about in a long time.

"Yes. And their house."

"Fin!"

He raises his hands. "I know, Pixie. You've made it more than clear you don't want me for my money. But I had to do it. They were struggling. There was no way your dad was going to get sober with that hanging over his head." He grips my hips. "You deserve a dad, Margot. One who's not an out-of-work drunk. It was in my power to help. So, I did."

"I'm going to pay you back," I insist, having no idea how long that could take.

"No. You. Won't." He's firm and determined. "You're my woman. You're going to be my wife. What I have is yours. All of it. Even my money."

I shake my head. "It's too much, Finley." I hate the defeat in my voice and the relief I feel for knowing my parents no longer have that burden to weigh them down. And me, for that matter. My heart defect wasn't my fault, but they did go into debt to save me. Realistic or not, I've always felt responsible for their problems as a result.

"It's not." He captures the back of my head, still gripping my hip. "If you had money, more than you could ever spend in a hundred lifetimes, would you help me? Would you help my family if they needed it?"

All the fight leaves me in a rush. "Of course I would."

"Then there's nothing else to discuss. I can. So, I did."

"And you paid for his rehab." I remind him. He nods. "And you're getting him a job. A damn good job I'm not sure he deserves."

"Maybe he doesn't—that's yet to be seen. But he went into debt to save your life. I will never stop helping them as long as there's a flicker of hope in your eyes when it comes to salvaging your relationship with your family."

"Gah." I fall into him, hugging him hard. "You're insane. You know that, right?"

His chuckle rumbles through his chest and tickles my ear. "I'm insane about you, Pixie. Only for you."

"Take me to bed, Finley. My legs are stiff, and I need to feel your naked body pressed to mine as you fill me up." My girl kisses along my neck.

And I have a steel hard cock in two second flat. "Does that mean…?"

"It does. Strip me bare—" Her confidence cracks right along with her voice. "—Only…" Her faces scrunches up as she sobs, "Please don't freak out. I couldn't handle you walking out on me again. Twice in a lifetime is more than enough."

"I'll never leave you again, Marguerite. I was an ass for doing it the first time. A coward for the second. There is no third time. The only *third* I am to you, is third guy you've had sex with." I stand up with her in my arms, her legs around my waist. "I sure as fuck will be the last."

"Promise?"

"I promise." I kiss her forehead as she leans forward. "I can't promise I won't get upset for all you've been through. For all you've endured. But it won't be because I think you're anything other than my beautiful Pixie."

On the bed, I kiss her until her tears have stopped, and she'd wiggling beneath me like she's trying to shed her skin.

Maybe she is.

My Pixie told me her secret. The cocoon of fear and shame is starting to be shed. My girl is sprouting wings like the effervescent fairy she is.

Her jedi skills in full force, she gets me naked while I've only managed to get her sleep shorts off. Her panties and t-shirt still in place, I pull back in awe of how she does it. "You've got to stop trying to sidetrack me from getting you naked."

She freezes, her sigh heavy. "Shit, I'm sorry. It's instinctual—automatic."

"I know, baby." I suck her bottom lip, then delve in, taking her mouth and playing with her tongue. "Take your panties off."

Her moan at my command has my hips flexing to fill her exactly how she needs it, and how I need to give it.

She reaches between us and works her panties down her thighs. I take over from there and slide them off the rest of the way. Her legs part, and I nearly surge home when I settle over her—my cock knowing its path to its favorite place.

But I don't. I can't. Not yet.

Dipping low, I kiss from her belly button down, across her hips. Then, lower to slide my tongue between her folds and kiss her clit, sucking and nipping until her fingers grip my hair, and she's begging for my cock.

Slowly, I push her shirt up and kiss and lick my way upward. Under the fabric, my hands grip her breasts and brush my thumbs over her stiff peaks.

"Fin," she cries.

I have to check myself. Remember how important this moment is. She's lost in the sensations of my touch. I don't even think she realizes how momentous this moment is, my hands on her bare breasts. But I sure as fuck do.

Bracing above her, my fingers carefully touch the beginnings of her scar right below her breasts. My eyes are trained on her, waiting for any signs of panic.

There's none.

Her hand flies to mine, kneading one breast as I lift her top with the other. Her moans grow as my mouth moves closer, first kissing her pale pink scar then moving to her ignored breast. I hesitate, taking a moment to get my fill of the sight of my Pixie's breasts. They're small but perfectly round globes with dark rose nipples.

It feels like I've waited a lifetime for this. I flick her nip before sucking it deep and teasing it with my teeth. She bows off the bed, her hands holding my head right where it is.

"Fuuuck," my girl exclaims as she wraps her legs around my ass, squeezing, urging me to fill her.

Not yet.

I switch to the other breast, tease and pull her stiff peak and quickly remove her top over her head, tossing it to the floor, hoping to never see her wearing anything like it to bed again.

Naked, my girl looks at me with no fear as my eyes slide down her body, taking her in and wondering why the hell we waited so long to be skin to skin. "You're fucking beautiful, Pixie. There's not a damn thing wrong with you."

On a cry that can only be described as wild, she attacks my mouth, pulling me close and rubbing against my cock, sliding me around her wet heat, coaxing, teasing—begging.

When my name flies from her lips as she breaks our kiss, I give her what we both need—my cock, filling her sweet pussy to the brim.

"Fuck, Pixie," I groan around our kiss. "So fucking good." I slide my arms under her shoulders, holding my weight just enough not to crush her but not so much that I can't feel her bare breasts against my chest. Her nipples brush my skin with every thrust of our hips.

"Yes!" she chants with every upward stroke. Followed by an, "Oh, fuck, yes," every now and again.

My sprite's dirty mouth has me drilling harder, grinding deeper, and savoring her mouth like it's my last fucking meal.

Clinging to me, she starts to shake, and her words turn to guttural cries. Her breathing is so harsh, I worry for her heart—that she swears is just fine. "Are you going to come for me, Pixie?"

"Yeeeeees!" Her mewl is loud enough to shake walls, wrap around my cock, and squeeze the love in my heart. "Fuuuck, yes!" she screams her release.

We've had mind-blowing sex before, and my girl can come like a champ. But *this* orgasm is big and torturous, fueled by fear, the depth of unconditional love, and the knowledge that we've found our forever after.

A few more pumps and I still, letting the waves of her contractions milk my cock as I bark my release into a kiss that I never want to end.

A forever I never saw coming

A future I can't wait to start with my girl, my Pixie.

# Thirty-Seven

IF THERE WAS ANYONE IN THE HISTORY OF TIME who ever said flying in a private jet is *hard*, they're flat-out crazy. I know it's old news to Fin and his family, but Sam was smiling like it was Christmas morning, just like I was—and like Matt's girl Gabby was.

Matt surprised us all by bringing a date to our wedding. No one mentioned it. Fin gave me a pointed look that said, *I'll tell you later*. Not that I mind. Not like I'm actually running this circus that's my wedding. I'm just the bride, a participant who needs to show up in white tomorrow and look as pretty as I can for my groom.

*My groom.* OMG! I still can't get over it. I'm actually marrying Finley Granger—yes, he told me his middle name he hates, that I secretly love—McIntyre.

Everyone came: my mom, dad, sister, her fiancé, and my brother. Then there's Fin's family: his mom and dad, Joe and Sam, Matt and Gabby. And Fin's brothers through choice not blood: Victor and Michael. Jace falls into all the categories. He's both family and brother by choice to Fin, Michael, Victor, Matt, and Joe. Plus, he's Sam's brother, essentially her only family since her mom can't seem to pull her head out of her ass enough to give two fucks about anyone else other than herself and her grief.

"You okay, Pixie?" Fin frowns at me.

"Yeah, why?"

He flexes his hand. "You were squeezing my hand like... I don't know... Just... Are you okay?"

208

I curl up tighter on my side, my chair reclined as I look at my man and kiss our joined hands. "Sorry, I was just thinking about Sam's mom."

His warm palm cups my cheek as his eyes soften and he turns toward me.

"She's missing out on so much. I just wish she could find the strength to get better. They don't talk about it, but I know Jace and Sam miss her, maybe even more than their dad. He didn't have a choice—he was killed. But she is choosing to live in her grief instead of loving the ones she has left."

His forehead meets mine as he leans over the arm between our seats. "I know, Pixie." His lips brush my skin. "Not everyone is equipped to deal with life's curveballs. She's getting help. Means there's still hope."

I guess there's that.

I sleep though the rest of the flight, still not feeling the best, but certain it's stress of the wedding and all of life waiting for me to decide what I want to be when I grow up—which is now.

If he wasn't more concerned with me having a seatbelt on, I've no doubt Finley would have me sprawled across his body sleeping like a baby. But as it stands, he wakes me up gently right before landing with sweet kisses and tender caresses.

According to Sam, Joe had additional cabanas built since their honeymoon, allowing each brother and family to have their own space. I can't imagine how much all of that cost. The McIntyre wealth is difficult to fathom and not be intimidated by or run for the hills.

Surprisingly, we get the big *cabana*—which is more like a mansion with enough bedrooms for everyone to stay with us, but Joe insisted we have it to ourselves. Even the new cabanas are the size of homes and not the pretty but modest grass huts I imagined (and like the name implies). Everyone will meet up later for a cookout on the beach.

But for now, I'm lazing by the ocean with Sam and Gabby while the guys swim, snorkel, and try to kill each other. You know, in that loving, macho-guy kind of way they do.

"You feeling any better?" Gabby asks.

"Honestly, not really. I think I could close my eyes and sleep for a week. I can't wait to spend three weeks here relaxing just like this. Doing absolutely nothing—except my husband."

Giggles ensue until Sam decides to play Debbie Downer.

"How long have you been feeling yucky and run down?" The concern is evident in her tone and the worry in her eyes.

"I'm fine, really." I tap my chest. "My ticker is just as good as yours."

"I wasn't thinking that at all." But her frown tells me she's thinking it now. "Really, how long? Usually you're full of pep and the last person to fall asleep on a trip."

True. "I don't know, a month or so. It's just graduation and the stress of getting engaged, married, deciding if I still want to be a doctor or not."

"The fact that you're doubting it should be answer enough." Sam hands me a bottled water. "Drink this. I know you wanted to be a doctor because of what happened to you as a kid. But it's okay to change your mind. Our dreams should grow as we do."

I've wanted to be a doctor since I had my surgery. I thought it was a cool job, and I wanted to help people. I wanted to make a difference. But there are lots of jobs that make a difference that don't require twelve more years of study. And just because a surgeon saved me doesn't mean I have to become one. "You're right."

Her eyes dart to Gabby before coming back to me. "Margot, when was your last period?"

"What?!" I thought she was going to want to talk about my career choice, not about…

Her eyes are wide in question. "Period. How long."

"Oh, shit," Gabby steals the words from my mouth.

"I can't—"

"You could—"

"But—"

"Come on." Sam stands, wrapping her sarong around her waist and jogging over to Joe. They have a quick discussion. His eyes dart to me before returning to her.

Gabby and I wait at the pathway, knowing Joe will tell Matt and Fin where we're going—even if *we* don't know ourselves.

In Sam and Joe's cabana, I stare at the box she hands me. "Why do you have these?"

She tips a shoulder. "Sometimes I'm late. I always have a supply with me, just in case."

"Are y'all trying?" They've only been married five months. I thought she wanted to wait a few years. It's hard to believe Joe's the only guy she's slept with. They've been together since she was seventeen. He insisted they wait until she was eighteen and no longer in danger from her father's killer—whom she and Michael shot dead—and she was confident in Joe's feelings for her. I'm not the only one who doesn't feel worthy of these incredible McIntyre men.

"We're not *not* trying." She beams. "It's fun thinking about, and practicing is… Just, wow."

We all laugh until my tears morph into sobs. "I can't be," I mumble behind the hand I clamp over my mouth to stop from breaking down completely.

They rush me, hugging me tightly. "You won't know until you take the test. Go. We're right here with you," Sam cajoles.

Gabby steps back and hands me a tissue. "You don't know me. But you're not alone." She motions to the beach. "And that man out there will be nothing but ecstatic to know he knocked you up. The McIntyre men are possessive Neanderthals like that."

Sam and I share a look. "Matt is like that too?"

"Seriously?" Gabby laughs.

"Yes. Matt seems more playboy than caveman." Sam taps the box in my hand. "Go pee. We'll continue this discussion so you can hear."

But once I get in the bathroom, my thoughts wander to the idea of having Fin's baby. Will he be happy like Gabby believes? Or will he pretend to be happy for me, but wish we waited?

I guess there is only one way to find out…

"Margot?" I call as soon as I close the door to our cabana.

I was on edge the minute Margot disappeared with Sam and Matt's latest squeeze, but when she and Sam returned without Margot, I was on high alert. Sam didn't even get a chance to speak before I inquired about my bride.

Now, I scan the rooms as I pass, making my way up the stairs to the master bedroom. The full-length, floor-to-ceiling accordion doors are open, and the breeze blows the thin white drapes that give a modicum of privacy between us and the outside world.

Not finding Margot in our room, I continue into the bathroom and spot her standing in the shower. The water is beating over her head, but she's not moving. Taking a second longer than I'd like, I strip off my swimsuit and step into the shower. "Pixie?"

Her head snaps up, her eyes wide and rimmed red.

Defcon alert level rises. "Why are you crying?" Is she having second thoughts? Is she hurt?

Thankfully she answers before I give life to every fear I have regarding her. "I'm pregnant."

My progress to wrap her in my arms staggers as I replay her words in my head. "Say that again."

"I'm pregnant." She bursts into tears, and though they mix with the shower, the pain on her face is evident.

"Fuck me." My gruff tone has her peeking up at me.

Her eyes widen. "Why are you smiling?"

My grin only grows. "Because you're pregnant."

"Yeah, but... Wait... You're happy?"

I back her to the tile wall, my arms slipping around her to save back from the chill. "So fucking happy."

"You... What?"

My head falls to her shoulder. "You're crying because you thought I'd be upset?"

She nuzzles into my neck, her warm hands sliding around my waist. "I feared you might be."

I kiss her quickly and pull back. "Are you done in here? Do you still need to wash your hair or anything?"

"I'm done."

"Good. Hold on." I scoop her up, grab a towel as I exit, wrap it around her back, and set her on the bathroom counter. Making quick work, I dry us both off, wring out her hair, and watch as she smoothly secures it in a bun on top of her head. Then I carry her to bed and lay her down in the middle, crawling over her to rest between her sweet thighs. Her eyes grow wide when she feels what she does to me against her pussy. "I'm the happiest man alive, Pixie." I circle my hips, reinforcing my current state of arousal. "We got pregnant without even trying." The pride in my grin is not to be helped. "Obviously, I have super sperm."

She smiles for the first time since she told me. "Obviously that's it. It's not that I have super ovaries or eggs, or a magnificent uterus to house our baby for the next eight months."

I kiss her nose and along her jaw. "Of course, it's that too."

"You're crazy, my almost husband."

"I'm crazy for you, Pixie. Stark raving mad." Changing positions, I flip us over and situate her so she's sitting astride me, my hand splayed on her belly—or would-be belly if she had one. My girl is a tiny thing. "Are you okay with this?"

She nods. "I should be freaking out, but my only concern was how you'd feel about it. You've already turned your world upside down to move to Austin with me. Having a baby now will only make it more chaotic."

"You mean more *wonderful?*" I start to explore her body, cupping her breasts, teasing her nipples. "My mom is going to be beside herself."

"In a good way or a bad way?" She grips my forearms as she starts to undulate over my hard cock.

"Happy. Over-the-top happy." I run my hand down Margot's stomach to rub slow circles around her clit. The catch in her breath has me wanting to sink into her before I'm sure she's ready. "At Joe and Sam's wedding when you were dancing with Matt, she told me to go get my girl and make her a grandbaby."

"She did not." Her head falls back, and I can feel her moisture coating my cock.

"Mom always knows." I pull my girl down for a kiss. "Can we stop talking about my mom? I'd really rather fuck my baby mommy till she screams my name."

"God, Finley. The things that come out of that mouth."

"Let me show you what else I can do with my mouth, Pixie." And my fingers, and my cock.

# Thirty-Eight

"I CAN'T BELIEVE YOU'RE FUCKING PREGNANT before we are." Joe's pout is pretty hilarious.

He's the biggest of the three of us, the youngest, and the first to fall in love. Though, I don't think Matt is far behind. He's trepidatious, though. He and Gabby have a history. I hadn't put two and two together until last night when she commented on how she'd never seen me so happy. I hadn't thought she'd seen me at all, as in, *ever* until meeting her on the plane.

Turns out they went to college together. We'd met a few times, given the three of us were at UT at the same time. I graduated two years before them, but during their freshmen year, they had a *thing*. She's the one who broke his heart—or more like he broke his own heart by being an idiot, thereby breaking both of their hearts in one stupid, idiotic move.

But who am I to judge? I've pined over my Pixie for over two years and finally just got my act together.

I grip my baby brother's shoulder. "I'm older. I don't have time to waste. Besides, I hear you're trying." I don't point out that *I* got the job done without even trying. No need to rub it in his face.

His stupid grin is all I need to know that he's enjoying the *trying*, and that he's not really upset, maybe more surprised. After all, Margot and I are moving fast, but it's been a long time coming.

"Aren't you a little worried, Brother?" Matt straightens my tie I know for facts is already straight.

I slap away his hand. Now I'm sure it's crooked, which was his intent all along. "Joe." I point to my tie, and he saunters over to fix what Matt just messed up. "What are you talking about?" I ask Matt.

"Your woman. She's a tiny thing." He flicks his hand, motioning up and down my body. "Aren't you worried?"

My scowl makes Joe laugh. "You're a big motherfucker, Fin. Margot is on the small side," he offers up what is plainly obvious.

"It's gonna be like *Aliens*, poor Margot trying to push your big ass baby out of her—"

I cover his mouth. "Don't say it," I growl. The last thing I want to hear is my brother referencing my girl's pussy. "Seriously, dude. Have some decorum. I'm about to get married, and you're talking about the mother of my unborn baby."

"Exactly," he mumbles behind my hand and then licks my palm.

I jerk my hand back. "You're so fucking gross." I head to the sink to wash my hands.

"You never learn. You cover my mouth when I'm trying to talk, I'm going to lick your hand. Been that way since we were kids. Wise up, old man."

"Pfft, old. I'm young enough to kick your ass," I remind him.

"Is that what happens when Gabby sits on your face?" Joe elbows Matt.

"Every damn time, Brother." Matt smirks, then sobers. "I wish," he softly admits.

His change of demeanor has me narrowing my focus on him. "Everything alright, Brother?"

He drops his shoulders. His gaze is out the window of Joe's cabana. "I fucked up."

Joe and I stand on either side of him and catch the object of his attention staring right back at him. The war in her eyes is as evident as it is in his.

"She's the best thing I've ever known. But she closed the door on me long ago. I don't know how to get her to let me back in." The ache in his words is something I can relate to.

"Sometimes you have to give her time to see how you've changed," Joe offers.

I turn Matt to me, straighten his tie and run my fingers down the edges of his lapel. "Sometimes you have to make a big gesture to prove you're serious. That you're no longer that idiot she knew in college."

"But what if I still am?" His green eyes meet mine.

My gaze flicks to Joe's same green eyes. He nods, encouraging me to continue. Meeting Matt's stare, I tell him the only truth I know. "You wouldn't be asking if you were the same guy." I motion out the window. "Gabby wouldn't be here if she wasn't holding out hope the guy she wants is somewhere in here." I lay my hand over his heart, its thunderous beat hammering away.

In the distance, I see the white drapes of my island home swaying in the breeze and know my girl is on the other side. Is she thinking of me? "I found my heart, my purpose when I found Margot. I knew I wanted a family… Someday. But until I surrendered to the power of our love, I had no idea how amazing life could be. My future is what I hoped it would be, but a million times better because it's with her."

"Fuck," Matt exhales.

"Exactly," Joe agrees, his gaze already out the window, trained on his woman.

"I thought I knew what love was. I had no idea." I hope Matt will know what that feels like someday.

But for now, it's time to find my Pixie and make her my wife.

I shake out my hands, nerves rattling in my bones. Sam, Gabby, my mom, and Jenny left a few minutes ago to take their seats. It'll just be Fin and me at the altar. No attendants. I feel a little guilty about it, but I didn't want Fin to feel like he had to choose between his best friends and his brothers to narrow it down to one or two since I only have Sam and Jenny on my side. It's just the two of us getting married. There's no rule you have to have attendants.

"You okay, Marguerite? You look like you might get sick." My dad hands me a glass of water. "Maybe this will help."

"I'm good." A tall figure draws my attention as I spot Fin walking toward the flowered archway altar with his brothers in tow.

"You're nervous." He tentatively takes my hand. "You're the strongest, bravest person I know." His eyes tear. "I hope I can be just like you when I grow up." He smiles and sniffles.

"Daddy." I rapidly blink, looking up. "Please don't make me cry." He's been quiet since we arrived yesterday. But whenever I'd find him in the crowd of our friends and family, his eyes would already be on me or my mom. His features have softened. The stress he carried so evidently on his face is gone. He looks healthy, has gained weight, and his color's better. But most importantly, he's the dad I remember: soft-spoken, gives loving hugs, and looks at my mom like she hung the moon. We have a long way to go, but it's a promising start.

He shakes his head. "I'm proud of you. Always have been. I was just too messed up to be the father you needed. But I'm here now." He guides me to the front door but stops before opening it. "Thank you for letting me give you away. It's an honor I don't deserve, but one I'm deeply grateful for."

I can only nod my reply. Words leave me, and all I can think is I wish Fin were here to witness my father's bloom. Fairy tales and dreams aside, I always hoped my dad would be the one to give me away. But years of broken promises and hurtful words ripped that dream from my mind.

"I love you, Daddy." I kiss his cheek seconds before Victor's voice booms on the other side.

"It's time."

"I love you too, Girly." He opens the door. "Let's get you hitched."

The sight of Fin standing next to the officiant, waiting for me, has my heart leaping and my feet moving a little faster.

My dad chuckles at my side. "Patience, Margot. He'll wait for you. I promise."

I don't know if I can wait for *him*.

The urgency to make Fin mine is so foreign, but not unwelcome.

I'd become resigned to the idea of never having this.

I'd settled for less, expecting a solo existence hidden behind a happy window treatment.

Then *he* came into my life, seeing past my emotional blackout curtains to the interior inside, where darkness dwelled, and hope came to die.

Fin dared to love what not even my own father could love about me, except it's not a hardship for my man. Fin truly doesn't see my scars—the one on my chest and the ones inside—as anything other than badges of honor. Proof that I survived, that I fought and came out the other side, stronger and braver than before. His words. Not mine.

"Pixie?" His brow creases, and his jaw clenches as he takes a few steps toward us.

My breath catches at the intensity of his presence, reminding me how formidable he can be.

He narrows his eyes at my dad and takes my arm. "Excuse us a moment," he says to the minister and pulls me behind the palm trees lining the beach. Out of sight and ears of our family and friends.

Cupping my face between his massive hands, he scans my face. "What's wrong? You look like you're about to cry."

I nod and smile as tears start to fall. "You love me," comes out on a sob.

"Jesus, fuck." He pulls me into his chest, his arms wrapping me in the security of his embrace. "Of course I do. Are you just now accepting that?"

"You love *all* of me. Even the broken pieces." My tears fall faster, and I'm having trouble breathing.

A growl rumbles up his chest and echoes in my ears. He sweeps me in his arms, moving farther away, then sits on the grassy sand in the shade of the trees with no thought of ruining his suit. "Pixie, you have no broken pieces." He cradles my cheek and kisses my tears. "You're perfect for me in every way, just as you are. If you didn't go through what you did, you wouldn't be the woman I love—you'd be someone else." He kisses my face and buries his head in my neck. "Now tell me you hear me before I whisk you away, forgoing the ceremony, and fuck you until you come to your senses."

I laugh on a sniffle and a stilted breath. "That doesn't sound so bad."

His smiling face comes into view as he lifts his head. "It sounds nearly perfect."

"Nearly?"

"I'd prefer you were my wife before we do the deed again. But if you need a quickie before the ceremony, I'm happy to oblige." He presses a hot kiss to my mouth. "But understand this, Marguerite soon-to-be McIntyre, I am marrying you today. So, we might as well do it now rather than later since everyone is already gathered, and quite anxiously, I'm sure. They probably think we're breaking up or something."

"Or something," Joe's voice gets my attention as he steps around a tree. "We thought you slipped away for a quickie."

My eyebrows shoot up. "And you came to... What? Watch?"

"God, no," he balks. "I came to be sure we're still having a wedding." He motions over his shoulder. "And you're right, they are anxious. But I assured them you just needed a moment to yourselves." He looks at me and then Fin. "Remember the kiss Samantha and I had before we actually started the ceremony?

"How could we forget?" Fin points to the two of us. "We had front row seats."

"Well, that... Was us taking a moment." He smiles and dips his head, turning to leave. "Oh, Margot—" he stops. "Don't doubt my brother loves you. You are the sun, the moon, and the stars all wrapped up in a perfect package made just for him." With a wink he disappears.

"That's—"

"My brother telling you to stop worrying and marry my ass already."

"Yeah?"

"Yeah." He steals another kiss before asking, "Will you marry me, Pixie? Make an honest man of me, ease the ache in my chest, and give me more babies than either of us know what to do with?"

"Finley." My mouth crashes to his, taking one last kiss before making this man mine forever—and ever.

When we break apart, breathless and way turned on, he smiles. "I'll take that as a *yes*."

"Yes, Finley Granger McIntyre, I will marry you. Then you're going to fuck me until I never forget you belong to me."

His eyes darken. "It'll be my pleasure, Marguerite." Lifting me to my feet, he stands, dusts off the sand, and links our fingers. "Let's do this."

# Thirty-Nine

THE SLOW CRASH OF THE WAVES ON THE BEACH LULLS my eyes closed. My wife is between my legs, stretched out on top of me. The warmth of the sun is like a blanket, yet we're shaded from its rays under the beachside canopy.

We said *I do.*

We partied sans alcohol, in support of Margot's father's sobriety. Plus, my woman is pregnant—with *my* baby, in case you missed that awesome news.

I made love to my *wife* for the first, second, third time.

Then we said goodbye to everyone this morning.

Peaceful solitude surrounds us. The only remaining souls on the island besides ourselves are the staff, whom Joe swears we'll never see unless we *need* to see them.

The nearest doctor on a neighboring island sent over prenatal vitamins. We're here for three weeks, and Margot was worried about the baby getting the nutrients he or she needs. Her mom reminded her that the vitamins are actually for the mother as the baby gets what it needs from her. A few phone calls later, prenatal vitamins were delivered with the boat that came to ferry our loved ones to catch the jet home.

For the past few hours, we swam, ate, and are now lying on a double lounger, soaking up the quiet and enjoying the stillness of just being together.

I slide my hand down the curve of her back, up her side, and down. She doesn't move, barely ticklish, but I'm pretty sure she's not asleep. Just wonderfully relaxed. Like me.

"This is heaven," I murmur.

"It is." Her soft breath cascades over my chest.

"Promise me we'll do this every year, maybe twice a year."

"Three times a year," she suggests.

"Sold."

"At least one of those trips should be with everyone. One should be just the brothers or the six-pack and their families. And then one should be just us." She pushes up. "I'm hot." She swipes her forehead, resting on her haunches, facing me between my legs.

I hand her a bottled water from the ice chest next to me. Instead of drinking it, she first wipes the wet bottle over her face, below her ears, along her neck, then rolls it to her chest.

"Damn, woman. Are you trying to kill me?"

She just smirks, twists the lid open, and takes a long chug, her throat bobbing with each swallow.

She *is* trying to kill me. I'm certain.

Lowering the bottle, she hands it to me. Her gaze drops to my lap, scanning my growing length. "Something on your mind, Finley?"

"Yeah. You." I drink the rest of her water, then toss it and the cap in the trash.

Leaning forward, she kisses me with cool lips that taste like the peaches we had with lunch. Before I can take it further, she sits back, her hands resting on my thighs. "I have an idea I wanted to discuss with you."

"Okay."

"You know I've been uncertain about wanting to pursuing being a doctor this entire school year."

I nod.

"I think I know what I'd like to do."

I nod again. "Okay."

Her hand falls to her stomach, rubbing slowly.

I sit forward, place my hand over hers. "Tell, Pixie. I'm all ears." And eyes, and heart for my girl.

"You're going to be the first brother to have a kid."

"Yeah." I smile every time I think about it.

"Joe and Sam won't be far behind."

"Right."

"And eventually, Matt, Victor, Michael, and even Jace will have their own kids."

"Uh, you know something I don't, Pixie? Some of those are sworn bachelors."

Her sweet smile has me joining her. "Just wait. They want it. They just don't know it yet."

Oh, Lord, those guys are in trouble. Between Sam and Margot, they're bound to be paired up in the next year or so. "Okay, for argument's sake, let's say they all get married and have kids. What does that have to do with you and being a doctor? Are you wanting to be a pediatrician?"

"That's not a bad guess, but no. I'm thinking something that won't require any further degrees or take me years to accomplish." Her hand slips from underneath mine to on top and presses.

My cock hardens to steel at the idea of getting her pregnant again and again.

She notices and leans forward, brushing her mouth over mine. "Hold on, babe. Let me get this out, then I'll take care of you."

I cup her ass and situate her so she's straddling my erection. "We'll take care of each other."

Her fingers flex on my pecs, and she sucks in a breath. "You're making it hard for me to think."

*Hard?* She has no idea. I pull the strings on either side of her bikini bottoms, and before she can do more than gasp, her pussy is bare, pressing against my clothed cock. "Keep going, Marguerite." As she speaks, I slide my hands up her sides and cup her breasts, toy with her nipples, and untie her top. Pulling the fabric free, I suck a nipple and roll the other between my finger and thumb.

"Finley." She flexes her hips, holding my shoulder and the back of my head.

"Tell me." I nip at her breasts and then slide my tongue over one peak to the other, kissing her scar as I pass. Deftly untying my trunks, I maneuver enough to free my cock. And when she rolls her hips back, I lift her just enough to thrust inside her wet heat.

"Oh!" she cries.

"Fuck," I growl as her whole body shakes in a mini orgasm. "That was just a warm up, Pixie."

"IwanttoopenadaycareatMCI!" she all but screams, biting my shoulder and starting to round her hips.

I couldn't have heard her right. Stifling her movements by gripping her hips, I peer into her eyes. "You want to open a daycare?"

She bobs her head, whining, her fingers biting into my skin as she fights to control her body's need to move and ram me home over and over. "Yes," she pants. "Don't you want to be close to our baby? If I open a daycare, get the best childcare educators money can buy, we could have an MCI-funded daycare for employees with children newborn to pre-school. If need be, I could get whatever certification I need. Or I could just run the place and offer age-appropriate science experiments and lessons—since that's my degree."

"You're serious?"

"I am."

"Pixie." I'm near speechless. My wife who's smart as a whip and could be a heart surgeon like she's been planning since she was a kid, now wants to change careers, move back to Dallas, and open a daycare to take care of our baby—my family's babies—so we can all be close, be a part of their lives instead of overworked fathers or mothers, who only get to see their kids in the mornings, evenings, and weekends.

"What do you think?" Her soft brown eyes are so big and hopeful, even if I didn't think it was a spectacular idea, I'd be tempted to lie.

Thankfully, I don't have to—given our promise of truth and… "I think it's an amazing idea." I capture the back of her neck and pull her close. "But… I think you should oversee the daycare. Teach whatever you want. Get whatever license or degree you want or need. I want you to enjoy our children too, not be stressed or bogged down by running a full-time business. We'll have managers, teachers, nurses, a chef, cleaning crew, whatever we need. You will be at the top, the director. Then you have the freedom to do whatever you want with your time."

"Okay, but no stuffy, highbrow educators who live and breathe by rules and codes of conduct. Of course, safety comes first. But I want a warm, welcoming atmosphere for the kids and parents. I want you and all the parents to feel like you can come and go. See their kids when they want or can with their busy schedules, and even have lunch with their kids. I want new mommies to have a place to breastfeed or moms and dads to bottle-feed their babies. I want lots of snuggles and love—everywhere."

"Margot, it's a truly great idea. We won't be the first corporation to have inhouse childcare, but we'll be the best. It could even be a recruiting point for new hires."

"I'm so glad you like the idea because I'm really tired of school. I'm ready to start my life, and that includes you and our little one."

"You won't regret not being a doctor? I don't want you to feel like you have to give up your dream because you're pregnant. We can make whatever you want work. *I* will make it work."

She shakes her head. "I'm not giving up my dream. The dream has changed. Being a doctor was what I wanted when I was a kid because of what happened to me. I wasn't sure I'd ever find this." She motions between us. "I want to make a difference, but I want a life. A family. A daycare will make a difference for MCI parents and their children. You've given me a whole new family, Fin. I want to help take care of them. Keep us close, safe, and loved."

Jesus, this woman. "Your heart, Pixie. It's so fucking big. I don't know how you carry it around in your tiny body."

She smiles and bites her lips, tears glistening in her eyes. "My heart's not big, Finley. It's my love. My love for you and everything you love."

"Later, we'll start a file with all your ideas and questions. But for now..." I kiss her soft lips. "I need to love you."

"Please." Her breathy reply is accompanied by her clenching my cock and swiveling her hips.

"Fuck, Wife, you're going to be the death of me." I wrap her in my arms and slide down the lounger, bend my knees and begin to thrust. She may be on top, but I'm in charge. Not always, but giving my Pixie pleasure, making her happy is my life's mission.

She bites my lip and tugs enough to get my attention. "Not the death of you, Finley. The life of you. We gave each other life, freedom to stop hiding, a place to be ourselves—imperfect and undone."

"Fuck, Pixie." No more words. I take her mouth on a tantalizing ride that matches the way she rides my cock—with joy and total abandon.

My girl.

My Pixie.

Sunshine is her color.

Bright is her soul.

And happy is her new creed.

*The End*

# *Epilogue*

## ∿ 3 Months After Wedding ∿

"**Y**OU WANT TO DO WHAT?" I FOLLOW MY WIFE around Hugs 'n Love, MCI's new inhouse childcare facility located on the bottom floor of both the Alpha and Omega towers with outdoor space in between. Phase One is opening the Alpha facility, which will later expand to Phase Two in the Omega facility, where the preschool-age kids will eventually reside. Currently, they will all be in the Alpha tower until space is needed and Phase One is running smoothly. Amazingly, most of the kids are currently infants and toddlers at MCI. I guess we had a baby boom the last few years.

My girl stops, and as she turns, I catch sight of her nearly five-month baby belly, and my cock twitches, wanting to remind her where that baby bump came from. *Yes*, she helped. Still, it's my cock—it has a mind of its own. I don't control its macho actions. Pixie controls it, not me.

"I want to name our son Granger." Her voice cracks as she presses forward, her hand landing on my chest, her face overcome with emotions.

Fuck if that doesn't make me want to bend her over the closest desk. Or against a wall since there are *no desks* in a daycare! Her office!

"Finley? Are you listening to me?" She's morphed into annoyed, my response not quick enough for my demanding pregnant wife.

"Yeah, baby, you want to name our poor son Granger. What the fuck?"

228

Her hand flies to her belly like our innocent baby could hear my cursing.

"Pixie, even if he can hear me, he doesn't know what I'm saying. If he did, he'd understand my concern about you wanting to give our son a horrible name like that."

"Horrible!" she shrieks. My girl's hormones are out of whack, like crazy pregnancy mood swings out of whack.

Before she realizes what I've done, I've got her in her office, the door shut, locked, and her sitting on the desk. I had special glass installed that blacks out the windows at a touch of my finger... Done.

"Finley?" Her gaze roams my face as she bites her lips and her hips move of their own volition. She has no idea she's doing it. I'm telling you: crazy, amazing pregnancy hormones. She's horny all the time, can't get enough. Even when she's upset, like now, her nipples are hard, and her body is summoning me even as her brain is telling her otherwise.

"Yeah, Pixie?" I cup her face and lean down, waiting for her to realize what she needs. Release from the stress. Release from the hormones. Release from her beautiful body that is not wholly her own.

"Are we fucking or not?"

See, when she says it, it's not only hot, but it's okay for the baby to hear. But when I say it, it's crass and uncalled for.

"Yeah, baby, as soon as you take my cock out."

The trigger flipped, the haze is gone; her mouth smashes with mine, and I hold her in place as her hands work a little lower, getting access to what she needs—my cock.

Freed, my steel plops in her hand, and she strokes it like she's pumping a basketball full of air. "Jesus, woman, slow down."

"I need—"

"I know what you need." I pull her sundress up and over her head, take a second to admire her fuller pregnancy breasts, pull her panties to the side, and slide home.

"Oh, fuuuuck!" my girl cries.

I'm thankful we went for the sound-proofing, though the floor is empty, and opening day isn't for another month.

Pushing her back, I grip her shoulders and ram into her harder than I'd like, but just the way she swears she needs it when she gets all worked up like this.

"Finley, yes, babe, just like that."

See? Hard, deep, forceful. "I got you, Marguerite." I've always got her.

But when she bends her legs, holding herself open with a hand under each knee, I lose my mind. The sight of her pussy sucking my length, her juices coating both of us, and the sound of slapping skin has me thrusting faster and teasing her clit with my thumb.

Her first orgasm is immediate. The second one is mere moments later. But it's the third one that has me calling her name, promising her the world, and reminding me how much I love this heavenly creature in my arms. Crazy hormones and all.

Out of breath and cuddling on her couch, I kiss her silly.

"Granger, huh?"

She tips her head, her beautiful doe eyes seeking mine. "I love your name. All of your names are family names. You're the only son who shares names with your ancestors. I want to continue that tradition, but I don't want another Finley. You are my only *Finley*. I don't want to call our son that too. Granger is the only option unless you want to name him McIntyre Some-Middle-Name McIntyre." She grins.

I chuckle and kiss her forehead. "Granger McIntyre or McIntyre McIntyre are my only two choices, then?"

"Of course not. We could name him Dumbledore or Skywalker, but I think *Granger* has better sound to it, don't you?"

It'll never be boring with my Pixie.

"Granger it is, then."

"He sounds like he'll be the CEO of a great corporation someday." She snuggles in deep and closes her eyes.

"I hope he finds his *Pixie* before that day comes." I exhale and pull her closer, ready to hold her as she sleeps with our son growing inside her.

"Oh, he will. Don't you worry."

Worry? I have no worries with my girl by my side, in my heart, and her ability to remind me every day to take a moment to smell the flowers and feel the sunshine on my face.

*I hope you're ready, Granger. Your momma is going to love you silly.*

We both gasp, and her eyes fly open when my hand on her belly receives a swift kick.

## ⼁ 8 Months After Wedding ⼁

"Finley!" I cry. Our son is going to rip me apart from the inside out. "What did you do to me?"

"Fuck, Pixie. I'm sorry." He shakes his head, eyes filling with unshed tears. "It's too late to take it back."

"Take it back?! You want to take our son back?" The tears streaming down my cheeks only make me angrier.

"No! No, of course not." He presses a cool washcloth to my head. "You can do it, baby. You're strong. The strongest person I know. Only a few more pushes, right, Doc?"

"That's right, Margot; I want you to push with all your might on the next contraction," Dr. McGee says.

I glare at him. "All my might? You *think* I haven't been giving it my all?!"

Fin pats my hand. "I'm sure that's not what the doc meant. We know you're giving it everything you have. I'm sorry I'm such a big guy, giving you a big baby. But I promise it'll be worth it when Granger is here."

"Yeah, well, the next one you can push out of your huge penis!" I scream as the next contraction hits.

"Push, Margot," Dr. McGee orders like I'm not already pushing. "That's it. Just like that."

"You got this, Pixie."

I so do *not* have this.

I'm ready to go home.

"Push!"

I don't know who says it, but I close my eyes and push so hard, I'll probably crap myself.

"Holy shit," Fin's whisper has me opening my eyes. "I can see his black hair."

I start to cry. "I want him to have your eyes."

"Push, Margot. Keep pushing, then you can check out the color of his eyes yourself." Dr. McGee looks ready to catch a baseball as the nurse dabs my sweaty brow and looks at me with pity and encouragement.

Yeah, she knows. This shit is not for the weak.

Whoever said giving birth is the same pain as a man experiences when he's hit in the nutsack is a lying piece of shit—or a man, obviously. No woman would ever make that statement or even think to compare the two.

"One more, Pixie. You got this."

I do. I can do this.

I could be hit in the balls and give birth all at the same time. I am woman. Hear me roar!

And roar I do, until the pain leaves me in a whoosh as our little boy pops free. And his cry isn't nearly as loud as mine, but it sure is a beautiful sound.

"Jesus, fuck. I love you, woman." Fin kisses my temple.

Our eyes are trained on our little man as the nurse swipes him clean—a little—and places him on my chest.

"Welcome to the world, Granger." My strong man wraps us in his arms as best he can and whispers, "I'm so proud of you, Pixie. Thank you for giving me a son. But thank you most of all for giving me you."

At the sound of his daddy's voice, Granger stops crying and blinks, his blueish-green eyes looking right at us as if he can see us.

"He recognizes your voice, Finley."

Granger blinks again and starts sucking his hand when he hears my voice.

"He recognizes you too, Pixie."

"He's beautiful." I kiss Fin. "Thank you for our son. I'm sorry for being a bitch."

He rains kisses on my face. "You're perfect, Marguerite. Always have been. Always will be."

Yeah, I lucked out with this one. The life we have is not the one either of us saw coming, but we're so thankful it's here.

# Author's Note

I can't tell you how long I've waited to tell Fin and Margot's story. I wasn't a hundred percent sure where it was going, but I'm so happy with where they led me.

**Want more Fin and Margot?**
Sign up for my Newsletter and receive a free Bonus Scene!

Free BONUS SCENE: dl.bookfunnel.com/f8dndfsqny

Stay tuned for Matt and Gabby's story in *Until You Forgive*.
Don't miss out, add it to your TBR!
dmckdavis.com/all-books/series/until-you/uyforgive

# Did You Enjoy This Book?

This is a dream for me to be able to share my love of writing with you. If you liked my story, please consider **leaving a review** on the retailer's site where you purchased this book (and/or on **Goodreads**).

Personal recommendations to your friends and loved ones are a great compliment too. Please share, follow, join my newsletter, and help spread the word—let everyone know how much you loved Fin and Margot's story.

# Acknowledgments

There are so many people to thank, I'll never remember everyone. So just remember if you've ever read one of my books, commented on a post, read a newsletter, or supported me in some other way—I am deeply grateful and thank you from the bottom of my heart.

My husband and my kids are my life. They love me enough to support my writing aspirations that take me away from them at times, and still, they never complain, and cheer me on the entire time. Thank you, Boo, Honey Bunny Pumpkin Pie, and Doodles. (*They'll kill me if they see this!*)

Thanks to my mom, my sister (miss you every day!), and the rest of my family who love and support me.

Thank you to Teddy for being my sounding board and talking me off the ledge more times than she should have to.

Thanks to the readers, bloggers, followers, Diva members, and other incredible authors who support me in amazing, thoughtful, and giving ways.

Thank you to my amazing editor, Tamara, who makes me cry and breaks my heart so I can give you the best book possible. It's a tough job and she's always up for the challenge.

And last but definitely not least, to the readers, I thank you for buying my books, reading my stories, and coming back for more. It still amazes me I get to do this for a living, and you are the reason why. I am blessed because of you. Don't stop. Keep reading! And don't forget to leave a review.

Blessings!

# About the Author

D.M. Davis is a Contemporary and New Adult Romance Author.

She is a Texas native, wife, and mother. Her background is Project Management, technical writing, and application development. D.M. has been a lifelong reader and wrote poetry in her early life, but has found her true passion in writing about love and the intricate relationships between men and women.

She writes of broken hearts and second chances, of dreamers looking for more than they have and daring to reach for it.

D.M. believes it is never too late to make a change in your own life, to become the person you always wanted to be, but were afraid you were not worth the effort.

You are worth it. Take a chance on you. You never know what's possible if you don't try. Believe in yourself as you believe in others, and see what life has to offer.

Please visit her website, dmckdavis.com, for more details, and keep in touch by signing up for her newsletter, and joining her on Facebook, Twitter, and Instagram.

# Additional Books by
# D.M. DAVIS

**Until You Series**

*Book 1—Until You Set Me Free*

*Book 2—Until You Are Mine*

*Book 3—Until You Say I Do*

*Book 4—Until You Believe*

**Finding Grace Series**

*Book 1—The Road to Redemption*

*Book 2—The Price of Atonement*

**Black Ops MMA Series**

*Book 1—No Mercy*

*Book 2—Rowdy*

*Book 3—Captain*

**Standalones**

*Warm Me Softly*

# Join My Reader Group

www.facebook.com/groups/dmdavisreadergroup

# Stalk Me

Visit www.dmckdavis.com for more details about my books.

Keep in touch by signing up for my Newsletter.

Connect on social media:
Facebook: www.facebook.com/dmdavisauthor
Instagram: www.instagram.com/dmdavisauthor
Twitter: twitter.com/dmdavisauthor
Reader's Group: www.facebook.com/groups/dmdavisreadergroup

Follow me:
BookBub: www.bookbub.com/authors/d-m-davis
Goodreads: www.goodreads.com/dmckdavis

## d.m. davis
### SEXY WITH HEART
CONTEMPORARY & NEW ADULT ROMANCE AUTHOR

Made in the USA
Las Vegas, NV
20 April 2021